Emma B.____

The King's Idiot

Enjoy!

Emma Barrett-Brown

The King's Idiot

First Published Independently
Dec 2019 ©Emma Barrett, Plymouth UK

Cover Photography, Jay at McKinnon Images, Model: Sammy Lydiatt

Printed and Bound by KDP – Kindle Direct Publishing

This book is for Jay
And for Caroline as a thank you for all your support during
its creation.

Chapter 1

The stones of the passage were rough beneath Niamh's bare feet, damp from where the rains spilled down unheeded from the walls of the castle above. Her breath came in little panicked gasps as she ran, and her whole body shook. It was dark too, so very dark; Niamh could see barely a foot in front of her face and so was almost entirely reliant upon her over-stimulated ears as she moved, stumbling on into the darkness whilst the battle raged on above. The battle. The word still didn't seem real. Who, for the love of the goddess, would want to attack her father – he who was known as the most benevolent and kind king in all of Rostelis? She shivered and pulled her thick cloak more tightly about her, in the panic of her fleeing from the cosy room above, at least she'd remembered to grab for a cloak, despite how she'd neglected to slip her feet into her shoes. It had all been so frenzied: the screaming, the cries that the invaders were inside and that the ladies should flee! Then chaos as she was pulled to her feet and all-but dragged from her chamber by Maggie – her maid.

The Queen and the legitimate children, and even the other bases like her were likely already gone. Niamh and her maid had not been invited to join them in their prayers as the attackers had been spotted to the west, nor had anybody come to call for her as the attack was imminent. Not just for her bastardy – there were several bastards about the house, the king loved all his children equally – but more for her strangeness; Niamh was not well-liked, mainly due to her reluctance to speak unless she could absolutely not avoid uttering a word. It had always been thus; she was no fool, nor was she dim-witted or even shy, but mostly she chose to reserve her words, finding no peace in idle chatter. The King's Idiot, they called her – the dumb one, the mute. The royal children were especially cruel, taunting and jeering, and Niamh had found herself ostracised from their games and play on more and more occasions as she grew older.

Niamh set her jaw. She couldn't think of the other royal children now, possibly all slaughtered where they sat in prayer. She would never forget the panic which showed in the eyes of her elder brother, Laurin – he being of an age to join his father in the defence of the keep – as he'd run past her up the stairs, his sword shaking in his hands and blood on his tunic. He'd been the only one to bother looking for her, to check she was still alive. Neither would she forget the fear and panic on Maggie's face as Laurin waved them from the room, telling them to flee as he carried on upwards to check for any other stragglers. Her maid had looked almost like the ghost she would become just moments later as the invaders stormed the halls, sticking people with swords, even old ladies and bastard daughters.

Niamh bit back tears, there was no time to mourn now, no time to analyse the memories of her precious Maggie falling to the ground, and then the leer of the man who had caused the wound as his eyes fell onto Niamh – she just fifteen years old, blond and pretty as all the king's children were. Her face wore a few freckles which were inherited, she supposed, from her mother as the rest of the king's children had none. She was slender too, with blue eyes which glowed almost purple when she was animated or angry. The man was very rugged, old and garbed in leather armour which must once have been fine indeed, but now was barely held together at the seams. One of the savages! The Woldermen. Not subjects of her father, but heathens from across the border in the wildlands. Pagans who worshiped multiple gods and had little regard for kingship and property. It had to be them! Had to be! Who else would ever wish to remove the golden king from his castle? Niamh repressed a sob and continued on down the passageway. She'd escaped Maggie's fate or worse only by the assistance of one of her father's men, Josynne Shale, who had run his sword through her maid's murderer and then had thrust her through a door, down a set of stairs and then through the concealed wooden doorway at the corner where the passage met another. There he'd left her, shouting to her to hurry down into the darkness. All castles had these escape routes, hidden and forgotten. Niamh could only hope that her father had found his way out too. None of them had been prepared for an assault, nobody could even have dreamed that in a time of high peace, an army of wild men could take the Golden Keep.

Niamh shivered again and a lone tear fell from her eye, tracing a warm path down her icy skin. She put up a hand to touch the wall, to convince herself that there truly was a path, and that she did not merely amble aimlessly in the void. Another tear fell, and then another. Why could Josynne not have accompanied her? Why had he left her alone in the darkness like this? Was he even still alive? Were her siblings? Her father? Perhaps she, one lone girl, was the sole survivor of the golden reign? The pressure was too much to bear – not that she could ever be queen, illegitimate and considered dull-of-mind as she was – but the idea of it felt heavy on young shoulders.

As Niamh paused, panting, one hand on the wall to reassure herself of its existence, a sound came to her ear. Her whole body tensed, frozen in utter panic. There it was again, and again. Footsteps in the darkness. Niamh moaned. The sound was eerie and mournful, enough to make even herself shiver at its desperate sound. The keen of a lost spirit uttering its final plea before the night stole it away. The moan echoed into the darkness, causing Niamh to clasp her free hand over her own lips. The sound of her voice at all was alien enough, let alone a mournful wail in the darkness.

The footsteps moved closer, fast and paced as they echoed about her. Perhaps had the circumstance been different, she might not have heard them at all but in the otherwise silence, they were loud and clear. The owner was obviously well-experienced at moving in the darkness, the steps not stumbling at all. Already Niamh knew she could not outpace those footsteps and so huddled down into a crouched position, pulling the cloak she wore tighter about her. Her mind brought to her the hideous images of what was to come. No girl of her rank, even the bastards, were naive of how the women of the house might be treated in the case of an invasion. Hot-blooded men, Maggie said – or, had used to say – looking for the spoils of battle. The tears on Niamh's cheeks felt as though they would freeze and her fingers hurt from the clutching of the cape about her. A light caught her eye as she huddled, a strange blue fiery glow which moved closer with the footsteps. Niamh closed her eyes against it, not wanting to see the face of her attacker in the strange fire, but another strangled gasp of fear left her lips.

'What? Is somebody there?' a voice called out. Male, deep and from a mouth which was likely a little dry, for the rasp of it. The footsteps paused, though, rather than come closer.

Niamh, mute as ever – more so for her panic – simply cowered, she'd fight him, when he came upon her, that she'd already decided, but still her limbs shook.

'I said who is there? Show yourself!'

Still he came no closer and there was definitely an edge of caution in the tone. Niamh opened her eyes and cast her gaze upon the figure before her. Relief flooded her entire body.

The man was fairly tall and was dressed in the plain black long-trousers and tunic which bore the seal of the golden oak tree which denoted him a member of her father's mage council. His eyes shone with anger and worry below a head of ebon hair which was darted through with blues, braided at the front but hanging loose down his back almost to his middle. The light came from the flickering of a small ball of blue fire which the mage had harnessed within his palms – he was advanced then! And young to be so, thirty at the very most. Niamh did not know all of the mages, a council of twelve who kept themselves to themselves, but the name Helligan seemed to swim to her mind at the sight of him.

'Hark me now,' he said, 'Show yourself! I will give you no further warning!'

Niamh, still shaking but now with relief, stood from her hunched position and turned her face properly to him so that he might examine her features. The man's eyes ran over her, taking in her bare feet, shivering form and loose blond hair from where she had lost her gold and pearl hairnet. Niamh doubted she looked much like a daughter of the king, more like a maid in a stolen cape!

'You're one of the king's bastards, aren't you?' Helligan asked, stepping closer so that Niamh could feel the heat from his captured ball of strange blue fire.

Niamh nodded, still mute, still breathing too quickly but calming somewhat.

'My lady, I mean you no harm – I am one of your father's men.'

Again, Niamh nodded.

'What is your name?'

Niamh swallowed and wet her lips but panic had set her tongue to stillness and the word would not form. The silence pooled for a moment, but then Helligan spoke again.

'Ah, so you are the mute, I presume? Niamh?'

Relief flooded for a second time and again Niamh felt her chest expand without feeling as though somebody gripped her lungs in a cold fist. Again, she nodded.

'Come then, my lady, we have to be away before this passage is discovered and infiltrated.'

Niamh could do nothing but nod, despite how desperately she wished to ask all the questions which rattled about in her mind – of her family, of her father, were they all lost? Was the golden reign at an end, if her father's men had to escape through dark tunnels thus? The thought tried to surface, that perhaps her companion was just a coward – fleeing, but Niamh could not blame him even if he was – she'd seen the carnage of the attack first-hand.

Helligan lifted up the hand with the fire a little higher so that the tiny flame lit more of the surroundings, and then he put out his other hand for her. Niamh paused, she'd held the arms of her brothers, and of her father but that was a far cry from linking fingers with a stranger, flesh to flesh. Helligan glanced at her and the look was close enough to impatience for her to slide her hand into his, frightened to be left behind.

'We have to be careful,' his voice was low as he spoke, 'there are invaders everywhere, and likely they await the exits to these warrens.'

Niamh wanted to ask who they were, why they attacked, but instead she merely followed Helligan, her teeth chewing her bottom lip. Together they walked for what seemed to Niamh like perhaps another ten long minutes or so, and then she noticed the light of the fire Helligan carried began to grow dimmer – no, not quite – more that the tunnel grew brighter. The end must be close! Helligan glanced about them and then slowly closed his fist, extinguishing the flames.

'Carefully now, quiet,' he murmured, slowing his tread and pushing Niamh slightly behind him. She obeyed as he moved forward a few paces, paused, and then a few more. For a few steps more he moved thus, but then paused and muttered a cuss-word.

Niamh froze, peering to see what he saw.

'Stay here,' he murmured, 'out of sight!'

Niamh's stomach fluttered again with panic as she squinted her eyes and picked up on the three figures without. As Helligan had suggested they might, they had pre-empted escapes and were manning the exits. Somebody must have alerted them to the tunnel's existence!

Helligan crept forward, and where previously Niamh had heard his footsteps easily, now suddenly he seemed almost silent. His skin too seemed to dim, not translucent or invisible, just darkening, becoming harder to see. He did not attack though, merely crept closer and closer, one step at a time. The thing about mages, Maggie had once told Niamh as a girl, especially those who harnessed the energy of the elements, was that they struggled to fight alone; they were too noticeable, and by the time they had charged up any Magicka, a well flung sword could easily snuff them out. Niamh could now see how this might be the case.

Helligan's hand went to the wall beside him and Niamh watched as his fingers splayed, dragging in the energy from the very stones. That was the other problem with Elementalists – they needed a link to the power they tried to harness. A candle-flame could become a raging fireball, but without the candle, there was nothing. Helligan seemed to inhale, and then to exhale suddenly, and before Niamh's eyes had time to process, suddenly the men at the entrance were screaming as an invisible weight seemed to knock them from their feet. An earthquake of sorts, but localised and invisible. Helligan was advanced indeed, then! As the men scrabbled back up to their feet, Helligan pulled a chain from about his neck, holding it fast in his fist. As he did so, a ball of white fire tinged with blue seemed to form at his hand, growing larger and larger until he held there a flaming blue fireball much like the one he'd carried for light. He must carry a vial of water at his throat! Clever Niamh felt her eyes locked to his hands, watching as he worked; she had heard tell of mages who could create fire from a water source, but never before had she witnessed such a feat!

The ice flame glimmered in the darkness for the shortest moment, but then seemed to explode from Helligan's hand to engulf the figure closest to them. The man screamed, pulling at his clothing as the flames took him, then falling to his knees, dead. Niamh stayed put, but within she suddenly felt the burn of desire – not for him, but for the power he wielded. To be able to twist the elements thus, to defend herself rather than cower behind a rock and be protected. Niamh had never really had any desire to learn fighting beforehand, but suddenly it burned. She looked down at her grubby hands as Helligan dispatched another of the three figures beyond, and then the final one, with almost ease – not just those odd blue flames, but small icy spears too, which he seemed to produce from his fingers, not a part of him, but gathered for his use from the very air.

As the final man fell, Helligan seemed to slump slightly. Using Magicka had one final drawback – it was exhausting – or so Niamh had been told. Helligan paused for a long moment, catching his breath, and then looked to Niamh.

'Are you well?' was his first question, despite that he had fought alone whilst she lay hidden. Again, something almost akin to shame coursed through Niamh to have huddled so like the royal sop she was whilst he'd risked his life. She wet her lips and nodded, her mouth too dry even for a thank you. Helligan pulled in another calming breath, and then put his hand out again.

'Come,' he said.

Outside, the day was bright, too cheerful a day for the deeds which were carried out in its duration. The tunnel let out to a cave-like entrance which was situated on the other side of the moat, close by a small stream and hidden within a dell which bordered the edge of the king's hunting grounds; gnarled oak trees which linked together to form green statues in the bright sunshine. All about, the scent was of the forest: peaty mud, wild garlic and the soft sent of the odd flowers which poked up through the soil – the musky scent of the galderflower, sweet red buds of briar roses and even the occasional burn of Crimsonflame where the water of the stream dried out enough to allow them to grow. The flowers glowed an eerie orange as the tiny flames burned at the edge of each petal. They were not hot to touch though, an illusion which was fabled to have been a gift from the Wondering Man, Rostalis's old god, to his beloved daughter – known as "The goddess" or "She of many faces". Out in the sunlight, Niamh blinked several times and then swallowed again – ever her mouth seemed to dry, especially when panicked. She took in a deep breath, and then whispered the words, 'Thank you.'

Helligan, who had exited just ahead of her turned to glance at her face. 'You do speak then?'

Niamh nodded, but cast down her eyes.

'Then I consider myself privileged to have heard your sweet voice,' he said.

Niamh allowed Helligan to lead her to the edge of the dell where they had emerged. There she could turn and look behind her at the castle where she'd been born, and which throughout her life, she'd rarely left. She gasped in horror at the sight before her eyes and felt Helligan's squeeze where he still held on to her left hand.

Smoke was the first thing, wafting in gusts from the wooden and thatch rooves of the houses in the bailey which were aflame still. The keep might have been colloquially called the Golden Keep, but in truth it was still wood and stone, and wood burns. Niamh and Helligan stood some distance from the walls themselves, but still Niamh could see the blood which had spilled from the fallen bodies all about. They'd been slaughtered in the bailey as they'd tried to flee – women, children and men all tangled together in a jumble by the gate. Here and thereabout, a body fell at more distance – those who had almost escaped. Niamh hiccupped back another moan of panic, her heart thudding. Nobody could have survived from the main keep – surely? But then she and Helligan had – so there must be hope! There must be! Dimly she wondered if Helligan had a wife, or children, still within. Most of the mages stayed aloof from such attachments, dedicated to their crafts, but marriage was not forbidden. Did he stand now with nothing but a snivelling child by his side whilst within his wife was raped and tortured, murdered? Niamh glanced up, there was certainly pain on his features, pain akin to hers.

'No, I have no family to remain within,' he said, somehow sensing the unasked question in her face. 'I just feel for the poor victims.'

Niamh tightened her grasp on Helligan's fingers, he squeezed back but then released her, his eyes still on the smoke which billowed free. 'Your father escaped, early on, with the first wave. I know not about your womenfolk, I am sorry.'

At least her father was safe! Niamh felt that one hard lump dissipate at least. Her father was everything to her, he who had taken her in despite her bastardy, and who had raised her as a lady despite that she was illegitimate. He'd done the same for the others too, allowing them all the luxury of their status without hesitation. "King's children are royal despite the mother's tie," he'd say, "and name me a king who does not yearn for a large family!" a good man, he, beloved by his subjects for his kindness in rule, for his care of his people. Niamh's eyes burned at the thought, at the sight of Aurvandil, the Golden Keep, burning in the bright sunshine.

'Come, we have to go,' Helligan said at last, 'we can help not by lingering over-long here. We must find your father and the others, and try to see if we can ascertain what has happened.'

Niamh nodded and moved to follow him, but was distracted by a movement from the edge of the trees closer to the castle.

'Look!' she managed, needing to get his attention, and then pointed to the movement.

Helligan cussed again and once more, he reached for his amulet. The figures came closer and closer, not just three but a band of them – seven or more – all pointing and shouting. Helligan turned to Niamh and now his eyes were panicked.

'Run!' he hissed.

Niamh turned to do so but then realised that Helligan had not joined her. Her feet tangled as she faltered.

'Run I said!' Helligan's voice peaked slightly and then he spun back to the invaders. Niamh pondered for a flustered moment longer, but then let out a sob and obeyed. As much as she enjoyed the image of fighting by his side, she had no magic, no skills at all and would likely be a hinderance. Helligan could handle himself well enough and she'd just get him killed!

The ground under Niamh's feet was slushy from the water which drained from the moat into the rivulets which became streams until the coast. As she ran, Niamh's bare feet slapped so hard in the wet mud that they became almost painful but despite that, she relished the soft wetness on their torn and bleeding soles. Twice she slipped but did not turn to look back until she was sure she had gained some ground. When she did turn though, her heart sank, and then plummeted down into her stomach. Helligan had fallen. How, or even what had conquered him, she did not know, but his form was prone, slumped on the ground. All about was the evidence of his fight, crystal ice in the trees and the fallen bodies of three of the men – at least he'd taken some with him! Niamh's eyes scanned in a panic, but the assailants seemed not concerned with her, moving to stand over Helligan's body in what appeared to be deep conversation. Niamh shed a tear but paused just a moment longer, then pulled in a deep breath and fled into the forest.

Chapter 2

The sun glimmered out over the marshes beyond from the small window by which Niamh sat, making the sloshy mud lakes seem to shimmer on the horizon. The view was somewhat unbroken, aside from the obvious presence of the guards who were posted every few feet about the perimeter walls of Anglemarsh Keep. Niamh's eye counted soldiers – an old habit, especially since the events which had led to the destruction of the Golden Keep, despite the five years which had passed since that day. In her hands was the obligatory embroidery of a lady, but she wasn't really attending to it, more that it was something to fidget with, something to occupy her hands. The tower in which she sat was the west tower of a small keep, some twenty miles from where the Golden Keep was being rebuilt even still. The remains of the royal family had resided there in the years since the sacking of their previous home because it was the closest of her father's three castles. Of the royal children, Niamh was the sole survivor aside from the eldest, Laurin. The Queen and her young children, as well as those she had sheltered, had been found in the aftermath. Their bodies showed evidence of blade-wounds but at least they were unmolested, and not desecrated or torn up by axes either – just sleeping with bright red gashes at their throats. That at least was a comfort to Niamh's poor old father, who was suddenly so aged.

Niamh's father often spoke of returning home once the restoration of the Golden Keep was finished, but ever he seemed dissatisfied with the work, demanding whole towers be torn down and rebuilt. Niamh couldn't blame him really; she didn't really want to return there either. It had been five long years since her flight through the tunnels below with the mage, Helligan Darkfire – a man her father recognised at once from her descriptions of him – and yet for Niamh, that terror, that terrible flight could have been mere days past.

A knock came at the door and a wrinkled old face appeared around it. Morena was her new maid. She was an ancient creature who had once tended the king's sister, in her youth. She was primly dressed; blue cotton gown with only the scantest of embroidery and a white kerchief bound tightly about her hair. Still, in her age, she was a handsome woman.

'Your father wishes to see you,' she said.

'Certainly!' At once Niamh lay down the embroidery and stood. The old maid clucked and came to brush down Niamh's sumptuous green velvet gown with its golden thread. A few loose cuts of embroidery thread clung to the fibres but were quickly chased off by the maid's ancient, wrinkled hands.

'Here, braid your hair behind you,' Morena said, moving to do the task herself even as she spoke. As an unmarried girl, Niamh was still given the freedom to wear her hair loose, but thus was not acceptable below where her father held court. Niamh, at twenty years of age, was now somewhat old for marriage – most girls of her station making that great leap at sixteen or seventeen, some as young as thirteen or fourteen – but Niamh's father liked to keep her close, especially after the disaster. Niamh's hair was quickly braided and tucked away under a net, tamed, and Morena flicked some rosewater at her too, then helped her into some soft cloth slippers. Finally properly adorned, Niamh allowed Morena to lead her from her chamber, down two cold corridors to the stairs, then through those to the door of the great hall where her father was with his advisors. She took in a deep breath, and then pushed the door.

The great hall was quite plain in contrast to the vast throne room of the Golden Keep. Where that had been ornate, gilded and vast, this room was a small chamber of brick. A few tapestries hung at the walls but the room was devoid of ornamentations. Rather than the great throne of gold on its dais, was a simple wooden seat, set slightly above the room but not very much so, and covered with soft furs to cushion her father's aching, aged limbs. There was a contrast too, in those attending. Her father's court at the Golden Keep had been a vibrant place, buzzing with courtiers young and old. This hall had a handful of older courtiers, but none of the youth. The middle of the room was taken up with a large table on which were a handful of wooden pieces which stood to show the strategic placement of her father's armies. The sweetly simple life of peace was long gone now – the war with the Woldermen had spanned years, with both sides maintaining a front enough to defend, but not to advance.

'Sires, The Lady Niamh!' a voice to her right announced as Niamh stepped into the chamber. Her father looked up from where he was in deep discussion with his men. There were no mages anymore – most had gone over to the other side, drawn by the wild magic which flowed through the marshes. The two who had remained had both been executed as a warning to the others – a deed Niamh had trouble stomaching especially after Helligan's rescue of her. Would her father have spared him, had he returned alive? She liked to think so. Her father had never been cruel before.

'Niamh – come,' her father beckoned her over to the table.

'Sire,' Niamh's voice was a little dry but still she smiled as she walked over to the table where her father and his men sat in planning.

'Here, come and join us!' One of her father's men spoke too, beckoning her. Lord Shale, the other knight who had aided in her escape. He was perhaps the youngest of her father's remaining attendants, late thirties or so. He was quite a handsome man, with dark eyes and a wide smile. His hair too was dark and shaggy-long. Unlike most of her father's Lords who dressed well and fashionably, Shale lived in plain clothes, with no frills, he didn't shave enough and his nails, whilst clean, didn't tend to show the fussy manicures that most of her father's men favoured. Of all her father's lords, Niamh was fondest of Lord Shale.

Niamh did as she was bade, moving to take one of the hard uncomfortable chairs by the edge of the table. She sat and was brought a glass of wine which was a little too tart for her tastes but a good distraction to keep from having to speak again. Laurin, her half-brother, appeared too just minutes later – looking as puzzled as Niamh felt – and he too took a seat opposite her. Niamh smiled, her brother was a handsome man, blond as were all the king's children – they took after him, but fairer even than she was. His skin was pale too but not sickly, and his frame slender but wide enough at the shoulder to fill his fine jerkin. He smiled back at her, and his smile was wide, showing rows of perfect white teeth.

'Children,' the king said, 'I have asked you both to come to me as I have made an important decision regarding your futures.'

'Marriage?' Niamh hoped the panic didn't sound in her tone.

Niamh's father's old eyes took hers, blue beacons looking out from a face which looked too old, beneath a head of hair now white rather than the gold it had once been. He examined her as his comrades chuckled amongst themselves, but when he spoke, his voice was gentle.

'No, not for you dear girl, I could not bear to part with you now. It is of the succession I wish to speak.' He put up a hand to fuss his beard, but then seemed to realise what he was doing and quelled the stray motion. Niamh stayed silent, waiting with pounding heart. Her father waited to see if she would speak but when she didn't he continued. 'Niamh, I have thought long on this and I have decided, with the advice of my lords, that I am going to legitimise you.'

Suddenly the air felt as though it had all been sucked from her lungs. Laurin exclaimed, a happy congratulation but Niamh could barely hear him. She murmured and put a hand to her chest. All at once, the dim candles seemed too bright, the empty room too crowded. Her father looked to her brother, opposite.

'Of course, Niamh, you will follow Laurin for he is not just my male offspring, but my true legitimate son as well, and, God preserve, he *will* marry soon and bring with him a brood, but if he does not, you would be the next in line.'

'Sire...' she managed, somewhat breathless.

'It is for the benefit of us all,' her father said, 'I cannot leave the dynasty uncertain and with only one... one living son, this is as it must be.'

'But... but... Magda?' Niamh asked, naming her new stepmother.

'Yes, father, I am sure your lady wife will be blessed with another son any day now!' Laurin added. Their father had remarried two years after the tragedy, his wife a distant cousin who was also widowed, and who brought with her three children of her own, all daughters. So far, the royal couple had produced but two stillborn baby boys.

'Magda is very much the catalyst for these discussions, to be frank. This morning she officially informed the court that she is no longer of a child-bearing age, and that her courses have not run for three consecutive moon-cycles. I am afraid that I will father no more children.'

Niamh wanted to ask that if that was the case, had her father no mistresses now, but could not find the words to do so. Instead, she looked at her hands and counted backwards from three-score in an attempt to calm herself.

'My advisors are drawing this into law now, as we speak. I am proud to call you a royal princess now, Niamh, and I hope your brother will accept you now as a true sister of the blood.'

'Yes, sire, gladly!' Laurin grinned, his eyes twinkling. Bless Laurin, ever she had loved his soft gentleness — especially since the sacking of the Golden Keep. Still Niamh's voice was absent though, her chest hurt and her eyes watered. The last time she'd felt such high emotion had been years hence, when finally from her flight into the forest, she'd stumbled upon the band of bedraggled and furious courtiers who had escaped the violence and who had taken her back to her father and brother at Anglemarsh.

'Have you nothing to say, girl?' a voice from her side: Jahlyn Carver, one of her father's older advisors, a man in his fifties at least with a mane of white hair which fell behind him and a scar which covered most of his left arm.

'I… thank you, father…' she managed.

'It is a convenience to you both,' that was another of her father's advisors, Anric Nordemunde. 'You do us as much of a boon as we do you.'

'Hail Princess Niamh!' came another voice, and then another. Niamh bowed her head to show her gratitude. Her father put a hand onto the back of it, gentle and strong. 'You must consider your life changed from this moment on, child,' he said, 'A true princess now, you must learn policy and diplomacy. You must learn to lead, and to manage men. Your brother will guide you and teach you where I cannot!'

Niamh bowed her head, 'Yes, sire.'

'And you *must* learn to speak to people!'

'I… yes, sire.'

Niamh's father held her gaze a moment longer, the worry obvious in his eyes, but then he nodded too. 'I have a gift for you, to mark this wonderful day,' he said, then stood on legs which were not so strong as once they had been. He moved across to where the table was, then behind to the door of his private antechamber. Niamh, unsure of how to proceed, followed him to the door but not beyond – that was her father's private space. He remained within only moments, though, and when he returned he had in his hands a bow. The weapon was very ornate, delicately carved from what looked like a nice springy ash, but with a darker stain on it. The edges were carved into elegant furls which broke down to flowers on the ends which were tipped with gold. Niamh felt a smile beam through. She'd taken up archery in the aftermath of the sacking of the Golden Keep – the memory of Helligan made her want to learn some defence, still convinced that she could have saved him, had she known how. Magic was not for young ladies, however, or ladies in general, in fact but Niamh had found archery to be more acceptable, and had found to her own, and everybody else's surprise, that she had rather a talent for it. The bow was the most beautiful thing she'd ever seen. She accepted the gift and then swept down before her father in a curtsey of gratitude.

'Treat it kindly! It is an ancient thing, worth more than money can buy. A relic left over from when the elves walked this land.'

'I thank you, father, for a beautiful gift,' she managed.

'It was Shale who had it acquired for me to give to you,' the king nodded at the man.

'Thank you, Josynne,' she almost whispered, using his first name to loan him favour despite her lips drying up, 'it is beautiful.'

'Use it well, in defence of our kingdom,' he said as the king returned to his previous seat. Niamh, feeling dismissed all but ran from the chamber, out to the courtyard where the butts were set up.

Chapter 3

The rain lashed down on the slippery stone and grass grounds
of the courtyard, rendering the ground even more treacherous
and unsteady than it usually was. The downpour had started
suddenly, but the grey skies had been threatening such all day.
Niamh hunched down under her cloak, the hood pulling up
and her body already soaked through, her left hand, however,
held fast to her bow whilst the right held an arrow ready to be
hitched. Her training for the day was not complete and she
refused to go back inside until she'd completed the full three
hours. Lifting the bow, she hooked the arrow in and drew, took
a deep calming breath, and then released. The arrow flew, true
to target right until the end where a gust of wind knocked it to
the side so that it hit the very edge of the target. Niamh swore
and pulled another arrow. This one she adjusted slightly for the
direction of the wind. Her hand's steadied and her back
tightened.

'Left a little more, and up slightly,' came a voice from
behind her. Niamh turned her head to see Josynne Shale at her
shoulder. He too was wrapped in a cloak, his long hair pulled
away under a fur-lined hood which was already wilting in the
rain. His gloved hand came to move her arm slightly, lingered,
and then released it, poised slightly higher than it had been.
Niamh smiled. Lord Shale was once of the best archers in her

father's employ, possibly one of the best in the kingdom, and it was he who had taken over Niamh's training in the half-year since she'd acquired her bow. His wife, Lady Betha Shale, was the second cousin to Niamh's father, and so he had a distant line to the throne too, through her. Niamh forced herself to concentrate, and then let the arrow fly. Still not a clean shot, but it was closer.

Niamh lowered the bow and turned to Lord Shale with a shy thanks.

'Anytime, Princess. Your father is looking for you now though, I said you'd probably be out here, despite the weather!'

Niamh nodded and threw the bow onto her back. She was trying to be accustomed to carrying it thus, liking the comfort of having the weapon there, especially since there were rumblings that the Wolder army was moving closer again. Niamh hated the Woldermen, not for their wild ways and strange magics, not even for their sacking of her childhood home, but for the murder of Helligan Darkfire, for the murder of her siblings and the strain to the kingdom which had once been such a happy and peaceful place to live. Even thinking thus darkened her mood somewhat as she followed Lord Shale back inside and allowed the servants to take her cloak and bow.

'I'll inform your father that you will attend in an hour, after you have freshened up?' Lord Shale said, a glance at the wet patches on Niamh's blue gown and then up to where her braided hair was falling loose of the golden hairnet she'd tried to contain it in.

Niamh changed quickly, allowing Morena to pat her down with drying rags before slipping into a clean dress. Her wardrobe had improved with her status, but so had her father's expectations of her ever seeming immaculate. Morena helped her to slide rings onto her fingers and then let loose her thick yellow hair to be brushed and then refastened under the golden net which was encrusted with gems. The Golden Keep might be gone, but the king still wanted to children to be seen as bright and sparkling. Once dressed, Niamh made her way to the great hall. She took in a deep breath, she hated the ceremony of it all, but then pushed open the door and entered.

'Princess Niamh!' the royal proclaimer announced as she stepped inside and as ever, despite how she tried to repress it, the barking of her name made her wince.

'Ah, at last!' the king said, beckoning her over to the table where he stood with Laurin and his favoured Lords: Shale, Nordemunde, Carver, and Jansen, and another man Niamh did not recognize. Besides these people, the throne room was empty. Queen Magda was elsewhere but ever she was, uninterested in matters of state unless they involved those of celebrations or tourneys.

'Father, Laurin, My Lords,' Niamh managed, it would likely be the full extent of what she spoke unless called upon specifically.

'Daughter,' her father said, tapping a chair next to his own. Niamh sat herself down and focused on looking interested.

'My children, my lords, today is a blessed day indeed,' The king said, smiling wider than he had done so in many a year. 'May I introduce Lucius Mangeli,' he indicated the stranger, who simply nodded. 'Lucius is a mystic, a priest from Aireshire,' the king continued, naming the land just across the sea, 'one of the priests of the new religion, but also a sage and respected historian.'

There was a general mumble amongst the persons present, but Niamh kept quiet.

'Lucius is here to assist us with our problems with the Wolder, loaned to us from the court of King Julius Porscii himself. He and I have spoken long of an artifact in his possession, ancient and powerful, which might be the key to our success. At his extreme generosity, Lucius here carries this artifact with him today, to loan to us.'

'An artifact?' Laurin asked, 'What sort of artifact, father?'

'A weapon son, an ancient weapon. It is said to be a dragon-caller.'

'I… but the dragons left this plain long ago, with the rest of the fae. Do you claim you could… call them back?' That was Lord Shale, and to Niamh's eye, he seemed a little heated.

'Perhaps. We have now, in this castle, the item itself but it is ancient and unknown… we know not how it… well, how it works…'

Niamh's lips set. This "Artifact" had sounded too good to be true, now she was seeing the reason for that.

'And you will what… help *us* to discover its secrets?' Lord Nordemunde asked, of Lucius. Nordemunde was one of the older of the advisors to her father, quite a hot-headed little man with iron-grey hair and watery eyes.

'I seek the knowledge for my own lord and king, but with your assistance and new view-points, you might take a temporary ownership of the item, in order to win your war…'

'Do we have any notion of how it works? What is it? Can we see the item?' Lord Shale asked. 'This all seems very… abstract.'

Lucius stood. Taller than most at the table, he had a black braid of hair which was tied with golden thread, and clothing of white linen, decorated with gold - plain, to the eyes of those used to the extravagant court-wear of the Golden King's reign, and yet still obviously well-made and valuable. His hands were littered with rings and his eyes old, somewhat tired. The man was no bent historian though, with a straight back and good stature as he gazed down on the old king and his children. Niamh thought to herself that he was quite imposing really, especially for a scholar.

'The artifact,' he said, 'is known to us as the sphere of Gual. It is a plain glass sphere about the size of my hand, and would appear to be a depleted magical item. It seems to me, from my estimates of its age and design, to be an item which was forged back before the great split where the magic-dwellers of this world departed.'

'Surely that is just myth itself,' Lord Nordemunde scoffed, 'Bedtimes stories for children.'

'Some say it is so, my lord,' the scholar continued, unoffended by his words. Niamh tried to remember the stories, given as such: that once, not in the dark ages, but still a thousand years earlier, the little people and the humans lived side by side, magic dwellers, elves, halflings, even giants and dragons in some tellings of it. Together they'd lived in harmony, before the big rift – a war between the mortals and the magic dwellers. This war had raged for a hundred years but had been a true stalemate with the technological advancements and mechanical war-machines of the humans being enough to hold back the Fae folk, and yet the strong magicka of the Fae being powerful enough to resist invasion of their forests and marshes, moorlands and mountains. Finally a truce was drawn up, an end to the fighting which had led to the Fae folk leaving for another, alternate world. Elsewhere. Hidden by the veils of ancient magic. It truly was the stuff of legend, despite how some, especially the more common folk, fully believed it to have happened.

'The artifact was lost for three hundred years,' Lucius continued, unphased by the scepticism in the room. 'But then was said to be unearthed in a temple of the Fae gods in my country, and there left on display by the sisters, blind to the power they held. My king heard tales of this, of the myth of its origin, and so had it brought to us sixteen years past where I have studied it since. The sphere itself is of Dragonglass, I am certain, and thus it must be Fae. It is set into a carved bronze setting. It is quite beautiful, but it is dead of all power unless put into contact with a droplet of blood, in which case the glass glows deep red for just a second, and then goes back to clear.'

'Blood magic is powerful and dangerous,' again Shale was the voice of caution, but nobody paid him any mind.

'What do you suggest, to move forward?' That was Nordemunde, to the king.

'One of the reasons why my brother king, Julius has bequeathed the artifact to us, albeit temporarily, is that down on the edge of the Whites, there is a small temple of sisters who claim to have, amongst their treasures, a small vial of preserved dragon blood.'

'You think that that might be the key?' Laurin asked, his voice sounding youthful amongst the rest.

'I do.'

'But you cannot think to travel south? The Whites are filled with Wolder and you know the sisters favour the old ways. If you tried to take one of their treasures, you'd risk your men.' Again, Shale.

'Not if we send the royal children with them,' Lucius interjected. 'Something of a royal procession. The Sisters would never harm children… or allow harm to be done to them! Hence why I have asked for you today, Laurin, Niamh…'

'No!' Lord Shale stood, 'We cannot send them into danger! They are the kings only heirs!'

'Which is why the people will want to see them,' the king interjected, 'especially in times of unrest. Let the golden kingdom begin to bloom again, especially when the end of the war is nigh! Let them see the beauty and grace of their monarchs as opposed to this rabble of wild men! Let them see the contrast! They will be a good distraction.'

'But father! That is so far a pilgrimage!' Laurin said, 'It would take us weeks or more to make the journey and retrieve your artifact!'

As the prince spoke, Lucius sat himself back down and cast an eye over Niamh. She, sensing the uncomfortable feeling of being examined, looked back. The man nodded to her and smiled, then lifted the wine pitcher and poured himself a glass. Niamh ran a finger over the rough wooden surface of the table, unsure of what she thought of the events before her, of what she was being told. It all seemed very unlikely, and yet the tales of "before" were well-documented, widely believed. She did not mind going out on parade. Despite the risks, they would be well-protected, not just by her father's men, but by the common folk too. The king might have lost the love of his people somewhat in the war-torn lands, but the two remaining royal children were still regarded mostly with indulgence.

'I am willing,' she spoke, her lips dry.

'Good! Good girl!' her father beamed, 'Son?'

'I was to be wed, next month...'

'You will return in time for the great day I am sure, if not then a short postponement....'

'That saddens me father, and to be so long away from my lady...'

'When you are the king, you must become accustomed to being away from your lady,' Lord Nordemunde reminded Laurin.

'Indeed, yet I see fit to indulge you. If the queen agrees, you might add the lady Kyran and her sisters to the party,' the king added.

Laurin's frown lessened somewhat. He was betrothed to one of the new queen's daughters by her first marriage. A beautiful girl of auburn hair and doe's eyes.

'Laurin, will you come?' Niamh asked, her soft voice seeming to echo.

'If I must?'

'You must!' the King said, 'You son, will be in command of these lands one day! We must let the people see the future king, a handsome king, a brave king.'

After the meeting, Niamh slipped back up to her chamber and reclaimed her bow. If she was going to be leaving the keep, she was damned sure she wasn't going to be a sitting duck. From the window of her chamber, she could just about make out the spires of the Golden Keep. The damage was now almost completely mended and her father's men spoke of little other than of going home. Niamh allowed her eyes to rest on it for a long moment. After the royal procession, as it was to be called, the family were going to finally go back, her father had agreed, and she wasn't sure how she felt about that. Yes, the Golden Keep was more luxurious by far, and yet it was harder to defend, as time had already shown. It was more of a target than Anglemarsh too, especially once they were back within.

Niamh allowed her eyes to linger for a moment longer but then slipped the latch on the old wooden door and made her way down the steep stone steps to the side door. Outside, though, there was already a figure at the butts, bow raised and arm outstretched Niamh paused, allowing the door to close with a soft thump behind her. Lord Shale was already out at practice. His form was perfectly on point, his arms moving gracefully to reload the bow and fire two, then three arrows into the perfect centre of his target. Niamh stepped forward and saw his shoulders tighten. He'd heard even her soft step.

'My lady,' his voice floated over.

'My Lord Shale… Are you well?'

He lowered the bow and turned to her. His face was like stone, angry. 'No, my lady, no I am not well.'

'Oh?'

Shale seemed to sag. His handsome features were clouded. 'My Lord King says I must not accompany you on your fake pilgrimage,' he said. 'None of us are to, and so you will be less protected than you might be.'

'I… I am sure we will be in no danger.'

'And I am sure of the opposite,' he said. 'Do you think that it is sensible to risk the Wolder armies for the sake of some *artifact* which sounds more of a children's toy than a real weapon? Your father has lost all sense…' he flushed redder but did not apologise for his almost treasonous words. Perhaps secure in the fact that of anybody Niamh was the least likely to repeat the words.

Niamh slotted an arrow into the string of her bow and walked past Shale, she fired first one, and then two arrows into the centre of the target, crushed in amongst his own.

'I know you are good, but what when the target moves?' Shale asked. He moved to her side, 'what if it breathes and feels? With a life, with a family. Shooting a target is not like killing a man!'

Niamh said nothing. Lord Shale had been a young squire in the first Wolder wars, before her birth, he'd seen combat at least, and had ended lives.

'And what if they come closer than a bow will allow. I have taught you well to shoot an arrow, but what if one comes for you with a sword, an axe?'

Niamh's shoulders slumped. She looked to the ground briefly, then up to his face.

'My sweet lady,' he said, 'I cannot bear to send you thus, vulnerable.' He stepped closer again and put a hand on her shoulder, moving up to her cheek to pause and caress. Niamh allowed the intimate gesture, enjoyed the feel of it, but then stepped away from him, taking the hand gently in hers, kissing it and then releasing so that he was no longer touching her skin. She adored Lord Shale, had done since childhood, but he was married and father to two children, his familiarity was not chivalrous.

'I am...' she paused, as ever her words sounding stuttered, 'I am touched by your concern, my Lord – Josynne – but you must desist and trust in my father. He is our Lord and must be obeyed.'

'I am sorry, Princess,' he whispered, and then turned and walked to the edge of the courtyard, his own bow now thrown back onto his back. 'Now...' his voice grew stronger again, 'Now, I am going to throw a sod into the air and I want you to try to hit it as it moves....'

After supper, still distracted by the events of the day, Niamh made her way down the corridor from the grand hall and up into the dusty turret which contained what had survived of her father's library. The collections were uncared for now, since the sacking of the Golden Keep, and far less in number than they had been there. It had been her father's new bride who had requested the books be moved to Anglemarsh, but reading and learning had never been the priorities of King Hansel, and so despite the king moving the books to please his wife, the library had quickly fallen silent; librarians an unnecessary expense. To Niamh, this made the lonely tower a place of relief, of solitude from a busy household. She was not forbidden either, nor ever scolded for vanishing into the dark and dusty rooms. Everybody knew that if the princess were to be absent from court, that was where she would be found.

Niamh ran a hand over the books. Old and dusty, the spines of leather and cloth caused contrasts under her hands. Just over a thousand years of history. That was all this kingdom had, just that. Other lands, like the one from whence Lucius Mangeli hailed could trace their existence back for two, even three thousand years, but the legends had it that Rostelis was the land of the mists, and that the humans had settled there later, sailing overseas from distant lands. The stories went that before then, the land belonged to the fae creatures: dragons and sprites, sylphs, pixies and the little people. Just stories, but stories some believed with a fervour. Even the goddess was said to be of such origins, otherworldly and Fae; that was in part why the old religion was fading, disliked by some. The deity of the enemy. Niamh ran her hand over another shelf full of spines and then selected a volume at random. This she took to an old abandoned desk close to a window so that there was a little of the remaining daylight spilling in, and flicked open.

There was no mention of Lucius Mangeli's artifact within the pages – from Niamh's brief skim reading anyhow, but the tome was still worthy of admiration: page after page of beautiful drawings, interspersed with passages written in a neat but archaic hand. There were the dragons, the most noble of the fae races, followed closely by their almost rivals for the elite position, the elves. Elves were separable into three classes, the book informed Niamh, pale-skins, nightlings, and common. The common elf was the most humanesque, whereas the pale-skins were the most fae, often not speaking any common tongue and more likely to be enrapturing. The nightlings were the darker of soul, who practiced the old magics and were dangerous even to other elves. These creatures could change their shapes, becoming wolf, bear or even boar, if they wished to appear threatening. Niamh paused at the picture, a lurking creature hidden within a briar who had tangled hair, sharp teeth and red eyes. She shuddered, it looked dangerous indeed.

The next page showed an illustration of three giant bear-like beasts, all stood upright and bearing weapons. Bugbears, the caption called them. Niamh thought they looked wise, despite that the caption named them as a violent and feral race.

'You are studying hard, daughter?' a voice came from behind. Niamh glanced up to see her father standing in the doorway. He looked old, tired, and slightly out of breath for the stairs. Her heart soared for him and she smiled and stood, indicating the chair for her father. The old king shook his head and told her to be seated but smiled an indulgent smile as he did so. 'Don't be up too late, sweetheart,' he said, 'you've a long journey on the morrow.'

'Tomorrow?' she croaked out. Of everyone, her father dried up her voice the most.

'Mangeli thinks it wise to move quickly. His presence in our kingdom is likely already noted by his rivals. If they guess why he is here…'

'Father, why is he here? What is this artifact?'

The king raised an eyebrow, likely at hearing her speak so clearly. He paused a moment and then moved more-so into the room, pulling up another chair and seating himself beside her.

'The thing is, nobody quite knows,' he said. 'and until we can get it to work, nobody will. I have heard tell of it before, though. It is said to be the merging of human technology and fae magic, and it is this item which is said to have been the turning point in the final war.'

'Between them and us?'

'Yes, between us and the fae. It was powerful enough to frighten them all away, off the other realms and away from man.'

'How?'

'It is said, that it can summon the very dragons themselves, and thus bind them to the will of the holder.'

'It can do so much?'

'I am sure of it.'

'And you believe the dragon blood is what is required for it to work?'

'I believe it fervently.'

Niamh sighed and shook her head, unsatisfied, but then found a smile for her father.

'You look like your mother when you smile,' he commented, standing suddenly and moving his chair back to the window. 'Go to bed, sweetheart. More will be revealed once the item is retrieved, I am sure.

Chapter 4

The town of Dusksettle was a small walled-in town, more of a village really, which sat quietly at the foot of The Whites. Unlike the bustle of the city, there was little of activity save for the callings of animals and the clanging of farm machinery. As the royal party approached the gates, the armour of the guards gleaming in the corn-scented sunshine, a cry went out and the common folk gathered like a swarm of ants to a dollop of dropped jam. Niamh felt a real smile take her lips as the gates opened and two children – obviously highly honoured, came forth to deliver a spray of wild-flowers and blossom. Laurin sighed and rolled his eyes as Niamh dismounted to greet the children.

'Welcome to Dusksettle, Princess Niamh,' the smaller of the two children said holding out the flowers as the other uncomfortably chewed on the end of her little blond braid.

'On... on behalf of us all, I thank you,' Niamh said. Children, like animals and, occasionally close friends like Shale, were easier to speak to. 'Is there lodging for the royal party?'

'Yes, Milady, the inn is prepared for your ladies, and the tower for you...' the child glanced up shyly at the menfolk and guards, 'others...'

'Thank you,' Niamh smiled, then found a little silver coin in her pouch. 'for you and your... sister?'

The coin vanished like magic and with a brief smile, both girls turned back to the gate and their waiting family.

'You know, that coin will be a half-year worth of income for that family,' Laurin said, when Niamh had pulled herself back up onto her sweaty horse. She decided not to bother answering that one and spurred the horse on.

Inside, the town was hot and dusty for the lack of rain, despite that the nearby mountains were topped with white snow. It was a strange contrast. The party's horses were too numerous for the local stables and so were put to field with the cows which grazed out the back of the walls. This done, the party gathered in the small inn, enough to fill it to bursting. At the table closest the window, Niamh sat with Laurin and his betrothed, Kyran. The younger two girls had already retired for the night.

'Where is the sphere?' Niamh asked of Laurin.

'Lucius took it over to the tower.'

Niamh had not been best pleased to find that Lucius was to be their companion on the journey, but it had been agreed, apparently at another meeting the children had not been privy to, that the sphere must be taken down to the sisters, along with its keeper, to try to persuade the sisters to part with the dragon-blood and there-in remove the need to steal or otherwise remove by force, the vial from the sisters.

'He will stay to guard it?'

'Aye, sister, and me with him. The inn is for the womenfolk...'

Kyran put a hand on his sleeve, 'As prince of the realm I am sure...'

Laurin shook his head, 'I'll remain with the men as Father would do. I am to be king, and so I wish not to be regarded as one of the "womenfolk" if I can help it!' Laurin smiled that smile which reminded Niamh of her father, one she too occasionally held on her features. His blue eyes gleamed and his floppy hair caught the last beams of sunshine coming in the window, glowing almost white for its fairness. Niamh looked down at her calloused hands. She didn't really want to be associated with the soft womenfolk either, no longer a helpless and feckless maid, but a warrior in her own right, especially with her bow on her back, but she had no idea how to word that thought to Laurin.

'All will be well, sister,' Laurin said, misunderstanding her look, 'I will not be very far and we are safe here, walled in… and besides, we do nothing to provoke attack!'

Niamh nodded and lifted her glass of barley-ale, draining it, then stood and nodded to Laurin. 'I will see you on the morrow, brother,' she said.

Laurin stood too and, after briefly kissing the hand of his betrothed and then saying goodnight to the few men who remained in the inn, drinking too much and over-eating of the town's meagre food supply.

Upstairs, there were three rooms, Niamh and Kyran were to share one, whilst the younger two shared the other. Niamh presumed the innkeep himself and his family used the third. The room was quieter but still stank of beer. It was well made up in anticipation of their stay with soft blankets and a bedspread which must have been the innkeeper's best. A jug on the table held wine and there was a plate holding cheese and strange black berries still attached to the green of their stalks. When Niamh put one into her mouth it was firm and very sweet.

'Are they good?' Kyran asked doubtfully. Niamh nodded and offered her the plate. She poured herself a glass of wine too, finding that also to be sweet and ate a sliver of cheese. Kyran poured her own wine and sipped cautiously, then smiled and nodded without forcing conversation. Of all the Queen's daughters, Niamh liked Kyran the best as she knew when to leave Niamh alone to her thoughts. She went to the window and looked out. There were some lights over the wall, where her view gave her sight, like distant torches, but other than that the village was still. Niamh moved back to the dresser and released her hair and began to brush it with the brush from her case.

'Laurin seemed very drunk,' Kyran commented at last, when the silence was so deep it was almost stifling. 'Do you think he is well in the tower?'

'Likely a little sore in the gut, but he will survive.'

'Do you think that...'

A noise from without distracted Niamh and she put up a hand to still her soon to be sister-in-law. 'Hush!' She went to the window and looked out again. 'What the devil?' she murmured, seeing the torches now bobbing closer, more and more of them.

'My lady? What is it...' Kyran asked but as interrupted by a sound outside. Niamh's blood ran cold – she knew well the sound of a Wolder battle cry, ingrained in her memory like a flashbomb. Not again! Surely she could not be this unlucky twice! From over the hill, a party of Woldermen soldiers seemed suddenly to come into clarity in the poor light, marching with weapons drawn and war-cries on their lips. This was no small raiding party, either, but a mass of a hundred or more men, all painted in vivid colours and dressed in the rags of armour which had once been fine. Had word got to them of Laurin's visit? Or did they come for the artifact too? Niamh drew in a long deep breath, using her nose to pull in the oxygen and allow it to escape out of her mouth.

'Go and wake the girls,' Niamh whispered, tying her hair back into something of a tail with her golden thread. Kyran glanced out of the window and let out a little panicked cry.

'No time for panic, go!' Niamh insisted, finishing her hair and putting on her shoes.

Kyran stuck her own feet back into shoes and then ran to the corridor waking the girls. Niamh waited impatiently for them to dress and tie back hair, put on shoes and the like, and then took the youngest one, Jedda's hand, whilst Kyran took Myrtle. Together they crept downstairs to find the innkeeper just cleaning down the surfaces, still apparently oblivious to the noise and light without.

'Is there a cellar?' she demanded, her manners lost in her near-panic, 'a basement?'

'No, milady, we keep the beer out the back here. Why?'

Niamh bit her lip, her heart pounding, 'Because… because I think we are under attack,' she whispered.

'Surely not…'

'Look out of the window…'

The innkeep did so, paling visibly as he realised the truth of it. He nodded at the room behind the bar, 'Ladies, this is the best shelter I can offer, but offer it I do.'

'Thank you,' Niamh whispered and ushered the girls inside, then took her bow in her hand and began the waiting for the door to burst open.

For some twenty minutes, the fight without raged on. Niamh was desperate to go and help, but if she left she knew she'd be leaving her sisters undefended – the innkeeper had spiralled from disbelieving, to indignant and angry and now had moved to pale and shaking, a kitchen knife his only weapon. She, unable to just sit, moved to the door and, with a shaking hand, Pushed it open. The invaders were still over at the other edge of the village, but the scene was chaos. Buildings were burning where fire had been put to thatch, and corpses lay all about on the ground, felled by the blades of the raiding party. Niamh gasped and put a hand to her nose. The stench was unlike anything she had ever before experienced, even in the sacking of Aurvandil so many years earlier: blood, piss, burning flesh and worse. For a moment her stomach contracted, trying to expel her supper, but then settled again albeit somewhat precariously. She forced calm and tried to analyse the situation more thoroughly. The corpses which littered the ground were all clad in the rags of the villagers, mostly men but a handful of womenfolk – likely those who had tried to fight alongside their husbands. All unfamiliar faces; none of her brother's men were in sight.

A shout sounded to the west, and then a cry. Niamh's hand grasped her bow with a movement that she was barely aware of, adrenaline pulling it from her back and placing an arrow in the line before she even registered the intent to do so. The cry was quelled at once though and the noise of the burning houses and baying farm-animals returned to the forefront of Niamh's senses.

'Niamh?' that was Laurin's voice! Niamh spun about to see her brother at the corner of the inn. He was obviously injured, clutching the side of his stomach.

'Laurin! What…'

'No time,' he said.

'Are you injured?'

'Just barely. I'm well – I promise! They have taken most of the women and children over to the other side and most of the men are dead. Our men are holed in the tower but it won't take them long to break through our defences!'

'How?'

'A mage! They have a bloody… a bloody mage with them!'

'A mage?'

'It must be one of the remaining council! I don't know who…' Laurin gasped in another long breath, he seemed sober enough now where only half an hour earlier he'd been fit to drop. '…but it's not safe for the… for the ladies… now.'

'Come with us!'

'I can't! I'd only slow you down, and besides, we're regrouping to try to defend the keep – they are… they're looking for the sphere…'

Niamh's gut seemed to contract to a point of pain. Responsibility was something easily desired but now given she wasn't sure she wanted it.

'Goddess protect you,' she whispered to Laurin.

'And you, sister.'

The word brought with it an odd warmth. Despite how life had changed since her childhood, still the now-accepted family bond felt somewhat alien. Suddenly the words seemed to dry up again and so she nodded curtly and turned back to the door of the inn. Just inside, Myrtle, Kyran and Jedda stood like pale-faced statues. The innkeeper had retreated back upstairs it seemed, out of sight anyhow. Jedda, the littlest one was but twelve, Myrtle older, but couldn't be past fifteen. Kyran, the most sensible was her age or more, but a lord's daughter, ill-adept for battle. Niamh opened her lips to speak but the panic of these lives being in her care was too much, overwhelmingly so, and so of course no words came. She inhaled again, and clutched her bow, then indicated the door.

'Come,' she managed, and then pulled the door open again. Laurin was gone, just a smear of blood on the white wall of the inn to show he'd ever been there. Still, the voices of the raiders were distant enough for safety but they seemed closer than before. Rounding up the villagers who had not perished with a ruthlessly systematic approach. Beside Niamh, Kyran shuddered just as Niamh had the first time, but she did not step away. The younger two crowded about, looking out.

Niamh paused at the door, pondering. The voices all seemed to drift in from the west of the village, and the raiders had come from that direction. If that was so, and they'd not posted watchers about the walls, she might be able to lead the girls out through the east. There were multiple breaks in the wall there from floods the previous year which had never been replaced, and woods on the other side which might lend some cover for escape. The path that was seemed clear enough too, and there were not so many bodies, especially around behind the bakery. They would have to be quiet as mice though; if the raiding party heard them, that would be the end of it all. The only other option was to make a break for it through the main gate and hope that the raiders either didn't notice them, or wouldn't care for the escape of a handful of girls. That seemed highly unlikely though, especially if they realised who she was.

Niamh wet her lips again, and then stiffened as another cry came from the west side of the village, a woman's scream and then a horrendous silence. The sound decided her, they had little time left to make an escape. The path was somewhat obscured by an alleyway which ran between two houses behind the bakery. Before them was the body of the village priest, but little else. The worst part would be the run to the bakery where they would be out in the open for a few moments. Niamh lifted her bow again and then stepped away from the door.

'Come,' she said again, and despite the fear in their eyes, and the tears on little Jedda's face, the ladies obeyed. It seemed a lifetime passed as they ran as lightly as they could from the inn to the wall of the bakery. Niamh's heart thudded, making her feel a little hollow, her arm was poised with her bow, ready to face disaster. No disaster occurred though and they were stood with their backs to the bakery wall, all panting with fear rather than exertion. At Niamh's feet, the little bellflowers still bobbed, some with broken little heads from her feet. For a moment she concentrated on them, trying to keep herself calm, but then she looked up. Jedda had stopped crying but her skin was almost as grey as the clouds which gathered above. Kyran looked a little heartier, her eyes gleaming and wide but her lips set. Myrtle, the middle one chewed on a blond braid, her chest heaving and her gown dirty about her feet from the dust they had churned up. Niamh tried a reassuring smile and indicated the houses. Kyran nodded.

From behind came another scream and then the wail of a baby. Niamh stiffened again and gripped tighter to her bow. Jedda began to cry again, but the tears were silent, little rivers down her already sticky face. Niamh ushered the girls before her, taking up the rear so that if the raiders did come, they'd have her to deal with before the children. Still, they arrived without mishap at the wall, somehow, and there was a large hole where the floods had washed away some of the stones.

'Go,' Niamh hissed, indicating the broken stones. The girls clambered through but Niamh did not follow. The rough stone of the wall was easily climbable, made more so by the scattered stonework and ragged broken edge of the wall. The wall itself was on a gentle slope, so that where they stood it was no more than perhaps 6 foot, but further around it would give a good vantage point. Niamh had done what was asked of her, she'd led the girls to the woods, but could she really go and leave her brother to his probable death? It didn't sit right at all.

Kyran's head poked back through the gaping hole, her eyes questioning. 'Princess?'

'Take the girls to the woods,' Niamh said.

'Alone?'

'Yes. Find help!'

'What about you?'

Niamh indicated up the wall, then glanced back to Kyran. 'I'll get Laurin,' she said, hoping that the girl would not argue overlong, especially in the face of her betrothed's likely capture, possible death at the hands of the heathen invasion. Kyran nodded and slipped back through.

The stones were rough on Niamh's hands as she climbed, her bow around her neck, and in some places so crumbly that she feared she might tumble back down. She made it though, somehow, and from above, despite that her position thrust her up to a place where she could be seen, Niamh felt infinitely more relaxed to have a good vantage point. To the north she could see little as the houses still stood taller than the height of the wall, but to the other sides she had a good view of what was unfolding. Behind her, the girls were fleeing into the woods, hands clasped together as they ran. They'd be safe now, somehow Niamh just knew. The south and south-east side of the bailey which contained the village was swarming with Wolderman. The villagers, however, didn't seem to have all been slaughtered, but most were being held in something of a makeshift pen where the centre of the village used to be. From where she knelt, lying low on the crumbling brick, Niamh could not see her brother but there seemed to be a battalion of his remaining men regrouping on the path which led to the tower where the sphere and Lucian Mangeli were housed. Laurin was likely close-by then.

Niamh's attention was stolen briefly from the tower, by a blue flash in the distance, right by the gate. Her heart pounded, thinking for a moment that the girls had been captured, but then realising that no, it was the gate itself, encompassed in a strange dark blue flame. The mage Laurin had warned of! Niamh lifted her bow from about her neck and shimmied forward about a quarter of a turn. The wall was higher there, and so she was more conspicuous despite that odd shrubs and plants grew up from the stony bricks to give her some camouflage. From this new angle, though, she could see the mage more clearly. Male, weren't they all? Tall and lithe, but hooded so that little more of him could be seen. He was moving slowly about the walls, and seemed to be setting that odd fire as a tail when he moved. Creating a barrier about the walls, Niamh suddenly realised. If the circle closed, there would be no escape for any of them and poor Laurin and his men, as well as the villagers and now herself would be left in the hands of this band of thugs. Niamh watched the slow methodological movements of the mage as he moved closer. One of his hands was on the wall and the other, the other was clutching something about his neck. A bottle, most likely, she'd seen that done before and it seemed an easy solution to the problem of needing water close by.

Either way, Niamh knew that she couldn't allow this figure to complete his spell, to trap them inside. She slid an arrow into position and, moving carefully that she was not seen whilst simultaneously praying to the goddess that the man would not look up, she pulled the bowstring so that it was taut, aimed, and let loose the arrow. Her heart took up thudding again, she'd never before in her life fired an arrow at anything more sentient than a rabbit or grouse. A thousand emotions pulled free, triumph, anguish, remorse, but amongst them was no seed of doubt – that arrow would meet its target. Then, at the last millisecond, the mage seemed to sense his incoming demise and looked up. Niamh couldn't breathe. Her whole body seemed to turn to jelly as the man balked, swerved his body backwards, and took the arrow not to his heart, but to his shoulder. Already another arrow was in the string, but Niamh didn't let it loose. Her lips dropped open and her breath left her body in an almost primal cry of anguish. In moving thus, to dodge her arrow, the figure below had knocked back his hood revealing his face. He was thinner than she remembered, just a little, and held a long scar from his eye to ear on the right side of his face. His eyes were dark, his lips pressed, and yet still, Niamh would have known that face anywhere. She barely realised the pain as something hit her from behind, somebody else's arrow finding a purchase in her hip, as her eyes drank in the ebon and blue locks, the dark eyes and creasing brow of Helligan Darkfire. Another arrow hit her, this time impaling her shoulder and knocking her forwards from her perch on the wall, down to the hard earth some ten foot below. More pain, enough to make her scream aloud, and then the welcomed blackness of the goddess's kiss: oblivion.

Niamh awoke in a haze of fever and pain. She was laid in a cart, blankets over her and the juddering of wheels making her body ache and scream where the arrows had pierced her flesh. The sky above was blue, the sun bright, but then a blink and it was dark again. Somebody put a cup to her lips, then bread soaked in milk; she managed to chew but then the hazy mists came back down again. Twice more she awoke thus, a journey of what must have been several days at least, for the turning of the hours. Then there was stillness, a damp cloth to her head and murmured tones. A male voice, concerned, and then the sheer agony of being lifted, moved. Niamh screamed aloud, clutching at her wounds but then a foul taste came to her lips and all was still again. The next time she awoke, everything seemed quieter, dulled. She was no longer in the cart but laid down in a soft bed with pillows of feather underneath her cheek. Her limbs felt heavy, so heavy, and her head thudded.

She tried to roll over and then moaned again at the pain in her hip.

'Be careful, there,' the voice came from across the room, male, aged and deep, almost a croak, 'you don't want to start yersel bleedin again.'

Niamh glanced across the room. It was dark and only a single candle burned on the table so the figure was difficult to really see. A male crone of sorts, ragged gown and loose hair under a cap. He must have been eighty or more.

'Who are you? Where am I?'

'You are safe now, although was touch n go for a while... missed yer vitals.'

'Are you a... physician?'

The old man chuckled, a deep throaty laugh, 'aye, maybe, Milady, maybe that's what you'd be callin me.'

Niamh breathed again.

'Has... has my father been informed?'

'Yer father? Now, why would we be talkin to im?'

Niamh fell to silence, the truth slowly dawning, she wasn't rescued, she was a prisoner, a prisoner of the Woldermen.

Chapter 5

Niamh lay still on the bed listening to the sounds of the birds outside chirping. Free to fly away in a way that Niamh envied. Her bandages had just been changed for a second time by the strange old man, and her skin was sticky with some kind of tree-sap that had been applied to the wounds. Since she'd awoken, three weeks prior, she'd seen nobody but the old man and a woman who was apparently just as ancient, his wife, presumably. The old woman was friendlier than her husband, but neither would answer Niamh's questions as to where she was, why she'd been taken.

The room was very basic in furnishing. The bed Niamh lay on was lined with furs, as was the floor, where it was not bare with just its straw. There was no wardrobe in the room, no cupboard or washstand. Every morning, Niamh's water was brought in a plain bowl, a bar of soft fragrant soap with it. After the sixth day, she'd been allowed to stand, and to dress herself again in her now ragged gown. She was still a prisoner though, that much was without doubt. There were bars at her window and the door was ever locked tight with a key carried only by the old man who tended her.

At first, the pain of her arrow wound was enough to keep Niamh to her bed, but as it began to heal, she'd found herself more restless and angrier.

After a few minutes, the door opened again and an old lady entered with a bowl of hot porridge. Niamh still did not know either of her captor's names, and so to her they were just the old man and the old woman.

'Ere, got ye yer breakfast, milady.'

'Thank you. Where am I?' it was the same question she asked over and over.

'Never ye mind that, just eat up milady, need to get you strong!'

'I know I travelled for days! Tell me to whence?'

'Sorry, can't say.'

'Please?' she said, 'I am afraid. How long will you keep me?'

'Don't rightly know, yer 'ighness,' the old lady said, then looked up at her husband where he stood guard at the door.

'Until we receive word you're to be moved,' he added. 'You're a guest 'ere, Princess.'

'I am no guest, I am a prisoner…'

'A guest, a guest of Lord Helligan,' The old lady said.

'*Lord* Helligan?'

'Commander of the rebels and leader of the free men.'

Niamh sat back down on the bed, her mind whirled, so many questions! How had Helligan become such? Had he always been with the Woldermen? Was he the one responsible of the sacking of the Golden Keep? If so, why had his own men apparently killed him? She glanced back up at the couple who dithered in the doorway.

'I demand an audience with Lord Helligan then,' she said.

'Fraid not…'

'No, no more excuses! Give him this message, that I demand to see him!'

The old man raised an eyebrow and then looked to his wife again, she pressed her lips. Niamh stood as tall as she could with her injury and practiced her royal glower.

'If you please, milady,' the old man finally said, and then both departed leaving Niamh to her honey-laced porridge.

The light outside was bright to the point of uncomfortable after days upon days of incarceration. Niamh squinted against it, hunched slightly, as she was led from the house where she'd been kept captive behind closed shutters and out into the marshes. Her feet, bare of shoes – which had never rematerialized after her abduction – were tender against the stony paths, leading Niamh to favour the muddier banks next to them. In time the paths themselves seemed to vanish and Niamh had to trust in the old man leading her to know the way through. The walk did not take very long though, out away from the tiny cottage which seemed to stand isolated, and into the centre of the deep thick mires; moving only as she was led by her captors for fear of stumbling and falling into a bog or mire. The terrain was dangerous too, more so than would allow Niamh to make a run for home, or anywhere else without the risk of falling in and drowning.

The small keep was well-hidden for a house it's size, right out past the point where any man could have been believed to exist. Behind it were row after row of canvas houses and mud huts, a semi-permanent resting place for the Wolder army. Niamh allowed her eyes to run over this encampment, right on the edge of the marshland but half-buried by forests beyond. She struggled to remember her geography, to place where the marshes met the trees thus, but she could not recall any such place.

'Come,' the old man said, taking her elbow 'him you seek lies within.'

Niamh nodded, biting at her lip, and then allowed herself to be led through a stone arch into the courtyard of the keep. There was no gate but with such a path to get there, she doubted one would be needed. The old man led her by the elbow to a wooden door but rather than knock, he merely pushed it open and bundled her into the bare hallways within.

The walls were obviously old, as unknown to her as the odd terrain without. Had there always been a small castle here? She didn't think so, and yet it was obviously very old. The walls were panelled wood and rugged stone, the floors straw over slate. Niamh paused to inhale some more oxygen, and then allowed her captor to lead her on, through the hallway, under an arch, and then into a large airy chamber where finally she came face to face with Helligan.

Niamh's eyes filled with water but she blinked it away. Helligan looked just as she remembered him, aside from the scar on his face. His hair was long, mainly black but shot through with blue here and there, braided in places too, as the Woldermen were wont to do. He was dressed in black leather armour over a white shirt and his clothing and hair were noticeably cleaner than most of the Woldermen. His boots too were clean, if worn, and the leather looked soft and supple. Niamh allowed her eyes to drink him in for a long moment before she moved them up to his face. The same bright blue eyes, the same high cheekbones, albeit now with scar. His face looked gentle, and that was the worst of it. Niamh set her lip. After weeks of being incarcerated, dressed in the same unwashed gown, she knew she did not smell or look anything like acceptable. Her long hair was loose and knotted, her gown was filthy and creased. Still, despite it all, she had the manner of a princess as she squared her shoulders and met his eye.

'My lady,' Helligan said.

Niamh held his eye. She refused to name him Lord, he was no lord in her father's court! … *but once had been*, a little voice at the back of her mind tried to whisper. Niamh ignored it.

'You have requested… no, *demanded* an audience with myself and my advisors…' Helligan said, 'here, it is granted.'

Niamh's eyes flit about the room. There were five of them in total, the unwashed lords, the wild men's clan leaders. Niamh took in each one with distaste; two older men, one fat and with a big beard, short and balding on top. Sat next to the fat one was a mousey, smaller man, his eyes were bright and seemed to take in everything, a scratched sword lay on the floor beside him but his obvious weapon of choice was the axe hanging at his hip. The other two men were younger, one of them seemed almost friendly, smiling, and the other was his opposite, dark of hair and darker of glower. She suddenly felt too shy to speak, her words drying up.

Helligan sat back in his chair, his eyes examining her.

'Speak!' one of the older men, the slimmer of the two, ordered. He seemed perplexed at her silence.

'That's the idiot, not sure she can speak,' the fat one chuckled.

Niamh closed her eyes, blocking them all out. How was it suddenly so difficult again? She sucked in a deep breath and a tear spilled onto her cheek.

'You spoke well enough to old Hogg,' Helligan's voice snapped her out of her trance, 'but not to me, now that you have my attention?'

'I think she just wanted you to look at her,' the fairer of the younger men said, 'these nobles – perhaps she thinks you'll bow before her like the young fops of her father's court do...'

'Niamh,' Helligan's voice again, ignoring his friends, 'Lady Niamh... I remember you... you spoke to me before, if I recall? You warned me to the men flanking us, back when we met last?'

The memories those words stirred caused a sudden pain in Niamh's guts. All the betrayal, the pain of having idolised somebody so obviously unworthy. Unable to find words, she used the element of surprised to dart forward, murderous intent firing her body. Her hand gripped the hilt of the fat Wolderman's sword before any could leap upon her. In a fury, she lifted up the heavy sword in both of her hands. She could barely believe the weight of the savage instrument, and to think this was usually wielded in one hand! Still, she managed to raise it up over her head, though, and there she held it, tendons aching already with the strain.

Some of the men chuckled, especially the mousy looking one, but Helligan eyed her with seriousness and the other younger man – the darker one – stood, ready to move should she try anything.

'What do you suppose you are going to do with that?' Helligan asked in that soft, calm tone of his. He was obviously not perturbed by her actions, 'run me down? Spill my guts onto the floor before all of my brethren here?'

It might have been the slight mockery in his tone, perhaps the laughter of his comrades, but a bright crimson fury came down over Niamh's senses. She hissed out a breath and then, with all the might she had, she drew the blade down towards Helligan. For half a moment, surprise showed on his placid features, but then he put up a hand to his amulet, and another to the blade of the sword. Such a blade, flung even with Niamh's meagre strength should still have done damage to Helligan's hand, perhaps severing a thumb and slicing a palm. For a moment Niamh felt triumph, but then it dissipated as no blood fell. Helligan's eyes turned dark and with gritted teeth, he squeezed. Then the blade began to freeze. The effect started by the tip, close by where his hand gripped it. The little particles of ice seemed to form initially atop the steel before invading its core. A crackling noise came to Niamh's ear as the blade slowly turned white, and then the crossguard. As the ice reached her fingers where still she gripped the hilt, a strange sensation began, a sensation so very cold that it burned. She cried out in pain and dropped the sword to cradle her injured hand. As it fell, the sword shattered, a million tiny shards of ice which fragmented and scattered all about her feet. Tears of pain swam but Niamh pushed them back, nursing her injured hand, and glaring at Helligan through dark eyes.

'Princess,' Helligan said, 'I have no mind to be the type of man who purposely causes injury or pain to any, let alone a young lady such as yourself, but do not believe even for a moment that I will balk to defend myself from an attack – even from you!'

Niamh wet her lips and pulled in a deep breath, then spoke. 'You betrayed my father!'

'Lo! The bitch does speak then?' Helligan's companion laughed but Helligan silenced him by lifting a hand slightly, palm up.

'What did you say?' he asked.

'You…' she sucked in a deep breath and suddenly her voice was stronger, more confident, 'You betrayed my father and all that is good – coward! Dog!'

The room rang with a shocked silence. Niamh herself was shocked at the words which had escaped her lips and retreated somewhat into herself again. Helligan's lips twitched once and then twice, but he said nothing.

'Lady Niamh,' the older man took up her attention, 'we have discussed at length your fate and despite that you attempted to end the life of our commander… now twice… it has been decided that you should be allowed to walk free,' he glanced over at Helligan's silent form as he spoke, giving Niamh the impression that Helligan had laid down this particular ruling. Her eyes moved to the bandage apparent under his jerkin, the result of her arrow. His mercy in the light of his injury was unexpected in a man of his type.

'We have no spare supplies to offer you though, nor a guide to take you back home or to your brother,' the Wolderman was still speaking.

'Laurin lives?'

'He does, he evaded capture.'

'I must get to him!'

'You might, but if you wish for escort from us, you will need to pay just as everybody else does.'

Niamh glanced down over her torn clothing. Nothing remained, not even a finger-ring. Hopelessly, she looked back up.

'We can give you work,' the aged Wolderman added. Still Helligan was silent, allowing his companion to speak, 'and you can earn the money to pay for a guide.'

'Yes.'

'Very well,' the man walked to the corner and picked up an old broom which had been discarded there. This he handed to Niamh. 'I am in need of a housekeeper,' he added. 'Kilm here's wife does what she can but this is a big house…'

Niamh stared long at the splintery old brush, but then reached out a shaking hand and took it.

'You are free to leave at any time,' Helligan finally spoke, 'your debt will be settled in three days, and then somebody will take you home… so long as you behave and do not make any more attempts at mischief or we will be forced to return you to captivity…'

Niamh inclined her head, humbled.

'Start with the courtyard,' the old man spoke again, 'it's dark so take a lantern…'

The courtyard outside of the cottage was cold and bathed in a darkness which the little lantern Niamh had been given barely brought a glimmer to. The wind had taken up slightly too, a chill in the air which made Niamh shiver as it touched the thin cloth of her gown. She grit her teeth, at least she was being allowed to work for her freedom. From the minute she'd seen Helligan still lived, Niamh had expected death for her attempt on his life. Above her a bird crowed, some sort of corvid for the old gnarled sound, and then a fluttering as it moved from one tree to another in the darkness. The old courtyard was eerie, and Niamh was suddenly reminded of a hundred ghost stories Maggie had used to tell of the wild-lands. Skeletal wraiths, lost souls, will-o-the-wisps out on the marshland. The mighty dragons, and lithe elven folk, before they left her world for another, eons ago. The marshlands too frightened Niamh, vast peaty bogs which could swallow a grown man whole, navigated only by the Woldermen, who knew the intimate secrets of their hidden paths and safe routes.

The door behind Niamh opened, letting out a scent of roasting boar, and a light which lit up the darkened path she was trying to sweep. Footsteps came through and then the door closed again, cutting off the sounds of the voices within, the smells of that delicious dinner she could not afford to partake in.

Niamh continued her sweeping, trying not to glance up as Helligan sat himself down on the empty barrel which stood beside the door. Her eyes were cast down and her hands trembled slightly where she gripped the rough, worn, handle of the sweeping brush. The work had been given to her to demean her, she knew that, but at least the splintery old broom was something solid to hold on to.

Helligan was quiet a moment, but his eyes burned her back so that she knew without looking that he was watching her. At last he spoke. 'I did betray your father, it's true.'

Still Niamh did not turn, did not give an inch, but had he been watching her hands he might have noticed the broom tremble again.

'Everybody at court considers your father such a good king, such a good man,' he said, 'he is kind to his subjects, he treats his inferiors with kindness, house his bastards... even the idiot...'

Niamh pressed her lips tightly together to hear his voice utter that long-forgotten word.

'Such a kind man, so benevolent. You do realise it's all illusion, don't you?'

Niamh's fingers gripped the broom tightly enough to make her knuckles turn white. She did not turn, still, but her shoulders became rigid, her lips pressed tightly closed about a mouth which suddenly seemed too dry.

'...or mayhap you don't,' he allowed. 'I suppose to his children too, your father is given the status of a good man – that kind and generous patriarch. It's easy to be blind to the faults of a loved one, isn't it?'

Helligan paused as though expecting some reply. Niamh gave him none but she was aware that she had stopped sweeping, stationery as he spoke, with the broom held tightly in her pressed fingers.

'They used to call you an idiot, but you are not that,' Helligan said, his tone softening, 'not by far, I think. None-the-less, a quiet maid like yourself, unobserved, unnoticed, you must be able to eavesdrop well?'

Niamh nodded, ever so slightly.

'Good. Then I want you to do something for me – call it recompense for the arrow…'

The traitor expected a boon from her? The cheek of it almost moved Niamh to speaking but she pulled it back and made a few motions with the sweeping brush.

'It is not a great boon, and it is more for you, in a manner, than for me,' Helligan continued, 'What I want you to do is this: Listen in darkened corridors, listen at doors, secret yourself during late-night meetings which don't appear on your father's list of appointments. Arm yourself with knowledge, Lady Niamh. Open your mind to the idea that all is not as it seems, and open your ears and eyes too.'

Niamh glanced at him from the side of her eye but she could not really see him well through the darkness.

'You will, if you do as I say, see the truth for yourself – a truth you might not wish to know, but one you need to know. Then, when you know it, when you have witnessed some of what I have witnessed, then cast your thoughts back to your old friend Helligan, whose head will probably by then hang from the gate, bird-pecked and rotten, and remember that we fought this fight knowing full-well that we likely will not win it… for justice, to fight tyranny.'

Niamh's lips parted, almost driven to speak in her confused frustration, but Helligan gave her no time to form words. Already he'd stood and opened the door.

'It matters not to me if I live or die, so long as I leave behind me those who will continue to fight. Don't ask me why, as it is not something I do easily or often, but I trust you. I ask you not to trust me in return, but to explore for yourself, and use that knowledge you discover as you see fit.'

Niamh still did not turn, but, almost unrealising, she inclined her head slightly.

'Good. That is all I ask. I bid you goodnight. Don't stay up too late, the floor will wait until tomorrow to be swept.'

Another pause and then the door behind Niamh opened and then clattered closed. Finally, she turned about to where he'd been stood, to view nothing but the darkened courtyard.

'Goodnight Helligan,' she whispered.

On the other side of the door, Helligan stood quietly. A smile almost touched his features as Niamh spoke his name. He paused a moment longer, but the girl had returned to sweeping so he stalked back up the stairs. The girl was sensible enough and he'd insisted they keep her there in order to try to make her see the truth before she went home. It was going to be a long three days.

Chapter 6

The turning of dusk to full darkness finally caused Niamh to pause, the settling of the cool night air on her shoulders enough to make her almost tremble with cold and the darkness making her chore near on impossible. She remained outside for as long as possible though, feeling shy and reluctant to return to the house and there possibly have to make conversation again. Finally though, she crept back in and laid the broom against the wall. The fire was now roaring, inside, giving off a fair heat, whilst filling the room with the scent of burning green wood — no coal fires for men of this ilk. The crackle and pop of it was soothing though. Beside the settle was a soft grey house-kretch, purring its gentle soothing purr, content in the heat of the fire. Niamh moved to pet the silky fur of its ears for a moment before going to the old wooden bench by the fireplace and settling herself down. There were voices beyond, in the other rooms but this little area at least was deserted. Niamh lay down and closed her eyes. It was warm, and although the bench was hard, it held a thin cushion which was enough to give a little comfort. The noises beyond began to blur, blending in with the crackle and pop of the fire, the purr of the kretch.

Niamh awoke the following morning to find a richly lined fur cloak draped over her form, wolf-skin lined by the feel of it, A plate of food lay on the floor beside her, two chuck legs, bread and butter and a glass of milk. She stretched and sat up, allowing the cloak to fall and pool on the floor whilst she examined the food and allowed her thoughts to settle. The milk she took up gratefully, enjoying the smooth coldness of it on lips which were dehydrated for lack of anything to drink overnight. Once the milk was done with, Niamh ate the bread and butter but wrapped the chuck legs in a handkerchief and slipped them down the back of the coal scuttle for later. She'd never been a hearty eater and it felt better to know there was supper waiting later, than try to work herself up to going into the dining hall when it was full of Wolder. She waited then, for the noise of breakfast to begin and then to die down, and then made her way towards the kitchens, hoping that the men would all be about their business. Likely there would be dishes to clean and her own wooden platter needed to be placed amongst them. At the door though, she paused. There was already somebody at work in the kitchens. A tall, thin woman with sharp eyes and wiry greying hair. She wore a pinny and was vigorously kneading dough. Niamh shuffled her feet together as the woman looked up.

'Aha, you are awake?' her voice was deep and rich, entirely unsuited to her appearance. 'I was told I was to have help today! How do I address ya? Prin'cess? Mi'lady?'

'Just, Niamh is fine,' Niamh whispered.

'Niamh, funny name... alright Niamh, well if you could get the bowls washed and the table cleared I'll give this bread a bit more of a going over and make a start on making the beds...'

'I... what is... your name?'

'Just call me Missis Kilm,' the woman smiled, 'This is my house and you are a welcome distraction from all these great oafs my husband has brought in!'

Niamh's lips pulled into a smile, she liked this woman already.

Niamh worked all day under Missis Kilm's dictation. Together they made beds, swept floors, milked the cows and then made butter and skimmed cream from the milk. Niamh was sent out to pick Jummel berries and when she returned Mrs Kilm showed her how to make pastry, how to blanch the berries and to remove maggles – the tiny worms which feasted on the fruits from within.

'Now, add yer honey to the mix,' she instructed, standing over Niamh, 'There, that's 'im, good! Now pour yer mixture into the pie crust.'

Niamh did as she was told, pouring the sweetly crisp stewed fruits into the pastry and then placing the last strips of pastry over the top in a lattice. Once set, the pie went into the great stone oven on one of the slabs to bake.

'There an I think we're done for the day,' the old woman smiled. 'Dinner is bubbling away, the pie is baking, the house is clean…'

Niamh nodded but was interrupted from having to try to reply by the door behind opening and one of the Wolder entering.

'Something smells god!' he grinned, then took up the lady for a kiss. Kilm then? Maybe? Probably? Niamh averted her eyes, especially as the old lady giggled like a girl at the newcomer's over amorous embrace. She pulled away though, and indicated Niamh.

'Prin'cess gone made us a pie,' she said, smiling at Niamh, 'quite the little bakeress she is!'

Kilm's eyes grazed over Niamh but she did not hold his attention long and as he and his wife moved to mutter amongst themselves, Niamh took the opportunity to sneak away. With her chores complete until after supper, she had a few moments to herself. First, she went to the well and drew out a pail of water to wash her face and hands. Her hair felt grimy but there was little she could do about that other than to dunk her head into the icy water – something she did not much like the idea of. Instead, she dried herself quickly on a rag she'd appropriated from the kitchen and then made her way back inside.

The smell of the hot stew which was being served in the dining hall was almost enough to make Niamh dare to go and join the menfolk, her stomach growling almost painfully, but already there was enough chatter and clamour coming from that direction to stay her. She moved to where she'd stashed her food and retrieved it, opening up the handkerchief and laying the food out on her lap.

'I wouldn't eat that, if I were you…' Helligan's voice drifted in from the doorway. 'Chuck meat goes bad fast and it's been by the fire all day so will be warm and full of the beginnings of rot.'

Niamh looked down at the meat. It did not look bad but she'd never had to judge food's freshness before.

'Come, come and have a good hot supper. That is not enough to sustain a working woman, anyhow.'

Niamh pressed her lips, tempted, but then shook her head, wrapping her spoiled meat back up and putting it down beside her.

'My lady, you have to eat!' Helligan said, stepping closer.

'I am well…'

'You are not! I won't have you starve under my roof you stubborn little creature – come on!' Niamh gasped as he reached in and gripped her wrist in his hand.

'Stop! Let me go!' she murmured but Helligan was having none of it. He pulled her to her feet, his grip on her not painful, but too firm to escape.

'No, I'll not have you starve yourself on my watch because you're too timid to eat in front of the men. Come on…' he hissed, pulling her with him towards the dining hall. Niamh marched on at his command, her lips pressed angrily but her growling stomach helping to command her. Inside the hall, all eyes looked up as Helligan led Niamh in, holding tight to her wrist.

'Sit,' he snapped. She did so, finding a space at the end of the bench, uncomfortably close to one of the bigger of the Wolder men. Helligan released her there but, still seeming somewhat annoyed, banged a bowl down in front of her, scooped out a ladleful of stew and then roughly tore a chunk of bread which he placed down beside the bowl. 'Eat!' he commanded.

Niamh's hands shook but she kept her eyes downcast, afraid to look up into the faces of the men about the table. Helligan stood still behind her, watching her. She nodded, wet her lips and then lifted the bread and dipped it in the stew. Nobody had given her a fork or spoon so she used the crusty bread, still hot from the oven, to scoop up the food and put it to her mouth. After the first mouthful was swallowed, Helligan moved to the other side of the table and sat down in front of his own bowl. There was food already half-eaten before him, leading Niamh to conclude he'd noticed her absence halfway through eating and had come to find her with a purpose. She took in a long, deep breath, and then scooped another mouthful of stew and began to eat.

After the stew was consumed, old Mrs Kilm vanished and returned with the now golden, crusty pie.

'Oh by the goddess!' one of the men exclaimed, 'is that sweet-pie?'

'It is! Baked for ye by the hand of a prin'cess…'

Niamh wished the floor would open up and swallow her as once more all eyes, Helligan's included, fell to her. She could find no words to explain that she'd only followed the other woman's instructions, that she'd never baked before in her life, and so she simply remained silent, glancing to the pie and then back to Helligan.

'Then we are privileged indeed,' Helligan finally said, 'Come, let us enjoy!'

The pie was good, sweeter almost than some of the honey pastries which were stock foods back in Anglemarsh and the Golden Keep before it. Niamh's piece was small but proved too rich for her, especially topped with milk-cream and yet more honey. She just about managed half, and as she pushed the plate aside was almost brought to laughing by the speed at which it was whisked away by her table-neighbour.

'Well, you weren't eating it,' he shrugged, scraping the wooden bowl with his spoon.

'You are welcome,' she managed, pulling a guffaw from another of the men across the table. Her eye caught Helligan's and he too was smiling. Niamh's heart thudded, it was rare indeed to see comradery like this at home. Everybody smiling, laughing amongst themselves, bickering... it was oddly comforting.

Later, as the night settled on the house, Niamh and Helligan moved from the dining hall back into the small room where she'd slept the night before. Helligan had with him a bottle of fine honey-wine, likely pilfered for it was a very good blend. He poured a goblet for himself and then handed her one too. Niamh drank, the sweetly thick liquid a reminder of home. She paused, drank another mouthful and then looked over at Helligan. He was already on route to intoxication, having indulged over supper of three cups of wine already. He was not boorish though, not like some of her father's men got, just thoughtful, relaxed.

'Thank you,' she whispered, nodding to the cup. He'd not shared any of this bottle with any of the others and so she guessed it to be of his own private stash.

'You are very welcome, Princess. A taste of home, somewhat?'

Niamh paused, inwardly cursing herself for having invited conversation. 'Yes.'

'You will be there again soon enough.'

'Thank you.'

Helligan lifted the bottle again, refilling her goblet before his own. Still the manners of a courtier, which almost saddened her. Her father's man, but her father's betrayer.

From the corner of her eye she saw the little grey kretch slip in through the door, pause and survey the room with yellow eyes. She smiled and clucked at it, making it come and rub against her leg. The little animal reminded her not just of home, but of the Golden Keep, when that had been home – she'd had a kretch of her own there, and it had given birth to a litter of kretchlets under her bed shortly before the Wolder attack. Niamh wondered suddenly what had happened to those poor beasts, had they been slain or had they turned feral? Did a little army of Feral Ketch still roam the lands, maybe? Most likely not, most likely they'd just died. Helligan's eye caught hers again, though, pulling her back into the present, he smiled then glanced down at the little furry body which had left Niamh to rub at his legs. The silence pulled. Usually silence was a place of comfort for Niamh, but suddenly it seemed less so, suddenly she felt uncomfortable. Helligan made no pains to alleviate atmosphere, either, not forcing her to speak. He seemed more interested in the kretch, and then when it slowly sauntered off in the direction of the kitchen, he turned to the flames of the fire, watching as they twisted and turned. He was closer to the fireplace than she, his comfortable, padded chair pulled up to the mantle. As Niamh watched, his hand strayed down and touched the edge of the fireplace and there began a small line of blue, emanating from his fingers to dance with the natural orange flame. Helligan the mage, so adept with his use of magic that he played with the flames for ought but entertainment. He'd had so much promise, such gifts.

'Why did you do it?' the question that burned deep within Niamh pulled free, aided perhaps by the wine she more gulped than sipped.

'Hmm?' Helligan looked up from his distraction, to catch her eye. His lips pulled into a smile but Niamh noticed for the first time that the smile did not echo in his eyes. Now that the wine was upon him, his eyes shone with worry, tiredness. It made him softer somehow, easier to talk to.

'Why… why betray us?'

Helligan took another swallow of his honey wine before answering, and then poured some more into Niamh's glass. She said nothing, not declining the drink – it was fine wine indeed and the glass and a half she'd already drunk was helping her to speak more easily. Helligan sipped again, and then held her eye squarely.

'The thing you must understand is that I never was your father's man. Above and before your father's authority, came that of the mage council and the council ever was its own authority. When your father decreed that I and my brothers take our wild magics to court I resisted, as did many of my brothers. We wanted no part of it and it was only through threats that your father had us with him at all.'

'Why resist?'

'Because your father sought to command us, to use us. That is why he summoned us to court but mages are not tools to be used and the magics we use are still wild. To be Wolder at court too... even before the war, your father was no friend to us, it was a daunting prospect.'

'You are Wolder... were, before?'

'All mages are... were. The wild magics we command are gifts from the old gods, given to their own people. You will never meet a mage who does not have the blood of the free-men in his veins... some say we are the last descendants of the fae themselves.'

'I didn't know.'

'And now you do. In the end, I went though, as I was ordered and there I rose in your father's affections – mainly because I was so powerful... in the end I found myself holding back, hiding what I could do from him for fear of how he would use me.'

Niamh remained motionless, listening.

'As I said to you last night, your father is not the kindly, benevolent man he would like the world to see. Some of what we were ordered to do was abhorrent – deeds I will not lightly tell of to a young lady like yourself.

'No, you wish me to know it, so tell me…' Niamh caught herself and flushed, glancing down.

Helligan paused, 'My Lady, I…'

'How am I to understand your stance if you withhold your motivations?'

'That is a fair argument. So be it. Your father… your father wanted me to use my magic to torture people. He wanted me – us – to become a feared means of interrogation and execution. One of my brothers he forced to roast a man alive, a common man, before his family. He was suspected of treason, you see, but I still maintain his innocence… another time he ordered me to inflict the illusion of pain on a prisoner, to torture him without breaking his body. I refused, despite your father's threats, and so he ordered one of my brothers to do it – he was not so strong.'

'You speak untruths,' Niamh's eyes were wet, her chest aching.'

'What reason do I have to lie to you, my lady?'

Niamh had no reply so looked down at her hands.

'I was ready to leave anyway, when the attack came, my brothers too. My intention in entering those tunnels was escape – not just from the attack, but from your father too. I wanted to just vanish, disappear and become another lost one in a burning city, but then I saw you in the tunnels. No matter if you were commoner or princess, I could not just leave a frightened maiden to die and so I decided to help you to safety first. You know what came of that.'

'And still, these Wolder nearly killed you…'

'They saw me as one of the king's men and so they attacked. When they saw my magic, Alfric and his band realised what I was, and so they sought to fell me without taking my life. They succeeded and took me to their home to be healed by their elder. There I awoke to the news that my brother mages had been executed without trial as accomplices to the attack – something they were not! I was… I was angry and afraid, when I was offered the chance to re-join the Wolder, to command the armies…I took it without hesitation.'

Niamh looked down into her wine. Helligan seemed so forthright and yet to believe him was to doubt her father. She could find no words to explain the inner turmoil so instead looked back up at Helligan.

'I know,' he said, 'you need not voice the thoughts running through that pretty head sweetling, I understand them well. I do not ask for your unconditional belief in me, but I hope you will open your eyes now and try to see what is in front of you.'

'I will,' Niamh said.

'Good. The hour grows late, I should go to bed. Here, to help you sleep…' he poured the last of the wine from his own goblet into Niamh's and then stood. Before leaving, he moved out to the door and returned with the same great-cloak that Niamh had slept under the night before. This he draped about her shoulders. 'Sleep well, Princess,' he said, and then he was gone.

Morning came quickly, the brightness of the sun peering through the eerie marsh mists. Niamh was brave enough to eat her breakfast at the edge of the great table again, a bravery made more so for the fact that the meal seemed less organised with the men just arriving when they came down the stairs, eating and then leaving. As Niamh finished, though, Helligan entered the room. Unlike the others who were bleary of eye and yawning, Helligan was alert, with the demeanour of one who had been awake for hours already. He was dressed well in his usual attire of black long-trousers, tunic and belt. His hair was pulled away from his face and he wore black boots. As ever, he was completely clean-shaven.

'My Lady, you have finished with breakfast?'

Niamh nodded.

'How is your head this morning?' he smiled.

In truth, the honey wine had left her a little sore but Niamh merely shrugged, unable to find the words, shy again now that she was once more sober.

Helligan chucked and put out a hand to beckon her. 'Come, I want you with me today.'

'Oh?' her heart thudded, panic making her guts shudder.

'No need to look so afraid! I merely wish to show you the barracks… all of my men think I am mad to let our enemy's daughter see our strength, but I think you will enjoy the day, as it is Osta today, and so there will be celebrations all about…'

'Osta?' Niamh whispered, but she stood and moved to Helligan's side, dropping into step with him as he moved towards the door, leading her outside.

'The day of festivity. Amongst the free people, it would be chaos to celebrate every name-day, birth, marriage, life-end, and so once every two moons, a day is put aside for celebration. A day where no man works, and the mead runs freely.'

'For morale?

'No, just for the joy of it. You have to understand, you've encountered very few of my people, and only ever in battle but we are a people of joy, of living life as the privilege it is. Death comes too soon for many, and so life must be celebrated!'

Helligan led her from the front of the house, down to where the trees met the marshes. Through them, Niamh started to see the beginnings of tents. As they passed through the trees, the sound of pipes came to Niamh's ear, pipes and what might have been a fiddle. She moved a step closer to Helligan, the jolly sound somewhat unnerving, but Helligan did not react, merely continued to walk, leading her through to where the army was camped. Her heart thudded. She'd not expected there to be so very many of them. An army which would potentially overrun her father's! Maybe Helligan had motive after-all to bring her here, she thought grimly, news of this going back would certainly give the king a moment's pause. Tent after tent after tent, all of the rough, home-spun tan variety, some large, others small just for sleeping, as far as her eye could see over the valley they'd found themselves on the edge of. Here and there, about some of the larger tents were little crowds of people, hay bales piled up and music spilling free. Not just men, either, but women too laughing and dancing, spinning children with them as they twirled.

Helligan took Niamh's hand and tucked it into the crook of his arm, another indication of manners borne at her father's household.

'I know you are shy,' he said, 'but don't be – just come and witness…'

Niamh nodded and allowed Helligan to lead her to the nearest large tent. It was of old canvas, surrounded by haybales with loose straw on the floors. Two men sat with pipes near the entrance, and as they approached, Niamh could see a table being laid out by an old woman, who did not look dissimilar to Missis Kilm, with a huge variety of berries, fruits, bread and meat, despite that it was only a little gone breakfast. Already too, the ale – cheaper by far than honey mead – was flowing, and jollity was beginning.

'Come,' Helligan said to Niamh, after greeting a few of the men and kissing the cheek of a dirty ragged girl of about ten years – 'sit, have some wine or some ale if you like…'

Niamh took a small goblet of light ale from the barrel at the edge of the room, doing like the others about her were, and just dipping the goblet into the barrel. There was a dead fly floating in it but she just scooped it out, sure that kicking up a fuss over a dead fly was a good journey to ridicule in this world. Helligan took a goblet too, drank it down and then refilled. He smiled again and that look was somewhat disarming, bringing a twinkle to his eyes and ironing out the sternness of his brow.

Niamh sat in silence, watching as the sun rose over the celebrations. At the news of Helligan's arrival, more and more of the soldiers and their wives seemed to cluster about that one tent, but Helligan, after initial greetings, chose to remain beside Niamh, just watching from where they sat on itchy hay bales. The assortment of men was more varied than Niamh was used.

Skin of the pale northerners beside tan, dark, and the greenish glow of the forest men – stained from years of living in the forests by the sap of the trees – or so her father told her. The men, and women too were all wildly kept, with hair of reds, yellows, black and browns – beards to match on more than half of the men. None wore armour, so all were clad in tunics or soft leather – mostly a little ragged. There was not a weapon in sight, and nor was there any squabbling above what she'd already seen in the house – that good-natured joshing. It was all so loud, more and more so as more and more of the camp gathered around them. Rough music overtook the pipers, and for some time the clashing and clanging of that rose to a din that Niamh wouldn't have been able to shout over had she even wanted to.

The feast was declared served at high sun, and just like the kitchens of the house, brought forth chaos – a mad dash to stuff faces with food after a little knocking and bustling. Helligan, who had sat quietly beside her throughout the morning glanced down at Niamh's face.

'Are you hungry?'

Niamh shook her head.

'Hmmm… is that that you're not hungry, or that you are shy of trying to get to the table?'

'More the latter,' she confessed.

Helligan stood without a word and took her hand, a gesture more familiar than she was used, but as he led her down, people parted to let her to the table. That people were curious about her was obvious and for the first time, rather than the image of a horde of invaders, Niamh began to look at individual faces, people – different motives to hers, different lives, but just people. She half expected the "Is that really the princess" whispers from children that she often heard in the capitol, but in fact the children here were quiet – awed.

It took only minutes to fill her plate and retreat back to the hay bales. Helligan glanced back but then pulled up his chair by the table, joining in the chatter and laughter and making

Niamh regret her retreat. She sat alone, on the outskirts and suddenly realised that she wanted to be a part of it all – something which she'd never in her whole life wanted before. At Helligan's side, an empty wooden chair beckoned. After her escape, it seemed a million miles away, a million steps too many, but then Helligan turned to check on her and those miles melted away, giving her the nerve to stand and return to the table.

'Ah, you've decided to join us, princess,' Helligan said, 'sit – eat – and after maybe some dancing?'

As afternoon crested and then began to recede, Niamh escaped back to her seat on the hay bales. She was giddy from the ale which seemed never to run out, and stuffed to full from chuck-meat and berries. The table was pushed aside and before her, the dancing had begun, with Helligan leading the revelries. Kilm and his wife had materialised shortly after the beginning of the feast, and Niamh recognised one or two other faces from the house. She found smiles for them, but despite the festivities, there were none really returned aside from Missis Kilm. She was still distrusted by the men, it seemed.

As one song came to a juddering halt, Helligan came back and held out a hand to her, 'Dance, Princess?'

Niamh shook her head. She'd attended some of her father's court-events which involved dancing but those were much less rambunctious affairs than this wild, intoxicated celebration. She would not even know how to begin! Helligan seemed to accept her decline for almost a minute, but then grinned and thrust out his hand again, his eyes glowed.

'Come,' he said. 'It doesn't matter if you don't know the dances – this isn't your father's court! It's all much more of a muddle!'

Niamh paused, adrenaline rushing through her. She finished her goblet of ale and then, taken by some mad frenzy, nodded and let Helligan take her hand.

The steps of the dance seemed to make no sense, and before she knew it, Niamh was breathless and dizzy, hot to the point of sweating in the fading evening sun and despite it all, giggling like a child, a joy she'd not known in so many years coursing through her. Helligan was a strong dancer, probably led by his time serving the king, and with him leading her Niamh managed to keep up, just about. The dances were indeed more of a muddle, too. At court every step was dignified and choreographed, a step, a turn, a clap, and so on, whereas here people seemed to just grasp each other's hands and let the music lead them, moving up through the other dancers, turn, circle, swap hands… and if you weren't in the right place at the end of it, then you simply re-partnered with whomever was closest; a huge bearded Wolder with masses of white hair and a big grin in Niamh's case after the first roundel.

After the dancing came more food, more ale, and then there was Helligan again, sat beside her on the bales.

'Are you having fun?' he asked, softly.

'I am. I don't understand why you brought me here though?' as before, with the liquor in her veins and the company of Helligan, Niamh's tongue loosened more so than usual.

'You seek motive in everything?'

'I do, for there usually is…'

'An understandable caution, I suppose, for one who lives at court. I do not miss it.'

'You claim no motive, then?'

Helligan pondered a moment, 'only in that I wanted you to see my people as they really are. I was well aware that your only experiences of us have been in battle, I wanted you to see that we are not monsters, but men too and how better for you to see that than to witness a celebration?'

Niamh inclined her head and allowed silence to fall as she pondered his words. If nothing else, certainly her fear of these men was fading, no longer faceless monsters, now Missis Kilm, Kilm, Helligan, another she'd danced with named Bron. As she pondered, she looked out over the now hundreds of men gathered. The light was fading but a large fire had been lit, giving out an ethereal glow about the camp. The air was turning cooler too, despite the fire, aside from every now and again where a gust flew the smell and heat of the fire in their direction.

'Do you not fear detection?' Niamh asked.

'Hmm?'

'So many men, the noise and the fire...'

'I suppose we have our own forms of magic which help to shroud us.'

'Wolder magic?'

'Fae magic...'

'You really do believe all the old stories?'

'Don't you?'

Niamh glanced up at his face, growing more shadowed in the darkness. His eyes glowed still in the firelight. She didn't know any more what she believed.

'I... surely they are just stories?'

'As I see it, the stories of the wars are only a thousand years passed. A thousand years is such a short amount of time for a story to fall to myth – in truth, what could shroud a civilisation's memories thus, other than fae magics? What else has such power to cause such confusion?'

Niamh nodded again, then looked down at her hands, the shyness began to return at his soft tone, his obvious enjoyment of debate. Niamh already felt more comfortable around Helligan than most but philosophical debate was still probably too ambitious. Helligan watched her for a moment, she could see him out of the corner of her eye, but then stood and faced his men. They, seeing his movement, paused to look over.

'Men, I am going back to the house. Thank you for your company today.'

A murmur went up and a few tankards clanged, but then Helligan was forgotten as they went back to their previous pursuits – something which would not have happened in her father's court until he had departed. Niamh stood too, if Helligan was going, she wasn't going to stay here with these strangers. He took her hand and once more tucked in into this arm, leading her away. At the house, deserted and quiet as it was, with most of its occupants still out in the field, Niamh hoped he'd pause awhile again, but instead he led her to her makeshift bed, said a quick goodnight and then was gone, leaving her with her thoughts.

The following day broke as though nothing had been different in the one before it. The sun was bright and by noon had turned scorching. Niamh stood at the gate looking out over the marshes as the mules behind her were loaded. Helligan had sent news with Missis Kilm of a supply run which would move close to Berry's Head, the village just south of Anglemarsh; a decent enough place to take a stolen princess to be returned and so she was released early from her bondage. She was wrapped up in a thin cloak that Mrs Kilm had found for her to keep the sun off of her fair-skinned shoulders and had managed to tame her hair but for a few strands which blew about and tickled her face. The scenery was serene and calming to look over, her body tired and aching from sleeping on the uncomfortable bench for three nights, with a day's work and then a day's drinking between.

Helligan came up behind Niamh, making her turn-about, and in his hand he held her bow. 'Here, I think it is time this was returned to its owner,' he said softly.

Niamh's hand shook as she took the item back. It felt a lifetime ago since she'd last held her bow, had aimed it at Helligan and let the arrow fly.

'It is no mere bow, an antique, I think?' he asked, 'The men pilfered it as loot but I have taken it back for you, it seems only right that it be returned to you now... I'm not giving you any arrows though...'

Niamh found a small smile as Helligan's hand went to his chest where she'd shot him. She could not fault him that, although she knew already she'd not fire against him again. The bow felt good in her hands though as he passed it back to her, something solid to hold onto.

'So, going home,' he said, gentle, 'how do you feel?'

There was a loaded question. Niamh wet her lips, but then closed them, unable to reply not for a lack of words, but for a lack of clarity on that subject. She had thought that she wanted nothing other but to be taken home but now that the time was here it was strangely as though some adventure was ending and nothing but dull mediocrity in its wake. It would be good to see her father, Josynne and Laurin, but to return to them was to once more be the enemy of the man stood before her and Niamh realised only in that moment that she wanted them not to be on opposite sides.

'I...' she sighed, closed her eyes, rebalanced her thoughts and then spoke again, 'I... do not wish to become your enemy again, Helligan Darkfire. No... no matter what my father... what my father says of you and your men, I know you are good...'

'Only in fairytales does good battle evil, sweetling. In reality, man stands against man and no man is truly good or truly evil. Your father and I stand opposed, we have different values and each considers our path to be the correct one. If the goddess is kind, she will favour the path of least bloodshed and pain for all.'

'So... so mote it be and blessings upon you Helligan...' Niamh paused, 'I... I will pray for your life, if not for your cause.'

Helligan bowed his head, then turned and walked back into the house. Niamh's gut contracted to see him go, her eyes trying to well up. Shocked at such a reaction, she turned and walked towards the men who were gathered making the final preparations for the trip to Berry's Head, near Anglemarsh where she would be left.

'Come, Princess... let us be off,' One of the men spoke, and then they were away.

Chapter 7

Berry's Head was a relatively small town which was situated just south of Anglemarsh, close enough that the spires of that smaller keep were not just visible, but detailed even in the dimming light. They had travelled far: through the wetness and coldness of the marshes out to the open fields with their buzzing bumbles and crowing birds overhead, from there they'd taken one of the winding dry paths which ran alongside the King's roads, but at a distance so as to be unseen, hidden by the wheat crop. Niamh sat on the back of a mule-led wagon throughout this journey, the wheels causing her to bounce around and have to hold on to keep herself seated in the thus far empty wagon. They'd travelled for several hours thus, and then stopped to eat yet more Jummel Berry jam and bread. The man and woman with her were the same as those who had held her prisoner before, but with Helligan's trust of them, Niamh found herself unafraid of them, if totally silent in their presence. They too, seemed to be content to allow her her silence, and didn't push her to speak.

At the gate to Berry's head, the bumping of the cart stopped. Niamh sucked in a deep breath and cast her eyes over a finally familiar surrounding. From within the walls, there came the sounds of the usual bustling marketplace, the children playing, business conducted and traders calling their wares. Chucks cawed and an old snoutlet grunted and oinked close enough that it must be just on the other side of the wall.

'King's men's ere...' the woman said, indicating the stables to their right which showed an abundance of horses in the black and gold livery of Niamh's father.

'What then? Go back?' the man asked.

An almost panic gripped Niamh. To be so close to home and then have it snatched away? No! She, driven by panic and adrenaline, all but leapt from the back of the cart and ran, not even looking back at the cries of the couple behind, up to the gate. There she was met by a town guard who put a hand out to stop her

'No beggars, Miss! Not until our royal visitors are done.'

From behind, Niamh could see the older couple dismounting the cart, both wary and confused.

'Please!' Niamh whispered, falling to her knees in the dirt. 'No beggar... I... let me inside!'

Another guard came closer, obviously drawn in by the commotion and Niamh was relieved to see the old couple falter without, watching with wary eyes as Niamh begged for admittance.

'I am no beggar!' she managed, more coherent as she turned to the other guard. He started violently, and his brow furrowed.

'Good Lord!' he exclaimed, 'Princess?'

Niamh felt as though her heart would explode with relief. She felt a tear brew but pushed it away and nodded. She stood shakily and a final glance showed her the couple who had brought her to the gate now making a hasty retreat.

'Bless you girl, Earlton, go and find the king's men!' the guard snapped to the other, but then Niamh's eye caught a sight of somebody, the best of somebodies, and before she even registered her flight, she was sprinting towards him. Lord Shale just stared, his face turning from bland to shocked and then delight. He caught Niamh up as she reached him and lifted her right from her feet, clutching her tightly to his armoured breastplate.

'Princess! Oh... oh ... is it really you?'

'Jos!' she sobbed, all of the stress of the last few days melting away. 'Jos... they let me go! They...' the words were lost in his shoulder as gently Lord Shale placed her back on her feet. He held her pressed to him a moment longer, but then pulled away and turned to his squire,

'Go and send a message to the king! And send for clothing! Food... the Princess is returned to us!'

Niamh steadied herself, a hand still on Lord Shale's arm but dropping to her waist to see Lady Shale emerge from the building beyond. The lady gasped and all but dropped her basket to see Niamh standing there, and then she found herself embraced again, the goddess once more thanked for her safe return.

After Niamh was well fed on richly filled custard tarts and huge haunches of Jaggerbeast, and dressed once again in her finery, she was led to a horse and given help to mount by Lord Shale himself. His hands shook under her boot but Niamh pushed up anyway and settled herself in the saddle. They were to ride not to Anglemarsh, Lord Shale informed her, but to the Golden Keep.

'The Keep?' she whispered, almost awed as the horse began to move.

'Yes indeed, your father relocated there after you left for your... mission. Your brother and sisters are already home... you missed the Royal Wedding...'

'Laurin married whilst I was... away?'

'Princess, your brother was convinced you were dead and your brother's wife saw you shot down.'

Niamh said nothing, but within her heart hardened a little, so had they not even looked for her?

'But... but I was not dead...'

'So I see, and I vow to you, I fought hard to have you recovered, dead or alive but it was too many... many resources for... for your father...'

'I know *you* would have,' she murmured, her voice so low he might not even have heard it.

The ride to the keep was thankfully shorter than the ride before, and more comfortable astride the little dapple-white horse Lord Shale had purchased for her to ride at Berry's Head. The Golden Keep was much as she remembered it, a motte above a bailey which was built up into towers rather than the simpler round castes. The gates were closed tight, and then those beyond the bailey were closed too, locking the royal family away from all including their own people. Within the royal gates, the grounds were lush and covered with bright green grass. Fruit trees bearing jims, apples and tart fel-fruits hung overhead causing the scent of blossom and some shade from the bright sunshine. Once within the keep itself, Niamh found herself almost pulled from her horse by her ladies and dragged upstairs to be made even more presentable. Finally, hours later, and once more a princess, Niamh was taken down to the great gold-lined throne room.

The hard soles of Niamh's shoes clanked on the stone flags as she opened the door to her father's throne room. A royal announcer called out her arrival, but it was needless for all heads were already turned to the door.

The king sat on his throne, once more the golden seat of his forefathers. The throne was not, and never had been raised up, but still sat betwixt the two golden pillars which went all the way up to the tall domed ceiling, higher than both the first two storeys of the castle. Before the king was a row of benches and the royal musicians who played ceaselessly even as she entered. There were large high windows all about the two walls which faced outside and by these were cushioned benches. The king's war-table stood in the far corner, covered in paperwork and the little markers which were sometimes used to represent armies, but which in this case were scattered. Several rooms lay off to the sides, but all were firmly closed and locked, rarely used in the previous occupancy and in some cases shrouded by large pillars.

Milling about the room were most of her father's court. There was some dancing apparently being led by Queen Magda, over to the right-hand side of the room nearer the musicians. Kyran and Laurin were seated at a bench by the window, the younger children absent. Lords Nordemonde and Shale were seated beside her father, but as Niamh was announced, Shale stood and came to greet her and welcome her in. Laurin too stood and came over to bow and kiss her hand.

'Sister, I thought for sure you were dead,' he sad, 'When poor Kyran said she'd seen you shot down...'

'A flesh wound,' Niamh murmured, pressing her brother's hand in reassurance, but her eyes on her father who had not risen to greet her. Queen Magda at least had the decency to leave the dancers and come forward, she took Niamh's other hand and between them, Magda and Laurin all-but led Niamh to her father, with Lord Shale trailing.

'Father,' Niamh whispered, falling to one knee before him despite that as princess of the realm she need not kneel to her father.

'Child. You are alive?'

'I am.'

Niamh glanced up to see her father's old eyes were wet. He stood and raised her up, flicking his wrist at the others to return to their seats. Once stood, Niamh stepped forward to be kissed by her father, and was gladly surprised to find herself embraced too, held against a soft velvet doublet. 'After your dear sweet brothers and sisters were taken from us, I thought that I would never feel grief again,' he said, speaking softly, just for her, 'how wrong I was to find myself, when they told me my daughter died bravely, protecting her family and our interests. I am desperately happy to have you home.'

At his words, Niamh's stomach contracted. Every word Helligan had said against her father suddenly melted and once more her heart hardened to him – obviously he could not be correct about her father. The king kissed Niamh's brow, and then her cheek, and the turned her about.

'God has seen fit to return my girl to me,' he said, his habit as ever to call upon the new god over the goddess, 'let us praise him in all his might, and thank him again for his mercy.'

A few of the lords murmured a thank you to the gods but Niamh's eye went to Shale, whose wife was a known patroness of the goddess temples, and she was pleased to see him murmur the more traditional gratitude to her. He caught her eye and winked, ever so discretely.

The rest of the evening was spent in merriment, but at last Niamh's yawns attracted the attention of her ladies and she found herself bundled up to bed, dressed once more in her soft nightgowns and put down into the bliss that was a feather bed.

That night Niamh slept like a baby, and much so for the next three nights, her adventures put firmly behind her other than when her father quizzed her well on the location and size of the Wolder army, questions she answered truthfully enough, but without any clarity. She could say there were a lot of men but could say not how many, nor even guestimate, for she'd not seen them all. Helligan, and more-so his kindness to her, his assertions, she kept to herself. There was her only conflict at being home, her only worry. Helligan's face haunted her, coming to her mind at the strangest of moments and pulling her back to her time in the marshes. He'd ever been so open, so earnest, and yet he must have been wrong! Either that or he must have been trying to make her turn coat on her father!

On her fourth night home, Niamh was more restless. She'd spent most of the day in the company of her new sister, Kyran, and then had gone out to shoot some butts for the evening, predictably joined by Lord Shale, who ever seemed to know when she was without. Later, after supper was eaten, she fell onto her bed but was unable to sleep. The night-time in the keep was quieter than the day, but still the castle always seemed abuzz. Niamh's chamber was only on the second floor, too, above the throne room and so the sound of the festivities below was tiring. That night, she tossed and turned until the music at last faded away, and then was on the verge of sleep when she heard a footstep descending the stairs. She sat up in bed. Why would anybody be going down the stairs at this hour? The servants would be abed and the lords and ladies should be retiring. Niamh sat up for a long moment, then frowned to hear another footstep go down, and then the creak of the throne-room door opening echoed in the vast halls of the keep.

At once, Helligan's voice echoed in her head, his talk of late-night meetings. She'd all but dismissed Helligan's warnings since her return but now, alone in the middle of the night listening to what sounded like people gathering below, Niamh suddenly found it harder to forget. She slipped out of bed and paced her room and then, decisive, put on her green silk gown which was discarded on the chest at the end of the bed, and pulled back her hair into its ribbons. She put on her softest shoes and then slowly, carefully, slipped out of the door.

Where the throne room of the Golden Keep was vast and filled with nooks and crannies, the king's war-room was not so much so, a small chamber fitted into the edge of the vast throne-room. Despite that the shoes on her feet were soft and quiet, Niamh kicked them off by the last stair to further hide her footsteps. The chill air penetrated deep into the old stones when the night's darkness seeped about, marred only by the odd flicker of a candle. The entrance to the war room was hidden though, lost in the shadows behind vast stone columns which went right the way up to the ceiling, decorated in gold filigree. Niamh's bare feet were cold on the hard, stone floor where she'd kicked her shoes off to hide her footsteps, but she ignored the discomfort as she crept further in so that only a stone pillar hid her from the rest of the party. Thankfully, voices carried well in the echoey hall and anti-chambers so that despite being somewhat removed from them still, every word was crisp and clear.

'And with the dragon-blood your boy took from the sisters before the attack?'

'It turns clouded, and then black.'

'I suppose any change is better than no change…. At least we know we are on the right track?' that was the voice of Lord Nordemunde, exasperated and tired. Niamh's brow furrowed. They were definitely having a meeting, at midnight, hidden away down here. How could Helligan have known? …because he'd once been a lord here too – she realised – and had probably been privy to such meetings. Niamh took a deep breath to steady her nerves, and then glanced around the pillar. Her father was at the end of the table, stood tall and talking about the Wolder problem – nothing unusual in that. Directly on either side of him were Lord Nordemunde and Lord Carver, again nothing unusual, those were her father's best friends. Lord Shale sat grave and quiet at the side of Lord Jansen, and then there sat three others. Gabe Horvel, a younger man than most present, of forty or so who was newly in the private circle of her father's friends – some relation or other newly arrived from Kingstowne in the south. Extravagantly dressed as southerners often were, but a pleasant enough fellow, he seemed to be more interested in a loose thread on his sleeve than in her father. Opposite him and Shale sat Queen Magda's cousin Norman Coss – a common man with a red nose who ever looked bored, and finally her father's financial advisor, Fallow Nightingale. The religious leader, Lord Gorren was strangely absent.

After quickly taking stock, Niamh pulled back again and tugged her cape about her against the cold. The Golden Keep was eerie at night, more so even that Anglemarsh had been.

'The way I see it, we have several issues;' Lord Carver was summing up, 'There is the insult of their stealing the princess first and foremost. How to work the sphere, the turning of The

Sacred Sisters to their old ways and the desertion of them to the Wolder camps…'

'…which is only happening due to the emphasis of my Lord King on stamping out the old religion,' that was Shale. 'If you were to be more open to ruling with dual religion…'

'Nonsense! The true god states that no other gods but himself should be worshipped! To tolerate the old religion thus makes the king compromised in his own beliefs.' Niamh could not see who uttered the words, but she could hazard a guess on Horvel – the southerners were much more for the new religion than the northerners.

'The bitches show nothing but contempt for the king,' that was definitely Nordemunde. 'If they would just convert…'

'They are the least likely of all to convert, surely you see that? They have dedicated their lives to the old gods and to the goddess…' again Shale, the voice of reason.

'And yet they have such sway with the people,' the king said, 'the commoners adore the sisters and they flock with them to the wild men's cause…'

Niamh stifled a yawn. The meeting was as dull as any less secret council meeting. She was contemplating escaping back upstairs when Lord Carver spoke again:

'What if we were to use that to our advantage – deal a blow to both the temple and the Wolder?'

'What did you have in mind?'

'What if we were to stage an attack on the sisters? Make it look like the Wolder had attacked a temple?'

'Hmm, now that might work…' Niamh's heart fluttered, that was her father's voice.

'If the men wore black and rags, a small party so as not to be conspicuous. Make it look savage – rape some of the women, slaughter the initiates…'

'You cannot be serious?' Lord Shale said, 'the sisters are sacred and the initiates barely women – children!'

'I agree,' another of the less familiar voices, 'You cannot condone such a heinous attack, my king…'

The voices rose into a hubbub, some for and some against the idea. The king spoke not, allowing them their discussion as Niamh lay back in shock against the pillar, her hands splaying out over the cold stone.

'Quiet now, quiet,' finally the king called the men to order. 'I think the idea as repulsive as any of you, but in desperate times, desperate measures must be considered.'

'You shame yourself!' That was Shale.

'You watch your tongue!'

'I will not! The job of an advisor is to advise the king! Not sit silently whilst he contemplates such despicable acts! Hansel, surely you cannot seriously consider condoning this?'

'Your words are noticed, Jos, but enough! I know my own mind!'

Niamh dared another quick glance. Shale was sitting with both hands splayed out on the table, his eyes flashed dangerously. Her father too seemed flushed, and the other Lords once again were beginning to take up discussion amongst themselves.

'What if we merely burn the temple?'

'What if the children were saved?'

'I suggest we simply flush them out, frighten them a bit…'

'But then we risk recognition…'

'… disguises….'

'murder…'

And so on, then, 'Enough! We cannot do this! I can never condone this!' Shale shouted above the hubbub.

'The council recognises your opinion,' her father replied, 'but we need not your permission. You are not the king, sir! Sit down!'

A general murmur of "Here! Here!"

'There is a temple out on the edge of the forest, between Anglemarsh and Berry's head.' Her father continued, 'It is small but is dedicated to the goddess Herodite – face of mothers. If that one were to be hit there would be outcry but with minimal loss to human life. There are but four sisters and three initiates there.'

Niamh felt her heart turn to steel as her father spoke. She could not believe he'd be so willing to sign off to the murder of innocent priestesses. Again the hubbub rose but her father silenced it.

'So we are for it, generally? With objections noted?'

'Aye!'

'Aye!'

'Nay!' Shale's voice rang out but was ignored.

'I say we send Sir Michael and his men,' Nordemunde said, 'They are unpredictable drunkards but likely not to… balk… at such a task.'

There was silence as the sentence was passed on the poor sisters. To be raped, murdered, desecrated. Niamh's stomach hurt.

'Other orders of business?' That sounded like Nordemunde again, but Niamh did not have it in her to look around the pillar.

'The invasion of Krall?'

Krall? Niamh did not know the name.

'If we were to attack there, then it would show them that their towns are not impenetrable. It might even draw them away from West Keep… I still fear an attack there,' her father said. 'It is a small village so will not be well-guarded but it would send a message…'

A Wolder village then? More slaughter of the innocents? Niamh's heart dropped further still.

'Indeed, Sire. Have we received any further information on the whereabouts of the village though? We've not had great success in actually finding them?'

'The bastards hide their dwellings well!' Jansen piped in. 'We of course know that it is somewhere near Berry's Head, south east, I am told. It'll be hidden well by the forests, I would say we know that much for certain at least.'

'There is a man who knows, and who has offered to guide us, but at a cost…' Nordemunde spoke.

'What man? What cost?' That was the king again.

'Sire, do you recall a man named Ondreich Highcastle? He was a minor knight here briefly but was banished from court and so defected to live out in the marshes with the wild men?' Nordemunde's tone was filled with distaste as he spoke.

'I recall, yes. Renamed himself Highlark or something?'

'That's the man. Well it seems the Wolder life is not for him after all and he wants to come back. One of my men has spoken quietly to him and he is willing to show us the secret paths to the Wolder villages hereabouts: Krall, Grull, Dragon's fort…'

'By the God! And you mention this only now? What is his price?' her father asked.

'The return of his ancestral home, gold, and a wife.'

'Reasonable requests. Any specific wife?'

'Yes, Sire, your daughter… the bastard.'

Niamh's gasp was audible, would have been heard if not for the instant raising of voices again, mainly in her defence this time!

'No!' Shale spoke again for the first time since the king had silenced him, 'he can't have Niamh! My Lord, you cannot!'

'My Lord, the princess is too valuable a piece to throw away on a low-import as this…' maybe Coss – the accent was northern at least.

'Indeed! She is legitimised now! Her marriage is no trifle to be thrown away.'

'Some foreign prince…'

'Ties with abroad…'

And so on. Then Shale spoke again.

'Sire, Highlark is old enough to be her father and more. He is a man famed for his mistreatment of his subordinates. He has had a wife already, or more than one if I hear the right of it, and he was not above humiliating them, beating them and even fucking them in public. He has raped several girls that we have heard of, and once beat a pageboy to death for refusing to pleasure him – that before he was banished from here. He is no mate for our sweet princess!'

'Would he take no other?' the king asked.

'I think not sire, perhaps one of the queen's daughters might amuse him awhile… especially one of the younger ones… but for a wife he wants the royal tie,' Nordemunde spoke again. 'Niamh is legitimate now, sire. He wants to take advantage of that.'

'The girl's a looker too,' Jansen piped in, 'She's a true prize for any man.'

'Please, my Lord, not Niamh,' Shale said again, his tone almost desperate. 'She is… she is worth so much more…'

'I know you are sweet on her, Shale, but you are married already…' that was Carver, 'she will have to marry sometime, and if it is of military advantage to the king, then it must be considered.'

'I know she must be, but find her a foreign prince? A lad her own age who she might have a chance of loving. Not this… this is…unthinkable… he is a rapist, a murderer… My Lord King, please? I will even set aside my reservations on the temple attack, if you will spare your daughter from this!'

'And yet, I think I must consider it at least,' the king said, 'There is a strange magic which hides the Wolder settlements from us. If this man has the secret, it could change the whole course of the war. For once we could move from defence to attack… Niamh is a good girl, but she is in the end just my bastard daughter, legitimised for appearance sake.'

'And if she marries him and then by ill fate becomes queen, do we really offer a crown to that monster?' Nightingale, the quiet one, spoke at last. 'He would cripple the kingdom in a year…'

'Niamh will never become queen. My son stands before her, and he newly-wed with a wife already in fruit…'

'I will have no part in this!' Shale's voice was accompanied by the squealing of a chair moving backwards with force.

Niamh glanced about the pillar and saw him standing, furious. Lord Nordemunde was rising too, his hand on his sword hilt and Lord Carver too scrabbled to his feet.

'Sit down! Sir!' he barked, 'Lest we have you removed from this council chamber!'

Niamh glanced about her, looking for somewhere to run and hide but before events escalated, the King moved to Shale's side, putting a hand on his arm and coaxing him back into his chair.

'My Lord Shale, your father was a dear friend to me and an excellent advisor,' he said. 'I take your council very seriously, and I too am loath to lose our princess to such a beast. I will offer him his choice of my lady the queen's children and I will adopt whichever he chooses, to make her legitimate too and to give the royal tie he desires. Should he refuse me, then I will have to consider Niamh... we need this man's expertise.'

'None of those poor little girls should be subjected to this man, My Lord!'

'I know it, and yet war brings the worst for us all... calm yourself, here, have some wine. If I can spare my daughter this, I will. You have my word, but if this is what it comes to, then I would give my idiot daughter to him a thousand times over. She is just a bastard, and he might be the end to this war for good! It's an easy trade!'

Chapter 8

Niamh closed her eyes, allowing hot tears to roll down her face as her father's words sank through her, into her very core and there settled in a painful lump. Helligan had been right all along. Her father was no benevolent king, but a monster, a callous man who was fully prepared to murder priestesses, Wolder women and children too… to offer her and her sisters up to a man so despicable it make her stomach hurt. She glanced around the pillar again to see her father dipping his quill, writing furiously onto parchments – the official stamp of his orders to carry out atrocities, to barter with Highlark and to order Sir Michael and his men to murder the priestesses of the temple of Herodite. A strange light-headedness overcame Niamh, a dizzying, oddly strained feeling. She tiptoed away from the war-room in something of a daze and out to where she had left her shoes.

Upstairs once more, Niamh sat down on her bed and stared at the walls. She and she alone held this knowledge, the outcomes of that awful secret meeting. She and she alone could do something to stop it. But what? She moved the dresser and lifted her own quill and ink. A few words on a piece of paper could change it all. To let Helligan know her father's plans… She paused though, at the thought of betraying her father and besides, how did she know Helligan and his men would even care – the Wolder had slaughtered the last queen and her children, after all! Their own innocents. The Wolder had ever been the enemy, right until the point that she'd been taken by them… Helligan – he was a turning point in her estimations of them, she knew that! Was she being tempered by her affection for him? Had it merely been the Wolder village and herself under threat she might have convinced herself but when her mind took her back to what her father had sanctioned, the attack on the temple – no… no she was not being biased! She couldn't write to Helligan though! What was she thinking? Just because she trusted him, didn't mean he'd trust a random note written by her! Getting it to him was problematic too, it would mean trusting somebody with the job of delivering it, directing them straight to Helligan's hideaway, to the bulk of the Wolder Army. That was as dangerous as allowing her father his plans. The Wolder army, vast as it was, was less by far than what her father could muster if he happened to know where they were. Surprise was the key to their successes.

Niamh scrumpled the letter with frustration and threw it into the wicker bin. What then? She could write to the temple, warn them, but what if they did not take her warning seriously? What if word got back to her father? That would mean a whipping or worse, even imprisonment for being a traitor. Niamh touched the little golden device on her dresser which counted the hours – its tiny wheels turned relentlessly, moving ever closer to… when? When did her father intend to carry out these evil deeds? How long did she have? Nobody had said.

Niamh stood again and paced her chamber a few times. Outside of the window, the night was at its darkest, midnight now gone, and the dark hours heavy on the world. After signing them, her father would have stashed the papers in the lockbox at the back of the war-room for the morning. Ever orders were given at dawn. Even secret ones? She wasn't sure but it was a good bet. If she could break into that box somehow, the answers would be in the scrolls.

Niamh paced her chamber again, indecision burning in her gut. The meeting would likely be over now. She could sneak down, take the scrolls… and then what? How was she any further on? *You know the answer* a quiet voice within spoke, *you know there is only one path open to you!* To take the scrolls to Helligan herself. To defect and to… to run away? The mere thought was terrifying and yet, her inner thought was right – there was no other path. Niamh, and Niamh alone could save those people.

Without even really realising that she'd made up her mind, Niamh began to open drawers, packing as lightly as she could. Small things, a few pieces of jewellery – more for financial reasons than attachment to the pieces – and finally her own personal items, a hairbrush, a handful of hair decorations, a bottle of scent and some handmade soaps. With this packed, she changed into a plainer gown than she was wearing and positioned the strap of the bag across her chest. Her long hair was tied away under a hood and her plain black travel cape went on over it all. Finally she grabbed her bow and quiver.

Downstairs it was dark and quiet. A few maids bumbled about but they were easily avoided. The rest of the house slept. Niamh dared not light a candle so fumbled her way slowly through the great throne room and into the anti-chamber. There a little moonlight spilled in through the stained-glass windows, enough to allow Niamh to make her way to the box and try the lid. It was locked of course. Niamh sighed and began to feel around for a key. It was unlikely that it would have been left out, but she had to try! She was startled though, by the sound of footsteps behind. Niamh gasped and spun about. A figure stood in the doorway, hidden in the shadows but definitely there.

'Who is it? Who's there?' the figure spoke. Niamh froze, her bladder suddenly full and her hands shaking despite that of all the men, it could have been worse – the voice was that of Josynne Shale. The figure stepped closer, coming into view and giving Niamh a glance of that lithe physique, those archer's shoulders.

'Jos…' She managed but then her tongue was too dry, her words lost.

'Princess?' his voice turned to gentle surprise.

Niamh stepped closer so that he could see her.

'What are you doing down here in the middle of the night, Princess?'

Niamh floundered; her stomach too tightly wrought to allow speech. She bit her lip and tried to control the shaking of her limbs.

'Princess?' he stepped closer again.

'I… the sisters…' Niamh whispered.

'The sisters? You… were you eavesdropping? Earlier?'

Niamh nodded, her body so tense, too tense probably to flee, should she need to.

'Then you overheard your father's plans for you too?'

She nodded.

Shale paused for a moment, then looked over at the locked box Niamh had been fiddling with. 'You were looking for your father's orders?'

She nodded.

'To go to the sisters?'

Niamh hesitated.

'To the Wolder?'

'To Helligan,' she managed.

'Helligan? Helligan the mage? He lives?'

'He is Lord Helligan… of the Wolder army… he… he…'

'He is the one who took you, and who delivered you home safe. Now that makes sense… he's an odd one, but he ever seemed just.'

Niamh nodded and then glanced again to the lock box. 'Will you tell…'

'No,' he said at once, then fumbled at his waist for his dagger. Niamh felt a moment of panic, but then it passed as the dagger was placed in her hand.

'Jimmy the lock with this,' he said, 'and throw it down the well as you leave. Your father's stables are well guarded but if you go to the edge of the keep by the smith there is a smaller stable there too which is less guarded. Leave the keep by the west gate – if you look like a commoner that will be easier so don't take a fine nag, the rougher looking horses are cheaper and so it's more likely you'd be able to own one of those, as a commoner. Take haste and may the goddess protect you.'

Niamh took in a deep breath and then stepped forward and kissed his cheek. 'Thank you,' she whispered. 'The goddess love you, Josynne Shale.'

'And you, Princess.'

Chapter 9

Escape from the Golden Keep was easier than Niamh had imagined, especially with Lord Shale's directions, and before morning had really come, she found herself out on the road riding past the capitol and towards Anglemarsh. That would be the final hurdle to pass, and then she was out in the wild lands once more. Her disguise was good though. She was wrapped up in an old horse blanket she'd found in the stables, her dress well-hidden and with her golden hair dulled by mud. She looked every inch the peasant, conspicuous only by the grey horse she'd taken. Despite Shale's advice, Niamh had wanted a horse she knew would last the distance and not tire before she reached her destination.

At Anglemarsh – the gate to the Marshes – Niamh kept her head low. The keep was less occupied though with the king's return to the Golden Keep, and Niamh's years of living there made it easy to navigate without too much worry for being caught. The journey back into the marshes, afterwards, was arduous but not enough to daunt her. She'd memorised the path on the way out and it was less than a day's riding to Helligan and safety. She reached the house just as day was falling to evening, and there paused to catch her breath, before dismounting the sweaty horse and tying the rein to the gatepost. She took the scrolls from her saddlebag and clutched them tightly in her fist – those, more than anything, were her key to acceptance. She had to hope Helligan had not moved on, that the little house was still his base.

As she approached the door Niamh heard the low murmur of voices, and the scent of meat cooking permeated the air, lingering and making her salivate – she'd not eaten all day. Perhaps they believed, probably rightly so, that nobody but their men could traverse the marshes and so nobody had even considered she might return. Nobody had cause to know about her sharp memory for terrain, keen sense of direction. Beside her, a chuck cawed, making Niamh jump almost out of her skin. She glanced down at the feathered bird and a moment's sorrow touched her gut to think that soon enough its fat little form would be on their dinner-plates. The rest of the Wolder army were still out behind too, hidden in the hills – Niamh could hear the distant clatter of an army at leisure in its tents beyond, the general murmur occasionally broken by a bray of laughter or the clang of swords. The Woldermen were a wild sort to lead too, it couldn't be easy to be their general.

Niamh put a hand down on the door, trying to muster the courage to knock, but that privilege was taken almost at once by the opening of the door – they must have seen her arrive. The door-opener was that same old man who had handed her a broom, a week which seemed a lifetime ago: Morkyl Greashion. The old man cast an eye over her with the suspicion due, and stood barring the doorway. His eyes moved out to the darkness beyond, looking for signs of danger.

'I am alone,' Niamh said.

'What do you want, child?'

'Helligan...'

'What do you want with him?'

Niamh paused, she'd rehearsed in her head all the way there, but now found no words to reply to his barked question. Morkyl did not bend though, did not move to allow her access.

'I have information,' she finally said, 'for you...'

'What information?'

'Please…'

At her plea the old man softened slightly and stood aside to allow her to enter. 'Helligan's out in the field, I'll have him sent for.'

Niamh nodded gratefully and managed a thanks. The old man indicated a wooden bench under the window, complete with an embroidered cushion, and so she sat, clutching tight to her scrolls as though they were the only thing solid in the room. The old man spoke quietly to one of the pages who nodded and slipped out of the door. The room turned to quiet. The three lords who occupied the house with Morkyl and Helligan conversed quietly in the room beyond, seeming content to allow Morkyl to handle the strange visitor. From the enemy camp too, Niamh realised suddenly, the familiarity born from her time spent there had dimmed her senses to the truth that she might be perceived as threatening, maybe they even supposed she was still her father's pawn, sent in to barter for their surrender, that her papers were terms. Her gut tightened more so.

Several long moments passed, minutes turning to almost an hour. Morkyl seemed content to sit and guard her, but did not speak again, for which Niamh was grateful. Finally the door opened and Helligan entered. He was dressed in his customary black, hair pulled away from his face at the front but loose down his back. He strode in and knelt before Niamh in a strange display of almost subservience.

'What is it?' he asked, his voice gentle but his eyes alert, 'what have you overheard?'

Relief flooded Niamh. She forced herself to look to him alone, and try to forget his companion behind. It was easier to talk to Helligan.

'My father plans to attack one of the temples of Herodite, in disguise as… as your men.. to… to cause damage to your reputation with the commoners and the sisters.'

'I see, do you know which temple?'

'It is… in the papers… she said holding them up. There is… is more. He… he plans to invade the marshes,' she whispered. 'A village named Krall. He seeks to enlist the aid of a man called Ondreich Highlark.'

Helligan swore and stood, his face showed that there was some meaning in her utterance of that name which was alien to her.

'You are sure?' he asked.

'Yes.' She handed him the papers as an extra assurance, her hand trembling to do so, in realisation that she was now branded a traitor too. Helligan took the scrolls and opened them in his white hands. His eyes skimmed the paper and then back to her.

'Where did you get these?'

'I stole them.'

'From your father?'

'Yes.'

Helligan exhaled again and then turned to Morkyl, 'call a meeting of the five,' he said, 'We need to move quickly!'

All about the room there was a din of noise. Niamh sat very still and quiet as the four marsh-lords squabbled and shouted under Helligan's mediation. They sat in the room adjoining, the forbidden room for her – until now – with her father's plans before them all. The eldest of the four men, Alfric McClaven, was convinced and ready to run for the marshes to protect his home and their families. He was a small man with beady dark eyes and a thoughtful expression which made Niamh like him better than the others. Morkyl was frustratingly neutral of opinion, as was a white-haired man who wore a scar across his nose – Jarlsen Mantle, Lord of the South Keep. The last one, a man she'd met before – Kilm – was scathing indeed, convinced that the whole thing was a trap.

'They obviously sent the girl because they know you would trust her, Helligan,' he said. 'This scheme is impossible! This is a scare-tactic and I say we slit the girl's throat and send her body back to them in response!'

Niamh murmured in fear but Helligan put a hand on her arm making her feel greatly relieved that he'd insisted on placing her next to him.

'We'll do nothing so hasty!' Helligan said. 'Lady Niamh, can you shed any more light on this for us? How did you come upon the plans? What did you overhear?'

Panic shot through her, but Niamh knew she had to explain, had to make them believe her. She took in two deep breaths and then focused her eyes on the table.

'Helligan told me to really listen,' she said. Suddenly her mouth was so dry, too dry. 'When I returned… to eavesdrop at doorways and to… to… educate myself on my father… so I…I… did. I heard my… my father and his m…men plotting this. My father's men advised him to… to attack the sisters of Herodite… they said that they… they are too close in thinking to… to you because you and they follow the old religion…'

'And the attack on my village?' McClaven asked, 'what of that?'

'One of my father's advisors spoke the name Ondreich Highlark… said he could lead a band through the marshland safely…'

'And what of your loyalty to your father, child?' that was Jarlsen Mantle.

'I… I…' Niamh swallowed and took a deep breath. 'I… I cannot stand by when… when innocents will die. The sisters! I too… I too follow the old ways and this is… even if I did not… to order rape, and murder of children…' She stopped overwhelmed, and looked to Helligan, 'you must stop this travesty!' she said. 'And I knew… I knew that you would help them.'

'You seek then to save the innocent?' Jarlsen said, 'idealistic and foolish motives, but believable I suppose.'

'Perhaps so, but at least my motives are pure!'

Niamh glanced to Helligan again, but Kilm wasn't content with her answer, 'But why? I understand why he wants to attack the temple! To stop the common folk coming over to us by making us look like savages... that I understand, but why would he attack Krall? There is no tactical advantage to losing half his men in the marshes and then slaughtering a bunch of women and children... we have no wealth, no spoils!'

'To stop us fighting for Helligan, don't you see?' Alfric said, 'to send a warning to us and to make us march our men home!'

'Which is a means just as well served by sending us a little girl full of tales,' Jarlsen said, suddenly siding with Kilm. 'To frighten the men into leaving, thus he has defeated us without bloodshed!'

'Just as I have been trying to say!' Kilm stated.

'Ondreich Highlark would not turn easily, either... he's no turncoat, he hates the king.' Morkyl cut in.

'This is true,' Helligan mused, making Niamh's heart sink – had she lost them all, even Helligan? He turned to her again and put a hand on her arm. 'What did your father have, that he could possibly think would bring the exiled knight back into the kingdom's rule?'

'He was...' Niamh broke off, not for lack of words, but more to bite back the lump which swelled in her chest. 'They have already negotiated with him... he wants... wants money and his... his old titles back and he wants... wants... me...'

Niamh expected chaos for her words, expected another shouted argument, but instead, the room was deathly quiet.

'Ondreich is old enough to be your grandfather and has already been married several times – with children to prove it,' Kilm said at last.

'He is, the men said as much but they... they didn't much think that that... that that would matter... my father said to... to offer my step-sisters instead... whichever he might... might prefer...' Niamh looked at her fingers and ordered herself not to cry in front of all these great lords.

'The queen's daughters are very young, are they not?' That was Alfric.

'The youngest, Jedda, is but ten years old.'

Voices did raise then, in disgust. A clamour of words but Helligan brought them to order with a fist to the table. His eyes were very dark. 'Niamh, have you anything else to say?' he asked.

'Only that... that I would... would not easily betray my... my father. I thought him a good man until... until this night past... I...' she paused and drew in a long breath. 'I beseech you to hark to my words, but... but if you do not, at least do not send me back... release me into the marshes that I might hide and protect myself. I too am now a t...traitor and I...' she paused for another long inhale, 'I beg your consideration. If you do hark me, then do not just save your own village but I... I beg of you... save the sisters too – do not allow my father to have them killed thus.'

Again, her stuttered, halting words reduced the room to silence. Niamh looked from each man in turn, holding their eyes as the panic in her body came more and more under her control. Finally she moved her gaze to Helligan. His eyes were dark, his lips pressed and his fury seemed to cloud about him like an aura. He swallowed and then turned back to his men.

'Have any of you a reply for my lady?' he asked.

The silence grew heavy, but then Kilm spoke. 'You have my sword, mage. I will trust your judgement, even if you will not hark my caution.'

'Aye,' Jarlsen spoke, and then the same from Alfric.

Helligan turned to Morkyl, his most trusted advisor. 'The king will know by now that Niamh has come back to us, and with his plans so likely he will change them. I say that we take a quarter of the men and spread them through all of the local villages.'

'Agreed. We can take a party to the temple and warn the sisters, and another to Highlark to have his head before the king takes him in. If we move swiftly, we can prevent disaster.'

Helligan nodded. 'I agree,' he said, then cast an eye back to Kilm, 'and the lady Niamh is under my protection now,' he added, 'if any harm should come to her, I will retaliate!'

Kilm bowed his head, despite how his eyes glittered with annoyance. 'This I abide unless we find she has been deceptive; in which case she will face Wolder justice...'

'Fine,' Helligan said, and then stood and stalked from the room. At once upon his leaving, the room descended into arguments again, but Niamh was relieved to hear that at least they argued about which men were to be sent, rather than against the order. As they argued it out, Niamh stood and quietly slipped away. Nobody paid her much mind, all too intent on the discussion about them. Nobody had given her a hint of what was to be expected of her now, either. She had no room to hide in, no purpose now that the message was passed on. Still her horse stood by the gate, saddled and ready, and no page had seen it to be his job to rub the horse down and stable him. It truly was an odd world.

Morkyl emerged from the anti-chamber just as Niamh dithered in the hallway, he cast an eye to her with suspicion. 'What are you doing out here?'

'My horse...'

'I'll have it stabled.'

'A chamber?'

'For you? No, the rooms are all full. You might retake your previous place by the settle if you wish!'

Niamh nodded, thinking that the sweeping brush was probably not far off again.

'Go,' Morkyl snapped and with real panic, she did so, all-but running into the small hall and finding her way to that familiar bench by the glowing embers of the fire. There she lay down her head and closed her eyes. Tears came but Niamh pushed them away, she'd done the right thing, and that was all that mattered.

The voices from the other room slowly ebbed away and silence fell as the night wrapped her fingers about the old house. Niamh lay on the wooden bench, her cloak about her shoulders. It wasn't too cold though; no matter the temperature elsewhere, the marshes were ever heated by the gasses they contained. The last embers of the fire helped too to keep her warm. Where before, she'd slept easily, exhausted by her adventures, that night she felt wide awake. Every dip in the slats of the bench felt uncomfortable beneath her body and her head felt unsupported to the point that the thin cushion of the bench might as well have been flat and made of stone. Her limbs ached from the ride there and she'd not yet taken off her wet boots so her feet were likely congealing inside. A fat tear fell and she allowed it, but just the one, the rest she pushed back down inside. One word echoed, two angry syllables: traitor. She'd done it, betrayed her own father and given the opposition valuable insights into his plans. His words came back to her then though, his bastard, a playing piece… to be married off for militaristic advantage.

Footsteps came from her left and Niamh sat up abruptly. She was far too jumpy to sleep, even in the relative safety of Helligan's hideout. The footsteps passed by the wall and down to the kitchen, then moved back the same way and started up the stairs. Niamh sighed and lay back down, forcing her eyes closed. In all likelihood, they'd have her working again tomorrow and so she needed to sleep!

The footsteps returned just a few moments later. Goddess! How much water did a man need to drink at night? Niamh lay still, her thoughts projecting angrily to the night walker. The steps paused by the door, though, and then a low creak as it slipped open. Niamh allowed a quick peek before closing her eyes again in the darkness, the shadows hid the figure but stature showed it was either Helligan or Alfric.

'Lady Niamh, are you awake?' Helligan's voice.

Niamh sat up in reply.

Helligan walked briskly into the room and offered her his hand, 'come with me,' he said.

Niamh did not reply but took the hand and allowed Helligan to lead her up the stairs, across a wooden floor which cut through a dark corridor which was barely lit by the single candle he carried. Here he walked her to a wooden door and produced a key. Her heart thudded, her fingers clutched tightly in his. As he worked the key, she looked up onto his face, he seemed determined, his eyes like steel.

Inside, there was little luxury. The floor held an old rug over the straw, and the bed was set with curtains rather than boxed in as hers at home was, by sliding wooden doors. Here Helligan led her, and indicated she should get into the bed. Niamh's heart raced, but once she was beneath the coverlet – still in her fine gown but at least minus the shoes – she felt her body begin to relax. With a thudding heart, she waited for him to join her. The court where she grew up left no room for naivety, Niamh knew well what it was a man sought in return for his protection and attentions.

'Sleep here, my lady' Helligan said, 'it's no grand chamber, but better than the bench, I think.'

'And you?'

'I will find myself a warm spot by the fire with a bottle of mead, I will do well.'

Niamh's brow furrowed, disappointment flooding her form along with an alien feeling of longing. Was Helligan really going to just go?

'Goodnight, then?' she managed. Helligan merely nodded and stepped away, drawing the curtain. There he seemed to pause for a moment, but then his footsteps sounded, taking him back toward the door. After all that, he really was just going to leave her alone to sleep? She sat up and put a hand in the bed curtain, feeling the softness of the velvet fibres in her fingers. Her heart thudded once, then seemed to speed up.

'Helligan,' she whispered.

The footsteps paused again, and then his voice from the other side of the curtain 'My lady, there are no conditions to your staying here,' he said. His voice sounded muffled through the curtain but still Niamh could hear the emotion in it. 'No conditions or... or... expectations...'

'I know.'

'What... what is it then?'

'Stay anyway? Come back to your bed, with... with me...'

'I... that was not my intention in bringing you here.'

'I realise that.'

'And yet you wish me to pause? To return?'

Another flurry of irregular heartbeats, 'Yes.'

Silence fell from on the other side of the curtain. Niamh closed her eyes, trying to still the arrythmia in her chest. A footstep, a rustle, and then the curtain was pulled to reveal his face in the darkness. Helligan moved to sit down beside her on the bed and took up her hand. Niamh expected a kiss but instead he lay it to his own breast.

'See what you are doing to me,' he said. Beneath Niamh's fingers she could feel his heart racing too. 'See the power you have...'

Niamh said nothing but allowed her breath to escape her in a soft hiss.

'I can read most people so easily, but you – you are an enigma, Lady Niamh...'

'Just Niamh...' she whispered, then lifted his fingers to her lips and left a gentle kiss on them. Helligan shuffled closer, putting up his own hand to touch her hair.

'You offer me yourself?' he asked.

'Yes.'

'An offer you have made before, to others?'

'Never.'

'I am not a man for such, not a man to dally with a lady and then move on. I remember how things are at court...'

'Never,' Niamh said again, 'my choice.'

'Your choice' Helligan murmured, '…but you have taken a man before? You are not chaste?'

'I am.'

'Oh… by the Goddess,' he murmured, pulling away and dropping her fingers. Niamh murmured but reached for his hand again, this time moving it to her own breast. Helligan's eyes were wary, but fast becoming clouded as he leaned forward, his hand no more a prisoner in hers, than she was in the house, and yet just as she'd stayed, he did not pull free.

'Niamh…' he said, then pulled in a long deep breath and put his lips to touch hers. Niamh ran a finger over his brow, sliding it into his hair. Her breathing juddered in her chest.

'Tell me, honestly, why did you come back?' he asked.

'Because of my father…'

'Not for me?'

'A little for you…'

Helligan closed his eyes and exhaled, his lips on hers still so that she could feel his breath on them. 'I hoped you would,' he finally said, 'It had to be your decision though.'

'I… I wanted… but I didn't dare! Not until I heard what my father planned… then I knew I had to be brave.'

'Thank the goddess then, for giving you a reason for courage…' He moved then, pushing her back down and covering her slight form with his own body. His kisses were unrestrained, his hands moving to pull at the lace which held her dress closed. Niamh's shyness melted away in his obvious ardour, and she found her hands moving to touch him too, unbuttoning his leather jerkin and pulling loose the shirt beneath. Helligan finally managed the lace and loosened the gown, pulling it down to reveal her shoulders and then the soft white under-gown she wore beneath. Her nipples stood firm and erect, little buds which exploded strange new sensations when his fingers brushed over them through the thin cloth. Niamh moved so that the kirtle slipped free, and guided Helligan's hand up under the cloth of the white undergarment. He murmured again, then moved back to kissing her, almost roughly pulling away the under-dress. Niamh, suddenly nude, expelled another breath and sat up to pull away Helligan's shirt, touching bare chest to bare chest. Her whole body trembled, as much with nerves as with the cold, despite that a chill did seep in to touch her skin. Helligan smelled of cloves and spice, it was heady indeed and Niamh buried her face in his throat for a long moment, letting that scent overpower her. Helligan paused, and Niamh felt his body shuffle away slightly, a glance showed her he was unlacing his britches and that was enough to make her face burn again.

'Come,' he murmured, 'I'll try not to hurt you but if you are innocent it might…'

'I know…'

Helligan kissed her again, then with tenderness lay her down onto her back so that she lay beneath him. Her fingers clutched at his arm and her eyes closed. Helligan did not prolong it, entering her with a hard thrust which tore away her virginity in a sharp stab of pain. Niamh gasped and dug her nails into his arm. Helligan paused but she shook her head,

'Go on, don't stop!'

Helligan murmured her name and then began to move, their bodies fast finding pace and rhythm together until his body was stiffening, his heavy breaths becoming gasps. Niamh clutched at him, holding him tight to her and allowing the pleasure to spill into her body.

Afterwards, Helligan was very quiet for some time. His arm held her to his chest until she stopped shaking, his kisses brushing her hair.

'Are you all right?' he finally asked.

'More than.'

'Good.'

They lay again for a few long moments of blissful quiet, and then Helligan kissed her again. 'What would you do, tomorrow, in my position?' he asked, rolling over so that his face was very close to hers on the pillow. 'Who would you send to protect the villages, to save the sisters from their fate?'

'Jarlsen Mantle,' Niamh replied.

'Without hesitation? Why?'

Niamh was quiet for a long moment, enjoying the intimacy, but also that he genuinely seemed to want her opinion — hers! The "idiot" was speaking and Helligan was listening!

'Not Morkyl, he is your most trusted advisor. Not Alfric, he is too likely to be emotionally led, and not Kilm because you would offend him to send him on such a mission.' Niamh's voice was strong, her words easy in her exhaustion.

'So by process of elimination then? Yes, I see your points well. I thought to send Alfric — the McClaven clan have ever been known for their loyalty but I agree, should his own home or family become threatened, I cannot guarantee he'd remain staunch.'

'It is to you to make the decision though,' she said, 'You have more experience than I in leading armies.'

Helligan pulled her to him, kissing her lips softly, then putting down his head over hers on the pillow. 'I will ponder on it,' he said, 'thank you for your council.'

Niamh murmured happily and closed her own eyes, Helligan's arms still tight about her. Suddenly the world seemed friendlier.

Chapter 10

The bed felt very empty and big when Niamh awoke, alone, the following morning. She could still feel the presence of him with more than just the physical ache and the spilled virginal blood she could feel about her thighs, but he and his clothing were both gone. Niamh stood and examined the sheet for a long moment, Missis Kilm would have something to gossip about, later, at any rate. She stood and put her bare feet down onto the cold wooden boards of the floor, and looked about Helligan's chamber. Her gown was still crumpled on the floor where he'd left it and without any other option but the ornate golden-laced garment, she put it on. She'd have to ask Helligan if there were any ladies clothes to be had, something less like a runaway princess's gown. At the corner of the room, was a basin of water, it was still warm but a little clouded by soap – Helligan had obviously used it already. Niamh considered trying to discover a process to acquire more water, but then sighed – to do such was beyond her in her anxious state. Instead she lifted the rag from the edge of the basin and dipped it into the water.

Once dressed, Niamh moved to the dresser where an old tarnished looking-glass stood and for a moment drank in her appearance. She wondered if she looked different now, if the time she'd shared with Helligan Darkfire showed on her thin features. She decided that she did look older, more worldly. Her eyes shone now with a hardness which was never there before, an inner knowledge of the world. If ever she'd had baby fat, it was long gone, and even her locks looked darker, less childlike.

Downstairs, Niamh was assaulted by the smells of freshly baked bread and the sweet scent of preserves. Somewhat cautiously, she made her way into the little dining area and was pleased to find that Alfric sat alone, a bowl of still-warm preserves was in the middle of the table, with two loaves laid out on either side. Alfric had already carved himself two hunks of bread and was dipping them into the jam as though it were a sauce. Niamh smiled shyly, Alfric nodded good morning and refilled his cup with the thin beer which also sat upon the table.

'Come, sit! Eat!' he said, ushering her to the chair opposite. Niamh obeyed and took a seat, then pulled the breadboard over and cut open the bread, breathing in its softly sweet scent. She used the rounded blade of the butter knife on the table to spread some preserve onto the slice. The smell was sweet indeed, the berries not ones she knew, black and bulbus still within the preserve. She took a big bite and murmured at the exquisite taste.

'You like that then?' Alfric asked, dipping his own bread into the bowl again, then putting it to his mouth.

'It's very good.'

Alfric looked surprised that she spoke so easily, but then smiled, his big ginger beard becoming a bit lop-sided as he did so. 'The berries are called Pomples,' he said, 'they grow wild on the edge of the marshes. Missis Kilm turns them to jam.'

'Such a bounty for the picking.'

'That it is, girl. Most of what we have comes directly from the marshes. A bit different from the gilded plates of the palace I'd imagine?'

Niamh paused, testing his words for spite or malice but finding none. She looked down onto her plate for a moment, aware that she was shredding her bread in her fingers, but then looked up at Alfric again, 'better,' she said. Another lop-sided beard smile showed her that her response was the correct one.

From behind came a clatter and then the door opened to show Helligan's form, followed by the other Marsh Lords. Niamh's heart raced but she forced herself to come back to calm.

'Alfric, Lady Niamh,' Helligan spoke, stiffly formal considering the night they'd just passed. 'I trust you slept well?'

'Aye, tis good lodging,' Alfric said.

'I did, thank you,' Niamh said, but her mouth was drying again at the now full room. Kilm was already moving to the table, his eye on the bread and preserve whilst Jarlsen and Morkyl were making their way to the kitchens, likely to beg a bowl of the local thick gator and okra soup they seemed to eat for every meal.

Alfric looked from Niamh to Helligan and back, but did not comment on how she'd spent the night in his chamber – surely they must all know; there was no free chamber, after all.

'And you,' Niamh said to Helligan, desperately needing some glimmer of emotion from him, 'did you sleep well?'

His eyes scanned her face, quickly enough that she doubted any of the others noticed. 'Wonderfully,' he said, his voice gentle.

Niamh held his eye for a moment, but then smiled and nodded, a slight blush in her cheeks making them feel as though they burned.

'We have a lot to discuss after breakfast,' Helligan said, 'I have come to a decision on how to proceed!'

The rest of the day was mainly taken in planning. Helligan pleased Niamh by offering the role of protector of the marshes to Jarlsen, as she'd suggested, but at the same time he was oddly distant, speaking to her much as he did to the others, not like the Helligan who had gently whispered to her the previous night.

'What do you say, Lady Niamh? You know your father's fortifications better than we do.' Helligan said suddenly, pulling her from her inner turmoil. It was just past lunch and still they were sat in the planning room – Helligan's equivalent of a throne room – actually a small cold chamber with a table in the centre but little of any wealth or extravagance about. Stone walls, a stone floor, tattered tapestries at the walls.

'I... sorry?'

'The West Keep, or Anglemarsh? Which is better guarded?'

'West Keep. Father fears your army will come over the marshes. Anglemarsh guards the road and has only a skeleton staff now that my father has left it again...'

'Good,' Helligan said, then went back to viewing the table where he had wooden figures set out to represent his armies.

'You plan to attack, then?'

'Yes, if he will attack our homelands, our priestesses, then we will strike back. I am sending half of the men out to take Highlark unawares, and to remove the sisters of Herodite from harm's way... the other half are hungry for a fight too, so I thought to give them one... a keep would be beneficial to us and a step closer to removing the king from his throne.'

'What when the golden king is gone?' Jarlsen asked, 'will you put the crown on your own head, Helligan?'

Helligan paused and glanced up to where the four Marsh Lords stood about him and glanced between them all.

'No, actually,' he said, 'I'm going to put it on his daughter.'

Niamh's gut compacted dangerously and her hand moved to the edge of the table. The noise about the room turned to a din as once more multiple voices seemed to erupt, Kilm's instant shouting against the plan, Morkyl asking for clarity, Jarlsen and Alfric both chiming in too, more positively for Niamh.

'Wha... what?' Niamh finally managed.

'It makes sense, I think,' Helligan said, speaking to them all, but holding her eye, 'I do not wish to be king, nor is it my right to be so. I have no claim to any relation of your father, Niamh. And my lords, do any of you have any claim on, or desire of the golden throne? To rule the whole kingdom? To try to win the affections of common men not our own kind?'

The group had fallen silent and none of them spoke to correct Helligan.

'As I thought. We just need to appoint a better monarch, one we trust to rule with true kindness and a respect for all men, not just for some. We need a monarch who will not kill off the marshes, will not allow some men to starve whilst others gorge themselves. Fair, kind, intelligent, and with a claim on the throne solid enough to prevent the common folk turning on them – deposing them! The people love Lady Niamh and her father himself legitimised her...'

'Her father's people love her, but what of our people?' Kilm asked.

'What if she was blessed by Morgana?' Helligan asked, 'would you accept her then?'

'Aye!' Alfric said, 'I would fight on those terms for the lady.'

'Are there any here who will not?'

Kilm glowered but did not object. Jarlsen and Morkyl were both silent too: Jarlsen more thoughtful, Morkyl with concern in his eyes but still – neutral.

'And Lady Niamh, should this all come together, would you accept these brave commanders and their men as your army?'

'I... yes.'

'Good, then it is settled! We'll go out and remove the priestesses from harm, and then you and I will take a trip to visit with Mother Morgana, my lady, and ask her blessing to crown you as queen.'

A long moment's silence fell again, but then Morkyl pointed to the table, 'Best leave one of those groups of men with the lady then, Helligan. I think you just made her a target of every soldier loyal to her father!'

'The lady in under my personal care,' Helligan said, 'it will take a whole army to get past me, we all know that! Now, what about if we were to march on Anglemarsh with a smaller troupe, drive them out, and then attack the West Keep...' and thus the matter was dropped.

Later that same day, just as the sun was starting to set, the raiding party rode out, not to raid, but instead to rescue the sisters of Herodite – those Niamh's father had earmarked for attack. Niamh herself was to stay behind, Helligan decreed.

'If your father knows his plans are scuppered he might still come in hopes of reacquiring you, Princess.'

Niamh nodded, downcast.

'If you wish to be of use here...'

'I know where the broom is!'

Helligan laughed aloud but shook his head, 'I was going to ask you to start drawing out a map of Anglemarsh,' he said, 'all the nooks and crannies, anything you think might help us to take it.'

That was better at least to being designated housekeeper! Niamh nodded and then moved to pour herself a glass of the delicious ice-cold spring water which was the product of the old well in the yard. When she turned back, Helligan had gone.

The night seemed to pull on endlessly. Niamh drew up the maps with enthusiasm, and then managed to compel herself to enter the big old stone dining room at about supper time, thankful that most of the group were absent. There she and Missis Kilm, as well as two older men and Alfric shared a crusty loaf fresh from the ovens with a broth of chuck meat, crispy carrots and an odd green vegetable which Niamh didn't recognise, but which was sharp and aniseed-like to the taste. All told, a quiet and enjoyable supper before the endless stretch of night. Niamh couldn't sleep. She didn't dare go to Helligan's chamber when he wasn't there so had taken up her old spot by the fireplace again. There she lay and waited, and waited. The little house-kretch, a creature she now knew to answer to the name of Pommel, snuck in around the hour of four and made its way over to where Niamh sat, jumping up and pushing itself against her.

'Begone, I have no meat for you!' Niamh muttered, pushing the animal away. Rather than be pushed, the soft little creature turned spikey, digging a claw into her leg rather than be removed. Niamh swore at the sudden sharp pain but then looking down into yellow eyes, found a tired giggle.

'Well, I suppose I am in your place,' she allowed. 'Come here then, Pom.' The Kretch stretched itself out and then curled up in her lap, apparently sleeping despite that one eye kept opening, watching her distrustfully.

Never before in her life, had Niamh known a night take so long to pass. She sat upright until dawn began to bloom, and then more slumped as it drew in the brightness of day. Missis Kilm appeared at about six and clucked at Niamh, but did not move her from her spot sat watching the door and willing it to open.

'Ye know, you get used te it,' she remarked, picking up the broom.

'Hmm?'

'Never knowin if ee's coming back after a raid or battle. It's torment at first, but that passes and ye get used te it.'

Niamh nodded and yawned, rubbing her eyes.

'Best ye can do for ee is te get yerself up in that comfy bed o his and sleep off the worry so you'm fresh-faced for im when ee do come back…'

Niamh nodded again, her eyes so heavy she could barely keep them open. She stood, ready to obey, but then was taken by the sound of a lupinite's bark. At once she was alert again, running to the window. There'd been no lupinites here, in fact no dogs or wolf-kind at all, but her father's men, she knew, used them in battle. At the window though, the panic was instantly relieved by Helligan leading home his army. He took up the helm, bloodied and with hair a mess about his face. Beside him rode his Marsh Lords, and behind them the rest of the raiding party. Niamh pulled in a deep breath, worried they'd been too late, but then caught sight of a white-clad, hooded rider behind the men. The first Sister of the temple!

'Ah, an there they are, right as rain,' Missis Kilm smiled, then moved past Niamh to open the door. Helligan, just arriving without, dismounted with a little grunt. He was nursing his side a little, but otherwise seemed well. The other men remained outside, and likely were to ride back to the camps, even Kilm who merely winked to his wife, declining to dismount.

'Come inside, bring the sisters into the house, the two who were injured can be nursed here. Niamh, Mm Kilm, can you fetch water and salts?' Helligan barked.

Niamh did as she was asked, following Missis Kilm into the kitchens and returning with a bowl of soapy water. Helligan took the bowl and laid it down as two of the sisters were brought in on make-shift stretchers, accompanied by four others. All were dressed in the robes of Herodite, the white linen with the red rose embroidered on the front. All were hooded too, and without a mark of paint on their faces. The sisters of Herodite the Mother were an order of demure sisters, but not all sisters were so.. All of the sisters acknowledged that they worshipped the same goddess, but the different faces of her were debated with each order taking a different face of the goddess. Most were as normal as any other woman, simply engrossed in their religious practice, and some were to the other extreme. The sisters of Demontia, the face of lust, for example, were little more than painted whores and the sisters of Helston – the war-like battle face, were battle-hardened and scarred. The sisters gathered there in the vast hall, however, were all disciples of the goddess of mothers, and therefore they were quiet and gentle – healers and nurses.

Helligan handed the bowls of water to the older sisters, whilst the younglings went to pray by the fireplace. Niamh dithered, but then found her hand taken by Helligan.

'Come with me,' he murmured. 'Bring water and a bandage.'

Niamh did so and found herself led back up to Helligan's chamber, supplies in hand. There he let out a long breath and the mask began to fall, showing that he was in some level of pain.

'Helligan, what...?'

'It was as I feared, your father's men waited in ambush. We were successful, I think we killed them all and if not we sent them packing either way, tails between legs.'

'Will all of the injured sisters survive?'

'I do not doubt their magics for healing, but.. I...' Helligan lifted his shirt to show Niamh a jagged wound in his flesh there.

'Oh! Let me go and fetch...'

'No, I want no stranger's hands on me,' he said, moving to sit on the bed with a little hiss of pain. 'Will... will you? There's a needle and thread there on the sill – I can make fire to cleanse the needle.'

Nerves rushed, making Niamh's belly hurt a little, but still she managed to nod. Helligan put a hand to his bottle of water and touched the candle wick, making it burst into blue flame. Niamh took the needle from the sill and ran it through the flame, then came back to sit beside Helligan. The wound was red and angry, the edges jagged and still oozing blood. Helligan glanced down as she used a cloth to wipe away the worst of the dried blood.

'A sword?' she asked.

'Spearhead. I'm lucky it came back out and didn't break off in there.'

There might actually have been less damage if it had, Niamh pondered grimly but she said nothing of it and continued to clean the wound with the salty water. Once all the grime was rinsed away, Niamh picked up the needle.

'This will hurt,' she warned.

'No more than it already does.'

Niamh said nothing but threaded the needle, just like a million times doing embroidery at home, and then plunged it into the wet oozing flesh of Helligan's wound. He murmured and when Niamh looked up, she saw his eyes fill with water, he waved her on though and so she continued. Once he was patched up, Helligan lay himself on the bed. He was sweating slightly, obviously still in pain. Niamh made to leave, her mind set on finding him something to dull the pain, but his fingers curled about her wrist, holding her gently in place.

'Stay with me?' he whispered.

'If you wish it?'

'I do. You don't look like you've slept a wink — I will take that as flattery in concern for me, but I don't want you tired on the morrow, close your eyes, sweetling, I'm home now, safe and sound... come, lie down here and sleep.'

Niamh allowed the tiredness to take her bones and did as Helligan beckoned, lying down carefully beside him and closing her eyes. She was determined to stay awake, in case he needed anything, but in the end, she was asleep before he was.

Chapter 11

The forest at the edge of the marshes was lush and green. In the distance came the rush of running water, and here and there the ground seemed a little marshy under the hooves of Niamh's horse. Niamh didn't mind it, a strong enough horsewoman not to worry for a bit of squelchy mud and besides, the dim afternoon sunshine which was beginning upon them was quickly drying it up anyway. Helligan rode ahead of Niamh, his steed of choice a dappled grey stallion which seemed a little wilful under his command, occasionally throwing its head and snorting, causing him on more than one occasion to put a hand down to the wound he still held on his flank. Despite her insistence that Helligan rest in the aftermath of being injured, it had still only been a week since he'd taken the wound and still it was raised and sore. Niamh's own horse was the one she'd taken from her father's stables. White-grey of coat with a temperament gentle and tame, and more than once she'd pondered offering to trade mount.

As they rode, Niamh patted the sweaty neck of the beast and murmured quiet words of encouragement – somehow animals were easier to speak to than people. Helligan kept a distance between them enough to disallow speaking, despite how often he looked behind to ensure she still followed. Despite the warming of the sun as the day drew to a close, the air was still chilled, chill enough that Niamh was bundled in a cloak which Alfric had gifted to her, a man's garment made of itchy wool but warm with a fur collar from a wolf, likely one killed by his own hand. Her hair was neatly braided, coloured darker with juice from some berries Helligan had found, and her gown sensible. Helligan too was dressed in commoner's rags, with a rough-spun tunic and his long hair pulled into a tail behind him and bound with twine. Even if they did have to stop for the night, as Helligan had warned they might, there was no way either of them would be recognised now.

Helligan and Niamh rode for hours, through the marshes to the forest, and then onwards through the trees, past two small settlements and then back into the trees. Soon they would break for the wide sprawling moors which led to the very edge of the mountains. The woman they were riding to consult, Morgana, lived in a shack about halfway up. From what Niamh could gather, the old lady was something of a sage for the Woldermen, an ancient old lady who was grandmother to more of them than could count. The air turned more chill as the sun sailed behind a cloud and Niamh's stomach growled. They'd ridden all day without stopping and her body was beginning to feel it. Helligan pulled reign and turned back to her.

'Are you tiring?' he asked.

Niamh nodded.

'I thought so, your horse's pace has slowed. There's bound to be an inn within the hour – shall we stop and continue tomorrow?'

Several questions occurred to Niamh; would an inn overnight be safe? Did Helligan mean to sleep or just to stop and refresh themselves? Did he even have any money? Typically though, her voice chose that moment not to come and so she merely nodded again. Helligan's eyes skimmed her face, but then he turned back again and coaxed his horse into a trot.

It was little more than twenty minutes before Niamh caught sight of a pillar of smoke rising at the edge of the trees.

Helligan moved towards it and they found there a small hamlet which, thankfully, had an inn. The building was not large and was a little run down, but they had a stable for the horses and, at Helligan's enquiry, rooms and food too.

'You seem wearied,' the old man spoke as a serving wench went to find a bowl of stew. 'Have you travelled far?'

'We have, my wife's mother is very ill so we are travelling back to Hailstone to visit with her.'

The inn-keep glanced at Niamh's face. Her hair was covered with an old scarf and her body, still shivering, wrapped in Alfric's cloak.

'You don't look much like a Hailstone lass...'

Niamh noticed Helligan tense but she found a smile, 'I have often heard such,' she managed, 'my father was from the south.'

'I see,' he said, handing over two mugs of thin beer, and Niamh and Helligan moved to the safety of the table by the window.

'I'm sorry if I am a little tense,' Helligan said, as soon as they were sat down, 'I dislike you being out in the open so unprotected.'

Niamh nodded and sipped her beer.

'Do you realise, that as word spreads of your joining us, you will become more and more of a target to our enemies.'

'I'm not foolish,' she said.

'I know you are not, I didn't mean to imply...'

Niamh caught his glance and shook her head, shushing him as the wench came and placed to bowls on the table. The "stew" looked more like lumpy porridge, but it smelled good.

'Eat quickly so we might go upstairs,' Helligan said, 'I am not comfortable here.'

Niamh sped her eating up a little, then stood and allowed Helligan to take her hand. At the doorway, though, the innkeeper stood blocking the path. Helligan tensed again and Niamh felt her own body stiffen in anticipation. Helligan was strong enough to protect her, she trusted him, but the image of last time she'd seen him fight came back to her – the explosions and then turning to see him fallen – prone.

'I wish for no trouble, friend…' Helligan said.

'And nor I, but you chose to come in here…'

'I wish merely for a room, to sleep, with my wife.'

'Your wife, eh?'

Helligan put a hand on Niamh's arm, 'my wife,' he said again, firmly.

'Thing is,' the innkeeper said, scratching his neck, 'thing is I don't believe she is that – you wouldn't be absconding, now, would you? You have the look of a soldier, and she of a lady… the child of some Lord hereabouts?'

Niamh felt relief, the man didn't know then, didn't recognise her after all. Helligan glanced back to Niamh again and then lifted one finger with his right hand, a blue flame began to form there.

'I am no soldier, *sir*, I am a mage, and unless you wish to see your precious inn burn, you will keep from trying to blackmail me,' he said.

The innkeeper's eye fixated on the flames, watching as they ran over Helligan's palm.

'However,' Helligan continued, 'should you keep your tongue and say nothing of what you have seen here, then you might find yourself… well rewarded upon my leaving.'

'I… might?'

'Indeed, and know this too, I sleep with one eye open, before you consider opening my throat and that of my good lady here in our sleep.'

The innkeeper paled further. Niamh watched with interest, she'd not realised how feared the mages were, a true rarity now. The innkeeper moved aside and Helligan closed his palm, extinguishing the flames.

'Key?'

The innkeeper handed it over with a murmur that it was the room first on the right.

Helligan took Niamh's arm and led her to the stairs. There he turned back though, 'Mind what I said,' he snapped, and then led Niamh up to the room above.

Inside the room was very plain, but the bed looked comfortable enough. Niamh sat on the edge whilst Helligan moved to sit on a wooden chair close by the window. His jaw was still pressed tightly and his eyes aflame with anger.

'W… was that sensible?' Niamh managed to choke out, 'there are not many of… of you…'

'I know. I lost my temper. I'm sorry.'

'I…'

'Get some sleep, Sweetling,' he said, 'I'll watch over you.'

Niamh, exhausted after the long hour in the saddle, did not argue. Her thighs were chafed and her back hurt, especially her lower back. Helligan's eyes shone. Even as the light escaped the room and night drew in, Niamh could see his eyes, the glower of his features and she guessed that if it were not for her presence, the innkeeper might well be dead and the inn in flames. For her, he tempered himself and that gave Niamh another small thrill in the depths of her stomach. Somehow, she felt, they worked together well to achieve a balance.

Niamh awoke to bright dawn sunshine seeping in through the curtainless window of the little room. The beams fell onto her face, causing her to crease her eyes up again and move away. Half-asleep, for a moment she pondered where she was, but then the memory came back to her and her eyes moved to the chair by the window. Helligan did not look as though he had moved. His stance was a little more casual, his body more relaxed and he had folded his arms over his chest. Niamh guessed he'd not even so much as closed his eyes as she'd slept.

'Are you awake?' his voice was soft, still tired.

'I am – you should have woken me!' she said, straightening up. She'd slept atop of the coverlet, and fully dressed too, but still she felt infinitely refreshed.

'I wanted you to rest up,' he said, then stood, still nursing that damn wound at his side a little when he moved. 'We should go.'

'Is... is something the matter?'

'No, I merely wish to be gone before the household awakens,' he said, moving quickly to the door and then opening it quietly, with caution. Niamh, trusting his instinct, followed his lead, carrying her boots in her hand to muffle her footsteps. The tavern was eerily quiet below, the day not quite broken and the occupants asleep. Niamh tiptoed after Helligan through the building and out to the stables where their horses was tied. Quickly Niamh pulled on her boots, her stockinged toes icy from the cold ground, and then mounted her horse. Helligan patted the horse's rear and then climbed up on his own steed.

'Come,' he said, 'quickly! – they'll hear the horses!'

Niamh nodded and followed Helligan's lead, spurring her horse on faster than she would usually dare.

The rest of the ride seemed to pass quickly, likely in the adrenaline of their escape from the Inn. Niamh's horse was unsure of the terrain as they began their ascent of the mountainous ground, and so it took all of her care to keep him walking normally on the rugged ground. Helligan seemed to have no such trouble with his horse, and Niamh inwardly took back her smugness of having the "good" mount. Finally they came to a small Wolder village, tucked away in a glade of green, fairly close to the bottom of the peak. Helligan dismounted and made his way through the village on foot; Niamh followed his lead. As they walked, eyes turned to look upon them, but nobody challenged their presence. At the edge of the village there was a path leading off into a glade of trees, this path Helligan took, then paused.

'Morgana is a very, very, old woman,' he all but whispered, 'mind her manner. She may seem unfriendly, but she is not – just cautious. It was she who saved my life when... well, you know when...'

'Oh!'

'I know this village so intimately, and the villagers look upon us with such suspicion, because I was brought here after I fell. It was here I learned of the goddess's new plan for me, my new path.'

Niamh nodded and then followed him around through the trees to a small shack. The place was obviously old, but had been repaired over and over, probably by well-meaning clansmen, Niamh guessed. Helligan took in a deep breath and knocked on the door. There was a silence for a few moments, but then an old voice croaked, 'Come on in, Helligan Darkfire.'

Helligan nodded to Niamh and then pushed open the door. He had to stoop slightly to enter, and Niamh found herself blinking against the darkness as they passed into the old shack. The woman herself was bundled in rags, very much a Wolder matriarch. Her ears hung with various jewellery beneath a cascade of white hair. Her eyes were old, wise, and her lips pressed thin.

'So you came back then?' she said, her hand flicking to indicate they should be seated on the pile of furs and skins opposite. Her voice was aged, deep and with the croak old vocal cords bring. Helligan moved at once and was seated, Niamh dithered, but followed suit, sitting uncomfortably close to Helligan after the distance between them since he'd bedded her.

'It is good to see you, Mother.' Helligan said.

'You are injured?'

'I am, a spear wound.'

'Humph. It's healing – you don't need me for that. I see you have company, a wife?'

'No, not a wife. A companion, one I have brought to you with purpose.'

Niamh followed the conversation, her eyes darting from Morgana to Helligan. He had called the old lady "Mother", and she wondered quietly if that was a title or an endearment.

'Shame – you could do with a wife! I suppose you are still aiding my boys in their march towards the golden king?'

'I am, my power as a battle-mage has led them to grant me the gift of leadership.'

'A battle-mage? Hmmpfh. Is that still what you are calling yourself?'

Helligan glanced from Morgana to Niamh and then back again, 'I... yes...'

'Do you still deny your heritage, or are you bashful before the lady?'

Helligan looked again to Niamh, and then back to the old witch, 'Mother, I...'

'A little of both, mayhap? But then I think you ever tried to hide things from me.'

'I did, Mother, you know why!'

'Hmmpfh,' the old lady said for a third time, then turned her eyes to Niamh, 'and who is this one, then? Your paramour I suppose, if not wife?'

Lady Niamh is not my paramour, she is a princess of the realm...'

Niamh's heart sank slightly, she'd hoped for more than a flat-out denial.

'A princess of the realm, eh? Their realm, I presume, not ours? I know of no princesses amongst our people with honey hair hidden under the mulch of Hiffer berries... so be it, but why then am I visited by a so-called *battle-mage* – lord of this rebellion – and *a princess of the realm* here in my humble hovel?'

'I was a princess, I stand with Lord Helligan now,' Niamh managed.

'We come to you for guidance.' Helligan added.

The old lady gazed at them with veiled eyes. She simply watched them for a long moment, then took a deep gulp from a mug which rested at her side. Her eyes were very dark, and her eyebrows showed that once her hair had been the same. 'Speak,' she finally said.

'I seek to dethrone the golden king,' Helligan said.

'Yes, yes, you do not need a direct line to the goddess to have heard of Helligan the War-mage and his crusade to free the Woldermen.'

'Then you know I am your loyal son, still.'

The old lady said nothing.

'I seek guidance in how to proceed once we conquer the Golden Keep.'

'I thought my sons had already done that?'

'No, The Golden Keep was sacked, but it was not held. The King regained his castle and has fortified it.'

'Then perhaps you do better to speak of "if", than of "when" you conquer the Keep.'

Helligan, the great Helligan Darkfire, looked somewhat abashed to be thus chastised, and then nodded, 'My apologies for my arrogance,' he said. 'The sacking of the Golden Keep was before my time... as well you know, Mother.'

The old lady took another long drink from her goblet and set it down, tapping the rim. Helligan moved to the fireplace and rummaged there for a moment, still stooped slightly for the low roof. He returned with an old glass bottle from which he poured another glass of what looked like spice-water for Morgana. He took a swig himself, a gesture which showed his familiarity with the old lady and her house, and then offered the bottle to Niamh. She shook her head and so Helligan replaced it where he had found it and returned to her side.

'Come on,' the old lady sighed at last, 'out with it, Helligan, you have not travelled all this way with your princess in tow merely to converse and drink. What do you want from me?'

'I want to know if you would offer me your blessing if I were to crown the Lady Niamh here as the queen, after her father is deposed – if he is deposed.'

'My sons won't cry for her without my blessing, eh?'

'Indeed, you have the truth of it, mother.'

The old lady turned to Niamh and looked her up and down. 'Come, quiet one,' she said, patting the space next to her on the pile of old furs by the fireplace.

Niamh did as she was told, taking a seat beside the old lady. The smell of roses almost masked the musk of the old woman's body odour. Morgana looked her up and down, and then took her hand in hers. She inhaled a few times then opened her eyes again and glared at Helligan. 'Leave,' she said.

'I…' his eyes moved to Niamh's face but she nodded, she felt no fear of this old witch, despite that perhaps she should.

Helligan's brow creased but still he obeyed, standing and removing himself from the shack. Niamh could guess he was not gone far though.

'Come closer to the fire, child,' the old woman said, her voice little more than a croak, 'here, warm yourself.'

Niamh did so, it was true the little shack had grown very cold in the minutes they'd been there and it was good to feel the flames on her skin, chasing away the ache of coldness therein.

'So, Helligan wants to make you queen, to unite the people and all live happily in peaceful unity, hmmm?'

Niamh knew not what to say so remained quiet.

'Hmm. No words for me then, strange silent girl? That is well, we will suffice without.'

Niamh allowed her eyes to really take in the old witch's face, focusing on her wise old eyes which still gleamed with a twinkle which could have been good humour, could have been mere vitality. The old lady allowed Niamh her inquisitive glance but then spoke again.

'I see I am but a curiosity to you, I suppose to one so young and fresh an old lady like me must be so. It is well, child. I see intellect in your eye, and kindness.'

'I try to be kind,' Niamh whispered.

'Kindness can be an undoing in a queen.'

Niamh looked again to her hands.

'As can timidity,' Morgana added. 'A queen must be strong, must be more-so than even a king, in order to command respect… but I see you are strong, within, hmmm, and you have bravery too. I see what he sees in you, but I see potential only, untapped. Your journey is just beginning.'

Niamh nodded, her eyes on the face of the hag, now, rather than her hands. The old lady put out a hand and Niamh took it. The hag's eyes rolled back, showing just the whites. She sat for some moments, and then seemed suddenly to snap back to the present.

'Yes. The goddess has a plan for you indeed! You might be a good queen, one day, but still I see trials before then, decisions to be made and weaknesses to conquer.'

Niamh's heartrate picked up but she managed to remain serene, nodding.

'Weaknesses include those of the heart... Helligan Darkfire. You love him?'

Niamh's tongue felt alien, her lips dry. She nodded.

'Then you more than any need to keep a level head. Helligan was brought to me on the brink of death; my sons were reluctant to let such a powerful man die despite that he apparently served their enemy. I revived him and I gave him a vision of the future, should the king he served be allowed to remain on the throne. I opened his eyes but I have never known whether my actions were for the good or not. I still don't.'

'Helligan joined your cause,' Niamh whispered, defensive. 'He serves you now!'

'Ah! So in defence of him you will speak? But no, not my cause. I am too old for causes!'

'Your people then, he... he joined your people.'

'Yes, he did but there is more to Helligan Darkfire and his motives than you, or any of my boys, yet realise. His secrets are not mine to spill, but I council you with caution.'

'Helligan is a good man!' Niamh argued, a little hot of temper.

'I never said he wasn't, child. That is how I live with the fact that I saved his life. But Helligan is not... he is not a normal man. He is torn between two worlds, and the Goddess only knows which he will chose. If he loves you enough, perhaps you can lead him through the mists.'

Niamh looked at her fingers, heart pounding. 'But he does not love me,' she said.

'He has told you thus?'

Niamh shook her head.

The old lady said nothing, but found a knowing smile. 'Look a little closer,' she said. 'Men are prouder about such things.'

Niamh said nothing, but managed a half-nod.

The old lady surveyed her again, her lips puckering slightly, 'Call him back in,' she said at last.

Niamh paused, she'd never once, in her whole life, called for anybody. She looked helplessly to the old lady, and then went to stand.

'No, call him in.'

Niamh's heart pounded, her lips felt almost numb but she took a deep breath and then called, projecting her voice as well she could for Helligan.

Helligan's return was so quick that Niamh knew her suspicions were correct and he'd been standing just outside of the door waiting. His eyes ran over her, his surprise written in them for her shout.

'Ni... Lady Niamh... is all well?'

Niamh met his eye, her fingers almost numb but an alien feeling of confidence was growing within. 'All is well, Helligan,' she said, 'Morgana bade me call you.'

Helligan looked from Niamh to the old witch with confusion but then focused on Morgana.

'You have my blessing,' she said.

'Hmm?'

'Your lady here, I give you my blessing to crown her as queen, if you succeed in your crusade. However, I see shadows in your future, son, I bid you caution but I cannot see your path because, as ever, you hide it from me.'

Helligan's expression turned intense as he looked at the old lady, then, oddly, he knelt and removed the bottle of water he wore about his neck, and this he handed to the witch. She glanced down into it, and then back to him, frowned slightly but then put the bottle on the ground beside her, tentatively, as though it were fragile like an egg. She put out her hand then and Helligan took it, but his eyes were darker than before, more cautious. The old lady sat in silence for a long moment, and then opened her eyes again.

'I wish you luck,' she said, her voice showing that she was more shaken than she appeared outwardly. 'I will beg the goddess for your success,' she took up the bottle and looked almost longingly at it, then back up at Helligan. He knelt and the old lady slipped the leather string back over his head.

'Come,' Helligan said to Niamh, 'We need to leave if we wish to get to the cover of the forest before the night completely falls on us.'

Niamh nodded and took his offered hand, but then turned back to Morgana, 'Thank you,' she whispered.

'One more thing,' Morgana said, just as they were leaving.

Niamh turned but the message was not for her.

'My son. You must never, ever, agree to rule this kingdom yourself,' Morgana said, 'that, my boy, that would be allowing this to go too far!'

'I know, I know it well!' Helligan whispered, 'Goodbye Mother.'

Chapter 12

The only light in the dark of the woods was the flickering blue flame of the small fire Helligan had lit. The only sound, save the odd call of an owl, was the little pop and crackle as damp bark was devoured by flames and the occasional snort of the horses, tethered as they were to a tree at the edge of the glade. Niamh sat huddled in her cloak, sending a silent thanks to Alfric for the gift of warmth he'd given her. In one hand she held a small cup of water and in the other a rabbit's leg, dark and gamy, but succulent at least, and hot in her fingers. Helligan sat opposite, his back against a tree and his eyes wary. After their adventures at the inn, they'd agreed to take their shelter under the trees for the return. Niamh had never been out of doors so late, especially not with the intention of sleeping thus. Her limbs felt energised, her body alert and ready to move at any given moment. Helligan, opposite, was already finished with his half of the rabbit he'd caught, skinned and then cooked on his magical fire, and had deposited the bones, now stripped of meat, into his saddle bag, for what purpose she couldn't even guess. Niamh watched him a moment, and then allowed her tired eyes to move back to the blue flames. They were mesmerising as they flickered and popped, their odd blue hue giving off something of a glow.

'How do you do it?' the words were out before she realised it and even Niamh was shocked to hear herself speak, not just to answer, but to begin a conversation.

'Hmm?' Helligan asked, shuffling closer.

'To make fire from water. How…'

Helligan was quiet for a moment, but then shuffled closer again so that he was beside her. 'Water?' he asked.

Niamh indicated the bottle at his neck.

'This? Oh, that's not water sweetling.' Helligan slid the leather thong over his head and showed the bottle to her. Niamh's fingers closed around it, holding it up to the light of the fire.

'Don't uncap it,' Helligan warned. She nodded and then shook the bottle gently. No, no liquid. Not water inside but a strange swirling mass, like a blue mist which moved and swirled. The mist gave off a slight glow, like a will-o-the wisp.

'Beautiful,' she murmured, 'So… so very beautiful.'

'It's an… a… well, sort of a focus,' he murmured, 'A spell within a bottle which links me to the elements. If I use it, it is not as powerful as if I am touching a true element. Fire magic is stronger with fire, water the same, but it at least renders me able to cast when I don't have access to an element.'

'Do… do all mages have these?'

'No. It is advanced magic.'

'How… how do you…' Niamh trailed off, unsure of how to word her question. Helligan put out his hand, it looked normal, like any hand.

'It's hard to explain,' he said, 'the elements are not singular, not isolated. Most mages never progress past the basics because they refuse to entertain that. There are five basic elements too, with spirit being the fifth, and this too is difficult for some to accept. This fifth, the chi which runs through the core of us all, this is what is, essentially within this bottle, and it is this which links all of the others together. A master of the chi, can master any elemental magic. I am not a master yet.'

A small glow started in Helligan's palm. Not a bright flame, just a simple glow, it spluttered and then went out. 'That is all I have,' he said, 'unless I use my focus. I am working on being able to produce magic from within me, but I fear it is beyond this human form to do so. Here,' he cupped his other hand about the bottle and closed his eyes, 'Here I feel it burning within, a strange yellow liquid energy, I can twist it, touch it, feel it…' the flame grew as he spoke, taking on that odd blue hue. 'It's blue because I resonate most with water,' he added, reading her question on her features, 'most of what I manipulate takes on water's might…' the flame died down again and Helligan closed his fist. 'Does that help you to understand?'

'I wish I could learn something of it.'

'I am no teacher, but I could try to help if you wish to learn?'

'A female mage?' Niamh laughed, another alien sound, 'perhaps not…'

'I see no reason why not. You could be the first.' Helligan smiled, his eyes softening and his expression becoming more as it had been on the night they'd spent together. Niamh's heart pounded suddenly and, feeling brave, she moved so that she was within his arms. Helligan clutched them around her, pulling her to him.

'You have no idea of what you are capable, if you gave up the fear of trying,' he murmured, but then settled back with his back against an old oak and fell to silence. Niamh's eyes closed, tiredness dragging her on towards the sleep her body so desperately needed, safe in Helligan's arms with her head on his shoulder. Even as she nodded off, she felt his head bow slightly, and his kiss on her hair.

The crunch of a footstep sounded in the darkness, half-rousing Niamh from her sleep. She was lying still up against Helligan's chest, slumped a little through slumber but held safe by his hands. The wind whipped about them, a cold blast which stirred their clothing, and then another footstep came. Niamh lifted her head as Helligan knelt up, moving her slightly to do so. His eyes cast over the dark forest whilst his hand moved with that instinct he had, to clutch at the little bottle of strange magical essence about his neck. His shoulders were very tense, every muscle firm as he held Niamh to him.

'Did you hear…'

'Hush Sweetling,' he murmured, pulling further away so that he could stand, leaving her sat against the tree. The shadows pulled in but then one of the horses whinnied, making Niamh jump.

'Who is there?' Helligan said, casting out a hand, allowing the blue flame to burn there again, lighting up the glade. The light was bright and from her position sitting on the ground, Helligan seemed quite the sight to Niamh. His long loose hair flowed inky black in the darkness, the light of his flame picking up the blue hues. His eyes were dark, inky pools in the darkness and his shoulders tight, taunt. He looked taller suddenly, more imposing.

'I said show yourself!' he said again. 'By the command of Helligan Darkfire!'

Still nothing, but then the sound of rustling in the foliage. Niamh shuffled forward, staying in Helligan's light but reaching for her bow. With it in hand she felt stronger and stood too, drawing an arrow but holding it tight. Another rustle came from behind, making Niamh spin about but Helligan used his free hand to gently steady her. 'Calm,' he said, 'It's just an animal… look, yonder…'

Niamh's straining eyes moved to where Helligan pointed. She could just about make out a low shape slinking away through the undergrowth. Helligan watched with her, and then bent and touched his hand to the remains of the fire, flaring them over the half-charred log.

'A wolf, Sweetling,' he murmured, 'it won't come any closer than that to my flame.'

'How could you tell? I could not see it…'

'But I could, come lie back down with me…'

'It had a person's footstep…'

'Indeed, there are more things than we know hidden in these woods, but what it showed us was a wolf's face and so it is respectful to treat it as thus.'

'I don't understand.'

'You don't need to, but it leaves us in peace and so we will grant it the same honour… come, sit back down… there is nothing to fear here tonight!'

Niamh did so, allowing him to sit back against the tree in his previous position as she deposited her bow back with the bags before she sat. Helligan gently drew her back into his lap, an arm about her. She laid back down with her head on his chest for a mere moment but then sat up again, too spooked to sleep. Helligan took her wrist and turned her hand over, running a finger up over her pulse. He paused and then put his lips down there too, kissing the vein. 'I will not let anybody or anything harm you,' he murmured, 'please, you need to rest, it's quite a ride on the morrow and I don't want you to be tired…'

'How can I sleep when I know not…'

'You are in no danger, I promise you…' Helligan leaned forward and slid a hand through her hair, around her head, and gently pulled her back to him. She did not resist despite the fear. Helligan's breathing quickened a little though, and as Niamh looked up to see the cause, she found his lips moving to cover hers, his hands moving to hold her as he kissed her, lying her down in the dirt. Niamh gave one more thought to the odd footstep she'd heard, but then Helligan was unlacing her gown and her attention was gone.

Chapter 13

"And so, that settles it then!" Alfric's voice rang out with a happy tone, echoing about the low chamber. 'We have our queen, men!'

Niamh's hands pressed tightly together, the enormity of the situation finally seeming to come clear. She and Helligan had ridden in just an hour earlier, and already the news of Morgana's blessing had spread to the keep, travelling faster even that they had. Her clothing still stank of horse and her hair tumbled over her shoulders where she'd not had time to re-braid it. In that moment, she realised, she probably did look more like one of them than like one of her father's people.

'Prin'cess, you must be hungry?' that was Missis Kilm. She had now more help than she could use, with the four sisters of Herodite at her beck and call along with their childish initiates. Women borne to serve, and now housed in with the rest to keep them from harm's reach.

'I… thank you…'

'Queen Niamh…' Alfric said absently, 'we should remember that now.'

'I still say the child has no experience of leadership,' Kilm butted in, glaring at Niamh and at his wife equally. 'You're asking us to follow a child into battle, Darkfire, why? What do we stand to gain from this?'

'I suppose you want the crown for yourself?' Helligan asked, his voice soft but not without edge.

'No! Frek that! But surely you are a better contender than this… this girl?'

'I will never allow a crown to sit upon my head, you know that.'

'I do, and yet I see no reason to it.'

'Lord Kilm, I appreciate your misgivings…' as ever, when Niamh spoke, heads turned and with them came the nerves which were thwarted only by spontaneity. 'I assure you, I intend to take my council from your good selves only. You need a monarch who might be accepted by your people and mine both. Your people will ever accept another of my father's ilk just as much as the common folk will never accept a Wolder king. I am your compromise, surely?'

The room fell to silence as Niamh inhaled and then exhaled a long breath in the face of what was probably the longest speech she'd ever given before anybody but Helligan or perhaps Lord Shale with whom words had ever flowed easier.

'She's right, you know,' Morkyl said to Kilm, speaking for the first time during the conversation.

'But you have no experience! You can barely even speak!' Kilm wasn't giving in without a fight, turning his words to Niamh herself.

'Words are empty and mostly full of air. I have experience enough, I merely choose not to shout it from the rooftops. I am my father's daughter, trained in… in matters of court.'

'But no commander!'

'No, and yet there I have your good selves to guide me. None of you were born commanders either!' Niamh could scarcely believe the words were coming from her lips, but indignation was driving her to speak more so than she usually would. Helligan's hand came down onto her shoulder.

'The Lady Niamh will ever have all the expertise and support she needs from me, and I hope from yourselves too,' he said, 'She is correct in that we require somebody who will be accepted by both worlds and for now, she uniquely stands in that position. Trust in my intuition, it has never betrayed us before.'

'Here here,' Morkyl said and Alfric too was nodding. Kilm cast an eye over Niamh again though.

'What guarantee do we have that you will not be another as your father? How do we know that you will work for us as well as for your own people?'

'Because my birthage gives me to them, but my heart, soul and passions to you. I am truly both now, I straddle two worlds and should I ever come to be given a choice, I could choose neither without heartache.'

'Hmm,' and when your affection for our commander wears thin, what then?'

Niamh glanced up at Helligan and wet her lips, she paused a moment to ponder but then turned back to Kilm,

'My lord,' she said, hoping she was correct in that he would respect an authoritative response, 'who I have in my bed at night is none of your concern.'

The silence which fell was so long and drawn out that Niamh felt her stomach tie itself into a multitude of knots. Helligan's eyes were wary, the other Marsh Lords too, but Kilm looked as though she had slapped him. She'd gone too far! She shouldn't have spoken thus… but then suddenly Kilm smirked. His dark eyes glowed and a chuckle escaped his lips.

'Well, I suppose that is me in my place!' he said and with his words, the rest of the marsh lords chuckled too. Kilm moved closer to Niamh and bowed his head, 'As it please you, my queen,' he said, then chuckled again and left the room.

Anglemarsh was the first target for Niamh and her men. Niamh herself rode with the men as they approached the keep, her grey dancer keeping pace remarkably well with the battle-ready stallions bred by the wild Woldermen army. The day was dreary, grey and overcast with little natural light. A thin mist of rain fell, leaving Niamh's hair in wet hanks after just two hour's riding despite the lightness of the drizzle. Niamh had never ridden with an army before, the scent of sweat and horse almost overwhelming despite that she and the rest of what she hoped would one day be her court rode at the head of the forces, the army behind. The noise too, was unlike anything she'd experienced or expected. Not just for the clanging of weapons and shouting and singing of the troops but for the stomping footsteps of most of her army who had no horses. Wolder did ride, and their mounts were formidable, but most had no access to them and so only a small portion of the army was mounted.

Niamh's heart pounded as the army settled into a rough circle surrounding the open marshy grounds before the keep. Despite that since the king's return to the Golden Keep, Anglemarsh's defences were lower, it was still the largest keep before the capitol and was therefore guarded well-enough. Before the army gathered a group of sisters and ladies, battle-dressed medics as well as the softer looking priestesses in robes, there to pray to the goddess for victory. Queen Niamh, as they all now called her, and her Lords still held the head of the procession, Niamh's breath now coming in little panicked gasps. At a dell by the edge of a forest Helligan paused again, stilling a whole army with the raising of his hand.

'You stay here with the sisters,' he said to Niamh. 'it will be safer.'

'I can fight – I have my bow…'

'I do not doubt your skill or your intent, but if you were to fall… you've never been into battle before, it's too big a risk for now. Help to make up a hospital here so that when the medics drag men back you can treat them… that is just as important a job and you will be seen as merciful and gentle – two aspects of queenliness which are no less important that ferocity and intelligence.'

Niamh nodded her head, not wanting to argue with Helligan's command. He knew more of it than she did and in truth she didn't really want to go further down into the battle.

'Bless you,' she managed to whisper, moving her horse closer that she could put a hand onto his arm, 'and I beg the Goddess to return you to me unscathed!'

'So mote it be,' he whispered. 'For you, my queen,' and then he took off, the army moving around Niamh and her ladies in an arc to follow their commander.

It was a different experience to watch the Wolder attack as her own men, rather than an invading army. Where before they had seemed wild, fierce creatures, now they were suddenly vulnerable in their leather armour against the iron and steel-clad knights of her father. Suddenly their calls left her belly hollow and panicked for their safety. The Wolder did not take long to reach the keep; Helligan, Kilm, Morkyl all lost in the crowd. There was no parley either, no negotiations, that was not the way of the Wolder, and so the attack was instantaneous, abrupt. Their tactics were what her father would have called dirty, too. Rather than laying siege, they carried tall wheeled ladders which could scale the walls, clambering up, pushing on even when hot oils and water were thrown over in an attempt to move them, easily avoidable by the wheels on the ladders.

Niamh swallowed and turned to view what was happening behind her. Furs were being laid out and bottles opened. Salve for the wounds not yet taken, for blood not yet spilt. The medics, strong brave women who rode amongst the army to pull them out when injured, would bring them there and then return to the battle. Niamh wished she could be down there too, at least that way she'd be able to see what was happening.

Greta was the member of the sisters who remained to make camp closest to Niamh's age and she, like Niamh, seemed awed by the battle – probably the first she had witnessed. She stood still and quiet, still wearing her robes of white with her brown locks loose to her waist and then cinched in there to stop them blowing about. Niamh clutched her hand in panic holding on to her as she watched the men charge into battle. The glade was at the edge of the forest, up on a hillside so that the ladies could view the battle. It was somehow oddly distant from the keep though, as though a barrier or haze was put up between them. The din was audible, the clanging of axe on sword and the screaming and shouting of men, but so distant it felt almost like a mummer's play. Niamh and her ladies were close enough to see the fighting, almost to recognise individual faces, but not quite. Close enough to see the brightness of blood beginning to flow, but not to smell it.

'A finely-led siege, my lady,' Greta observed, 'Helligan the mage is proving now that he is a fine commander and not just one of the king's lapdogs like the other mages were.'

'A mage is nobody's lapdog,' one of the older sisters, Dora spoke, coming to join them. She had given up her white robes for a blue woollen gown but still wore her frail white hair loose in the way of her order. 'Only the goddess can gift a man with such power, only she can guide their hands, and the goddess does not look well on this golden king…'

Niamh allowed the droning voices to dim as she watched for a sign of Helligan on the battlefield. The first group of medics were returning, so soon they would be busy, but in that moment Niamh couldn't think of anything but him. He was not visible aside from the odd flash of elemental magic here and there. Her eyes burned for a lack of blinking, her heart seemed not to beat, imagining him fallen, broken, but then, there, in amongst the din and roaring she saw a flash of blue colour the far right-hand entrance and her heart pounded, he was right in the thick of the fighting!

'Ohff! Did you see that? Lord Helligan always was the strongest of the mages,' Dora was saying, 'Powerful to the point that even the other mages were wary of him….'

'Please… a little quiet…' Niamh managed to mutter. Dora looked to where Niamh still clutched Greta's hand and her old face wrinkled into a gentle smile.

'He won't fall, child, not here. The goddess has a bigger plan than this for Lord Helligan Darkfire…'

The battle raged for five hours, almost a whole day. A dizzying amount of time. As the casualties were brought up, Niamh found herself busied by caring for them, running back and forth like a serving girl for the sisters who had more knowledge and less time than she. Salves were applied, wounds bandaged, the dead buried in the woodlands where they died as was Wolder tradition – or so Niamh was informed – and one stomach curdling leg amputation, and then suddenly the Wolder horns were blowing victory.

What?' Niamh gasped, the sound bringing back the eerie memories of her girlhood.

'Victory, my queen,' Dora smiled. 'Look!'

Niamh spun about to see the gates opening and Helligan riding out, sandwiched by horn-blowing Wolder – one of whom was staggering slightly as he tried to mount his horse, and had a look of Kilm about him. Niamh pulled off her apron and gloves and took to her own horse, clambering up without a care onto the bare back of the beast and turning it toward the field. She and Helligan met about halfway down the field. He dismounted and ran to her, lifting her down from the horse and crushing her in a hug. He smelt atrocious, sweat and smoke and goodness knows what else, and he was obviously still high on adrenaline from the battle. He kissed her cheek and then dropped to his knee before her. His hair was wild, his face dirty but his lips in a smile so wide it seemed to brighten all of his features.

'Your new home, my lady,' he smiled, indicating the keep. 'I gift it to you, in the hopes that you will be more comfortable here than in my humble house!'

Kilm, came next, already so drunk he could barely manage a horse, and clapped Helligan on the back. 'A good fight, a good one indeed,' he slurred, then glanced up at where the ladies still tended the dying, 'any whores about up there?'

Niamh just glanced at him, shocked,

'Likely my friend,' Helligan said, 'go and see what sport you can find, you've earned it! I will take our queen home...'

'Whores?' she asked, as the other Lords followed Kilm, all drunk and muttering congratulations but eager to be up the hill with the ladies.

'Many of the ladies who follow the armies have... services for sale. It's harmless.'

'...his wife...'

'Is used to it,' Helligan chuckled, 'the Wolder are not so prim as your father's people in matters of heart.'

Niamh said nothing, but allowed Helligan to help her back up on to her horse.

'Saddleless! You are becoming wilder every day my lady, more like the men you lead...' he joked.

'I was... eager to come down.'

'I see. Come, then, let me take you home!'

It was odd indeed to re-enter the great keep of Anglemarsh as its conqueror. Still the evidence of Niamh's old life lay littered about. The butts where she'd practiced her bow with Josynne Shale, the parapets she'd walked with her father. Even her own chamber, still complete with her dresses and embroidery where nobody had thought to pack her things when they'd moved. Niamh, finding thus, felt her heart harden again towards her father. Had he really cared so little for her that he'd not even had her gowns packed?

Despite the revelry below, or perhaps due to it, the silence above seemed blissful to Niamh. She moved about her chamber picking up forgotten treasures and putting them back down again. Memories flooded, but they were false nostalgia, tainted and cloying.

Niamh opened up the wardrobe and looked over the clothing choices therein. She wanted not to appear lavish enough to alienate the Woldermen who fought for her, but she wanted something which would give her confidence, make her seem queenly. The gowns of red, or purple and of incrusted gems she stripped out of the wardrobe. The gems could be reused and the cloth was too regal. That left her with more humble blues and greens, one of the brown and the rust-colours of autumn. This one she pulled from its hanger and removed the pomander there to keep away moths. It was pretty enough, but earthy too. She slid the dirty rags she wore off and pulled the dress back over her head. Yes, the mirror showed her it was humble enough, but fine. She pulled a brush through her long yellow locks but then used a golden thread to bind it into wraps like the Wolder women were wont to. Finally, she opened a drawer where her circlet lay and slid it into her hair. Again, extravagant in the company she kept now, enough to name her queen, but much more humble than she'd have worn at her father's court. The person in the glass was not somebody she recognised well. Her eyes were wiser, her skin browned from the sunshine and her lips harder. She looked older, wiser. Her eyes showed the wisdom of having lived, rather than having been taught. She sighed and closed the wardrobe door, cutting off the reflection – whilst it did not trouble her, it did not fill her with joy either, a reminder that girlhood was through and responsibility lay on her shoulders. Responsibility for the men who had perished on her behalf that day, for the widows and fatherless children those deaths had created. Niamh turned to find Helligan stood in silence in the doorway, the door itself ajar.

'You look very fine, my queen,' he said, admiration in his tones.

'Thank you.'

'It is the truth, you seem troubled?'

'So many died…'

'Of your father's men? We took few casualties thanks to your ladies…'

'Of both sides. Fatherless children are fatherless children, no matter who their fathers were.'

'Thus is the way of war.'

'It is abhorrent.'

'I agree… but so is standing aside whilst a cruel leader allows children to die of starvation whilst he lives in a keep of gold. A ruler who destroys the sacred forests and threatens to burn heretics of a religion nobody asked for. A man who would have sold you as one wife of many to an old letch in order to murder innocent Wolder women and children, priestesses, for no reason but to send a message. What we do is abhorrent, what he does is monstrous, and if we do not stop him… with the sphere in his possession, he is a threat to us all. You realise, of course, what it does?'

'Somewhat? My father said it can control dragons…'

'It can. And more though, it can rip away the… the barriers between the worlds and bring them back, under his command… if the stories are true…'

'By the goddess! And are they true?'

'I don't wish to find out. Morgana is afraid of the sphere and thus I am afraid. This is why we attacked when the sphere was at its most vulnerable. I knew I had to take it before any real damage was done! Before he discovered how it works… if it works!'

'And I shot you!'

Helligan smiled, a genuine smile which crinkled his eyes, 'Yes, you did! And so your brother escaped with the sphere, but I got you so it was worthwhile.'

Niamh's heart fluttered. Helligan had not been hers since that strange night in the forest and yet when he spoke thus, she could almost believe he did love her.

'Is my father really so corrupt?'

'Look into your heart, look at what you have learned of him – surely you know the answer to that.'

Niamh pondered and then looked up at Helligan again, 'Then we have no option,' she said, 'We have to take the Golden Keep and remove my father from the throne!'

Chapter 14

Most of the following three days were spent in planning. Helligan seemed to think a traditional approach to attack would be best whereas the Wolder Lords seemed more inclined for their trademark stealth attack, arguing that it had won them the keep before. Niamh sat quietly throughout these debates, silent but watching, learning the ways of battle planning. She was content too: it was good to be home at Anglemarsh, to dress again in her fine gowns and once again to have her own rooms. Even if they took the Golden Keep, she'd decided to remain at Anglemarsh as her home, if possible.

'I understand but I have two arguments to counter,' Helligan said, interrupting her thoughts through supper, where still the debate raged. 'Firstly, the king knows we are here. It won't be much of a stealth attack, and secondly, you might be able to take the keep, but you lost it again last time… we need to garrison, not destroy!'

Niamh chewed on her chuck leg, the greasy meat just about all her stomach would accept. Her eyes flit to Kilm, the master of midnight attacks so it seemed, and the orchestrator of the previous attack on the castle.

'I say we attack on the morrow,' Kilm said, 'we achieve nothing by sitting here bickering like old hags!'

'Agreed,' That was Jarlsen. 'Helligan is right, they know we're here but we can still attack with some element of surprise…'

'My queen?' That was Morkyl.

'I… I agree. The men are ready to fight, but I agree that we should meet my father in the battlefield.'

'Very good,' Helligan said, smiling at her.

'I have one other boon to ask of you all.'

'What?' Alfric asked, 'What is it my lady?'

'When… when we take the keep, please don't hurt any of the… of the women or… or children…'

'Of course not! What do you take us for?' Helligan said, his brow furrowing.

'I… I… when you, they before… The queen and… and most of the royal children…'

'Were murdered by your father's men to stop them being taken hostage,' Helligan said gently.

'What? No… that can't be…'

'I heard him give the order myself sweetling. It is fairly standard practice in war. The ladies are at much risk of rape or capture. It is not unusual for the court executioner to be stationed with the king's family to… to prevent such things.'

Niamh's chest hurt suddenly; her forehead suddenly clammy.

'It is true, my queen,' Morkyl said, 'I was there that night and not one o my men touched a hair on those children's heads. Taint unusual – I heard a tale once of a queen who threw all her babbies off the battlements to save 'em from capture…'

'So it was never… it wasn't you who murdered by family?'

'Of course not. We don't take well to such things, my lady. That is a king's game…'

Later, Niamh lay alone in her soft feather-down bed. The blankets were wrapped about her but nothing helped the coldness that seemed to seep from within. Ever it had been one of her foremost banes of contention with her new clan, that they had put her family to slaughter and yet discovering that it had been on her father's orders hurt all the more. She allowed a few tears to fall in the darkness, but then was pulled from her misery by the sound of footsteps without. She sat up and forced her breathing to calm as a knock sounded on her door.

'It's me,' Helligan's voice, 'Niamh?'

Niamh's chest released slightly but then closed up again.

'Come... come on in,' she managed.

The door opened and there he stood. He'd discarded his tunic and so stood bare-chested in the doorway. His hair was loose and his eyes heady.

'Am I welcome to enter?'

'Always.'

Helligan entered the room and closed the door quietly behind him, then strode over to the bed. Niamh knelt up as he did so, meeting him as he slipped an arm around her back. His lips kissed with a passion, his hands clutching at her nightgown.

'Helligan...' she murmured and he paused, moving to look into her eyes.

'Are you well?'

'Yes,' she murmured. Helligan kissed her again, then pulled free her nightgown, touching his naked chest to hers. His hands fumbled the laces of his leather trousers and his voice murmured into her ear, and then they were joined, the melding of two people, flesh on flesh. Niamh moaned aloud, raking her hands through his hair, her head tipping so that her own long hair tickled her back. Helligan clutched at her, his breath panting, and it did not take very long for them both to reach the climax where the limb-juddering pleasure rushed through them, pushing them together into a long sigh of content.

Helligan moved first, his hands gently guiding her down to the sheets, and then following so that his body pressed to hers.

'I did not know if you would come to me again,' Niamh confessed, once her breathing had slowed. 'After the forest you have been... absent.'

'I know I have, but not through any wish to remain so. I have struggled every hour we are together not to lift you from your feet and carry you off…' he replied, a slight smile pulling at his lips. He kissed her again and then put a hand on her arm. 'You understand though, that I should not…'

'No… I don't…'

'Because I am trying to put you on the throne! You are my queen and I am your commander at arms. I wish not for people to question my motives.'

'For people to think you wish to rule through me.'

'Yes, exactly that,' Helligan said, 'and that I cannot allow emotion to blur my vision. I should not be here…'

'I am glad you came anyhow,' Niamh said, laying down on the coverlet, 'Stay with me tonight?'

Helligan lay his body against hers and pressed his front to her back, holding her in his arms. He laid down his head on the pillow, 'As you command,' he whispered.

Niamh lay against him and allowed her stomach to unknot. The minutes passed slowly but Helligan's breathing did not become the rhythmic softness she already recognised as his being asleep.

'Are you nervous, for tomorrow?' she asked.

'Only a fool would not be.'

'I suppose.'

'You must try to sleep…' even as she spoke, she rolled over to face him.

'I know it, and I know victory is all-but assured and yet tonight I dwell on the men we will lose, those who will not come home tomorrow. I pray to the goddess to spare as many as she can.'

'Those she takes will go to her eternal embrace.'

'They will, and yet here amongst the living they will be mourned. Wives will sob, babies will go hungry without fathers to fend for them.'

'Thus is war, I suppose.'

'Indeed, and we fight for a just cause, I know. I have to keep telling myself that.'

Niamh closed her eyes but whispered a prayer herself to at least spare Helligan, to not let him fall.

The night thickened and finally Helligan's breathing turned to light snores as the moon moved to a position to allow its subtle beams to fall across the floor. Niamh couldn't sleep. For some time she soothed her heart by watching Helligan, his chest rising and falling in a perfect rhythm. Niamh had heard before that on the eve of a battle, when life suddenly seems so precious, that the soldiers were more likely to take a wench to their bed. Was this just that? Was Helligan simply feeling his mortality, the looming battle a *memento mori* which had led him to seek to bury himself in her? He'd certainly been urgent enough.

Niamh sat up and put her bare feet down onto the straw which covered the floorboards. The anguish built as her insecurities bloomed. They were indeed likely to win on the morrow, likely to wipe out the bulk of her father's armies. Then she'd be queen and Helligan and his band of Woldermen would be her advisers only, if not gone completely. Helligan was her whole life, but she was merely a chapter in his. The tears began to fall unheeded. Niamh didn't really cry anymore, had not done so in so long that the water on her cheeks felt alien, burning little rivers down her cheeks. She pulled on her nightgown from where it lay on the floor and stood, moving to the window. Helligan stirred, seemed to realise her absence and sat up too.

'Niamh?' he murmured.

'It is well, I…'

'Are you weeping?' he asked, and from behind her Niamh heard the movement of him on the goose-down and horsehair mattress. He paused again, putting on clothing, then came up behind her and slipped an arm around her waist.

'Please don't be afraid,' he said, 'we're so very close to victory now.'

'I'm not afraid of our losing, the goddess is on our side.'

'Then what?'

His words, his lack of understanding pushed Niamh into something of a pique. She pulled away and turned to face him.

'You don't understand at all!' she said, the words suddenly easier than ever they had been, something she would not consider until later when he was gone, 'you… you… just…'

'I what?' he looked mystified.

'You see me only as the heir to the throne, I think, as a part of your crusade. Another pawn…'

'I see you not as a pawn, my darling, you are my queen!'

The word queen just made the seed bury itself deeper. 'Not so! You have made me the focus of your life's work, I think, you have made me your pet project!'

'Perhaps in truth, I have somewhat, yes. I have made it the focus of everything I do to ensure that you get the crown you deserve… but I don't see how or why that makes you so angry!'

Niamh began to cry again, rubbing her eyes to knock free the tears. Helligan stood beside her, trying to move closer again, his hands trying to take hers. His eyes were dark with confusion.

Niamh shook her head though. 'Leave me be, Helligan!'

'Why? I don't understand!'

'Please, leave me be. You say I am your queen, then I command you, leave me now!'

Helligan's face tightened. His jaw set and his eyes showed no emotion. He paused, but then seemed almost to choke out the words 'of course, your highness,' and turned away. Niamh's heart broke a little further, but she said nothing as he left the room.

The dawn broke too quickly, a bright streak of orange which started in the east, a pink dart, and then the blue of a sunny day. Niamh did not sleep after Helligan left, but sat in the hard chair by the window watching the night give up her hold on the darkness as the light conquered, pulling in the day. The men were soon to set off, not quite a march – not Woldermen! But to go into battle none-the-less. The siege was breaking, victory was nigh, barring disaster. Niamh's stomach hurt and she felt sick. So much so, that the whiff of meat cooking below was enough to make her put a hand to her belly, nauseated. She stood and swapped out her nightgown for the gown she'd worn on the night of the last victory. If she was about to ride victorious into Aurvandil, she'd best look like the princess she was.

Below, the Marsh Lords feasted on seared rabbit, fowl and beautifully poached eggs. Custard tart and the staple bread and preserves rounded off the feast – a breakfast fit to be a man's last, should the goddess decide to call them home, and which was being served throughout the camps. Niamh doubted her father's men dined so luxuriously.

All eyes looked up as she entered, bedraggled and with dark circles under her eyes. Helligan too looked unkept and Niamh's heart thudded to think she'd caused him a sleepless night too, and on such a night! She hoped not. The other men looked much themselves – Alfric, tucking into his food, his beard soaking up the juices of the meat, Morkyl mopping up gravy with bread and Kilm sitting quietly, watching the carnage of his comrades eating, a chuck leg in hand but his clothing clean of food. Niamh moved in silence to the table and took up the most meagre of slices of bread. Skipping the preserve but adding a little butter, she took a small bite.

'You should eat more, my queen,' Morkyl said, 'it is likely to be the last we see this day and you need your strength.'

Niamh shook her head, but took another small bite.

'You do not look well,' Helligan spoke to her as Kilm and Alfric began to bicker about the quantity of food a man should consume before battle.

'I am well enough.'

'Your stomach ails you?'

Niamh looked down to where her hand still rested on her belly. Her eyes moved back to Helligan, 'I am a little nauseated,' she said.

'To be expected!' Morkyl said, 'Nerves... today is a big day for you as well, lass!'

'Indeed.'

'And yet nerves have not troubled you previously...' Helligan pushed.

Niamh shook her head, not prepared to discuss the night before, not yet. 'What am I to do, today?' she asked, changing the subject.

'You are to stay put! The window in the west tower will give you a view of the battle but you and your ladies are not to leave this keep! You are too precious a prisoner if you are captured! The medics will bring the injured here to be tended.'

Niamh nodded, breaking up the bread in her fingers.

The bickering between Kilm and Alfric grew louder and Niamh cast a cautious eye to the other side of the table, half-expecting them to come to blows over a damn chuck leg! Helligan followed her gaze, and then stood.

'Come, men!' he said, 'we must be ready for full sunrise – I do not wish to still be marching at noon when the sun is high!'

All three marsh lords stood at Helligan's words, food suddenly abandoned as a chill seemed to spread over the group. Niamh felt suddenly overwhelmed, her heart hammering to look from one to the other of her men, Helligan, Kilm, Morkyl, Alfric... she hoped desperately that this would not be the last time she laid eye upon them. She stood and took in a deep breath. They were fighting for freedom, for peace from tyranny, but they were also fighting for her! As their queen, she knew it was customary to speak and with the risk they were about to take in her name, she did not want to let them down.

'Fight well, my dearest men,' she murmured, then, her voice strengthening, 'and know that you have my deepest gratitude for everything. I will pray for each of you, and I will beg the Goddess not to leaving me mourning tonight. Our cause is… is so important, so much bigger than us, but still I beg your forgiveness for a woman's heart, that I would rather defeat than to lose any one of you.'

All four men stared, but it was Kilm who came first to kneel before her. He took up her fingers and kissed them, laying the small axe he always carried down at her feet. 'My queen,' he said.

Alfric followed, not kneeling, but bowing his head and touching her shoulder. Morkyl came next, also kneeling, and then finally Helligan. As her darling knelt at her feet, the other men moved away, allowing him to kneel solely before her. He bowed his head low, and then looked up into her eyes. His palms touched, but then drew apart, revealing a small blue flame in each hand. He inhaled a deep calming breath, and then exhaled slowly.

'I have no sword to lay at your feet,' he said, 'but I offer you all the magic I command, all the power I possess, and despite your sweetest of words, I would still willingly give my life for you, my Lady Niamh. My queen, tonight!'

Niamh put a hand down on his hair, hoping he did not feel the tremble of it. Despite what he had said previously about his lack of desire to rule, she could not allow him to go to his possible death without asking the most important of questions: 'My king, tomorrow?' she whispered. 'My… my husband?'

A murmur went out amongst the marsh lords, but Niamh ignored them looking down only into Helligan's eyes.

'You know I cannot be your king,' he said, his face burning with passion, 'but if you would accept me only as consort, I would gladly be your husband, my precious lady.'

Niamh broke away. This was too much, she'd been too impulsive and now the moment felt too short to find the words for all she needed to say. Instead, she merely nodded, eyes full. Helligan closed his fists, putting out the flames, and then stood. Before them all, he slid his hands around Niamh's face and pulled her lips to his. Twice he kissed her, soft and tender kisses full of longing, but then turned back to the three lords who watched on with curious eyes.

'Come men, we have a war to win,' he said.

Chapter 15

Despite that the room was dusty enough to be almost choking and cluttered with old abandoned furnishings, the view from the uppermost tower of Anglemarsh was more than adequate to see the battlefield below the Golden Keep. In fact, from up there Niamh could see for miles around, right out into the marshes until the view grew hazy, and then right over the city which sat sprawling, it's edges almost reaching the walls of the keep, but not quite. Helligan's plan was to assault the keep alone as the men had before in her childhood, without necessarily attacking the city.

'The city guard will be an issue if they come to join the battle,' he'd said, 'but I don't want to risk the civilians to a blood-thirsty Wolder army if I can help it.'

Niamh had to agree with the sentiment.

From where Niamh sat, a wrap about her arms and her gown demure and without frills, she could see her men gathered below. Her father's men gathered too, outside of the keep. This was no night-time stealth attack like before, nor was it a surprise siege, like that for Anglemarsh – no, this was a full-scale battle, more so than she'd ever seen. At Helligan's command, the Wolder were more traditional fighters, more lethal perhaps although Niamh hoped he was not completely ironing them out – the Wolder were so lethal because of how they fought. They would never make real soldiers.

Behind her, Niamh heard footsteps and turned about to see Sister Dora behind her. 'Is there anything we can do for you, my queen, before we go down to pray?' she asked. Anglemarsh still contained the old shrines in the basements and so Dora and her flock had taken over the ancient place of worship.

'I am well, thank you.'

'I have… if the effort fails and your father's men come to get us, I have a concoction of herbs – it would be painless.'

Niamh put her hand to her waist and pulled up her dagger – one she'd appropriated from the armoury the day before. 'I have this,' she said, 'it's more fitting for a queen.'

'As you will it, my queen, but it will not come to that…'

'No, our army is stronger than my father's, slightly more in numbers and without the constraints of a rigid army.'

Dora inclined her head. Niamh knew that as a disciple of the face of Herodite, Dora did not approve of battle but she hoped that after what her father had tried to do to the sisters, Dora at least understood why this had to be.

'Will you…' she paused, knowing that it was not quite seemly to ask, then asked anyway, 'will you light a candle to the face of Helston, for me?'

'The battle face?'

'Yes… I know that it's unusual for one of your sect but…'

'For you, my lady, yes.'

'Thank you.'

With that, Dora turned and left Niamh alone at the window. The army were gathered now, with Helligan visible at the front with the Marsh Lords about him. They seemed in great discussion. Behind them, spilling out for further than Niamh could have imagined, were the army. Vast, making a black and brown smear on the landscape before the keep. She could see too, the common folk from the houses between, few though they were, making their way in slow, sombre chains, towards the city. No matter which side those men and women supported, they were sensible enough to leave now. Somehow the thought made Niamh sad and she determined to ensure that these brave people were recompensed once they won – which they would! They had the upper hand!

It seemed to take forever for the men to move the relatively short distance from Anglemarsh to the Golden Keep. An army, especially one mainly on foot, cannot move especially quickly – even a Wolder one. Niamh sat up a little taller. She could smell bread baking down below but there was no way she could have eaten anything more and so rather than pleasant; the smell made her a little queasy.

There, they were almost face to face with her father's army now. Helligan, so distant as to be unrecognisable but for his place at the head of the army, rode forth and Niamh squinted her eyes to see her father ride forward too, glimmering obscenely in his golden armour. Niamh could not remember that last time he'd gone into battle himself and was surprised the armour still fit him. Helligan and her father sat face to face on their horses for some moments in negotiation – standard practice before a battle – but neither dismounted and Niamh already knew this parlay would not end with a solution. Her father would not surrender and Helligan would accept nothing less. Her heart thudded to think how easily her father could just cut Helligan down there as they stood vulnerable, but to do such would be ungallant and Niamh knew her father would not behave so in front of his people, no matter how much he wanted to. Besides, Helligan was likely quicker on the draw with his magics than her father could swing his sword. It was some relief too.

As she'd supposed, the negotiation was unsuccessful and Niamh saw her father's steed turn first. Helligan stood poised a little longer, as is usual, to allow the defender his ground and then he too turned and moved back to the army. At such a distance, it was difficult to tell which marsh lord was which, but they as a group were recognisable for the way they reconvened about Helligan, deep in discussion.

Then suddenly the battle was upon them.

The footmen went in first, more of them by far in Helligan's band than her fathers. The Marsh Lords separated and each seemed to take command of a branch of men, forming three distinct groups. Helligan stayed close to the front and then, all of a sudden, there was that splash of blue that Niamh was coming to recognise – a soundwave of types which Helligan could expel from his form. Blue Magicka, which devastated the men before him. From her seat above, Niamh could see that devastation more clearly than ever she had before, the shockwave knocking a good thirty or forty of her father's troops backwards by several yards. Not a killing blow, but enough to cause confusion. Her army, Helligan's men, were moving forward quickly, pushing her father back. In the area to the left, by the city, the Wolder army was holding back the city guard who had come out to fight, as well as holding back a group of men in yellow tabards over their armour – Nordemunde's men, if she could recall the banners. Dead ahead, Helligan moved in with his band, the smaller of the groups, but her father had vanished, likely back behind the walls of the keep. The third split was moving in towards the walls on the western side of the keep, perhaps scoping for a place to lay siege – Niamh couldn't recall all the plans.

The fighting continued heavy for some time, more than an hour at least. Niamh moved away for a few moments to drink a glass of water, but then her pounding heart led her back to the window. The skies above were brightening, the clouds moving so that the sunshine bore down heavy – this was an advantage for Helligan and his leather and mail clad men against her father's steel-plated army who would be baking inside. Her father was still nowhere to be seen, but her army were obviously doing well, making it almost to the walls and gates. Helligan had moved to assist the eastern side, obviously having more trouble from the city guards than they had anticipated. There was stronger fighting there still, more men. Niamh scrunched up her eyes, trying to see properly. There didn't look to be many men in plate there, but still the fighting was thick. She looked on, frowning, as Wolderman turned on Wolderman. Her heart hammered. Surely not? Surely there could be no turncoat amongst the Wolder? Why would any of the Marsh Lords fight for King Hansel Torrington after all the evil he'd committed against them? It didn't make sense!

Niamh leaned so far out of the window her balance was precarious, trying to make out what was happening. All of the Wolder army were now turning on that eastern corner and the fighting was fierce. Helligan was lost in the crowd but for the occasion spark of blue here and there as he fought. More men spilled from the city, her father's guard taking advantage now that the turncoat army was revealed. The western group had all but abandoned their siege and to Niamh's horror appeared to be fleeing into the woods.

'Oh goddess, please...' she breathed as more men seemed to turn about and flee, her army scattering. Helligan himself seemed to be moving further away, his magic showing only haphazardly, and moving away from the fight. Helligan would never give up and so that could mean only that he was injured... or captured. Even as she thought this, the gates opened and her father sent out another batch of men into the fray, easily overwhelming the remaining Wolder who had not turned coat or fled.

Niamh moved from the window, unable to watch any more. Her heart was heavy and the tears which refused to spill made up a painful lump in her chest. She gasped, and then again, stumbling to an old dresser which was being stored in the tower amongst the other clutter. Niamh stood for a moment, one hand on the dusty dresser and the other over her mouth. Her thoughts would not leave Helligan, moving away with his randomly fired magics. What had happened to him? Where was he? The others had fled, had they left him or dragged him with them? She panted a few times and then looked down at her own hands. She could do nothing, not now, to save the battle. They were beaten but, if nothing else, she could gather her men, find Helligan… or… or something…

Closing the sash, Niamh made her way down the icy stone steps in something of a daze. At the foot she paused, hazy, but pressed on and pulled on her inner strength.

Greta, one of the youngers of the sisters, appeared at the end of the corridor, a few paces from Niamh. Her lips were pressed and her eyes wide.

'Is it true?' she whispered.

'Yes…'

'Oh! I had hoped I heard wrong!'

'I… I need to go out.'

'You can't go out there, My Lady. It's too dangerous now.'

'Helligan… Helligan… fell….'

Greta gripped her fingers tightly. 'My Lady, I understand, but you cannot go out there! You would be captured or killed.'

'You don't understand… nobody can! I have to…' she blinked away some of the haze, 'I have to go down myself. Is there… a disguise? I can disguise myself?'

Greta bit her lip and glanced behind her at the stairs she'd just come up. 'I daren't send you out as a sister in garb – I think you'd be in just as much danger, my queen, but perhaps a servant or some such could loan you clothing?'

'Yes…' Niamh whispered, 'Yes, perhaps that would work? Could you…?'

'I'll ask about now. You go down to the great hall. I'll find you something.'

'I will need… need something to cover my hair too… it is too obvious.'

'I agree. Go, My Lady, I will gather some things and join you.

The king's men marched on, relentlessly, and they took no prisoners – spearing every moving figure with swords designed to end a life swiftly and without thought. The rebellion really was over! They had lost badly due to the turncoat. Niamh stood alone in the middle of the battlefield surrounded by the din of agonised groaning combined with the horse's hooves and the final clashes of swords in the hands of those still refusing to give in to the soldiers. Her heart hurt, her head pounded and still she could not fully comprehend what had happened. Smoke rose up in several places where small fires had broken out, perhaps lit by her father's men to begin burning the corpses they would never see fit to send home. Maybe Helligan was among them – the very idea made her guts clench. He'd fallen near the edge, over by the trees where there was no smoke yet. Niamh sucked in a deep breath and prayed her disguise would hold, that she'd simply look like another peasant seeking out her lost husband or son on the battlefield. She made sure not to run directly to the edge either, but to dither and to bend every now and again, as though she were seeking out somebody in particular. The grass beneath her feet was sodden, not just with rain but with blood and piss too – a foul stinking mess which soaked her shoes.

A group of soldiers came closer, looking down at Niamh curiously. She froze, staring up at them, but at least her father's men were disciplined enough to leave the women alone – more so than they would be had this been an invasion, Niamh was sure – but her father prized his reputation above all, so his men simply rode by. Niamh kept her hands firmly pressed as she made her way to the edge of the battlefield. There was no sign of Helligan's body there, there were no bodies there at all, in fact.

'Helligan?' Niamh whispered harshly, as loudly as she dared, but there was no reply. She stood, feeling lost, but then moved a little further into the trees. Still nothing, but then – no there was something! A bright red droplet of blood, splashed over the green of the grass. With so many dead, it could have been anybody's but somehow Niamh knew already that it was not just "anybody".

'Helligan!' she hissed again, and followed another splash of blood, and then another. The path was leading her away from the battlefield, away from the din and back into the softly green lush forest. Even as she moved on, Niamh felt the energy of the trees caress her, pulling away the stresses; in some ways she was more Wolder now than she was anything else. At last the bramble wall flattened and showed Niamh the outline of a figure, a bloody boot.

'There you are,' she murmured, clambering over the bracken to kneel beside him and pull his head into her lap. There was a sword gash across his face, from brow to chin across his nose but thankfully his eye was still whole. Nettles stung her and thorns draw blood from her knees, but Niamh barely noticed. Helligan was conscious, just about, but there was blood all about his lips, smeared down onto the leather jerkin he wore. The arrows, for he was pierced multiple times, sat up jagged and straight, pointing up at the sky. One was in his lung, obviously for the blood on his lips, another was likely in his stomach, for the angle it pierced his belly. Niamh held back the tears as best she could. An arrow in the lung meant death, as did one in the belly – to have both… well, there was no way he could survive.

'Niamh?' he managed. His voice bubbled in his chest, definitely an arrow in the lung, then.

'I'm here,' she whispered.

'Did we… win?'

The tears fell at last as she was forced to shake her head.

'Damn.'

Helligan's eyes rolled back in his head and his lips pressed together. Niamh broke out into sobs which were loud and hiccupping. This was close to the spot where she'd lost him before, she realised, back before she even knew him, when he was just a battlemage and she the king's daughter. A lifetime since. Niamh put her lips to his hot brow, noticing as her own tears fell down onto his dirty bleeding face.

'Please don't die,' she sobbed, 'I cannot bear this!'

'Niamh….'

'No! Hush, don't say goodbye! If you do then your rebellion, what is left of it, is for naught because I will… I will not be able to do this without you! I shall become as corrupt as my father! I vow, if you die! Bitterness and pain will mould me into the very worst queen, to rule with misery alone! I will live only to avenge you, my love!'

Helligan's fingers moved up to tangle into her hair, his grip was very weak though, hardly able to grasp the locks.

'I… I do not think you have it in you to be vengeful…' he managed, smiling, 'But it… it will not come to thus… I… Niamh I can…I can heal myself!'

'What?'

'Using my… my magic, I can heal a little. Enough…' he coughed again and thick black blood bubbled for a moment on his lips.

'Do it, then!'

'I need the glade!'

'The glade?'

'Yes, where the goddess resides, I need that – magic – I-I'm not strong enough here.'

Niamh struggled to her feet and slid an arm about Helligan's back. Mages needed an element to tap into the magic which surrounded them, if the glade would allow him to heal, then to the glade she would get him! Helligan stood, but then moaned and put up a hand to his chest. Niamh clung to him, holding as much of his weight as she could, and led him onwards through the trees. His glade was not far, the elder-wood where he went to pray to his goddess, and with adrenaline pumping, Niamh knew she'd have to be the one to deliver him there.

The walk was slow and arduous. The din of the triumphant soldiers fading more so, but still something of a threat for later. The forest would be combed for survivors, especially when they realised Helligan was not amongst the slain. Helligan's weight was heavy too, despite how he tried to assist her by walking. Almost his whole weight lay on her shoulder, and his hands gripped her so hard it almost hurt. Twice he had to stop to cough up more bubbling blood, almost falling with the effort of doing so. At last though, the dense trees began to part, giving way to the soft green of the glade. Helligan stumbled free of Niamh's hand and all but fell onto the grass.

'Thank you,' he gasped, but then caught her eye. Disquiet showed on his features but despite that, and his pressed, bloody lips, still he managed to almost smile.

'Niamh….' He said, 'I need you to… to remove the bottle from my neck and then… to leave…'

'Never! I won't leave you!'

'I… I can't have you here just yet. I need… need an hour, alone…'

'But why?' suddenly she was sobbing again, determination leaving her.

'It's… this is powerful magic and you are…' he coughed again, more blood coming up, and didn't finish the thought.

'I can't leave you…' she whispered, but already she was lifting the leather thong from his neck, setting the bottle down beside him. 'Helligan, please…'

'You must! Go!'

'Helligan…'

'Go!' he cried out, then took to coughing again. Niamh fought back more tears. If she didn't go, he was going to die. Helligan looked up at her, his eyes now dull with the agony of his wounds.

'Please, my love, trust me.'

Niamh knelt quickly to kiss his sweaty, dirty brow, but then turned and, much as she had once before, ran away. Like before though, she paused to glance back and there caught sight of Helligan clutching at the bottle she'd taken from about his neck, uncapping it. As he did so, a strange iridescent blue light seemed to emanate from it, seeping out to cast an odd blue glow all around his form. The sight was so strange she almost paused, but then took a deep breath and carried on, back to the keep. Whatever he was about to do, he didn't want her there!

Chapter 16

Back at Anglemarsh, Niamh finally broke down. Her father's men had not begun their assault on the smaller keep yet but already she could see them regrouping as she slipped past in her disguise. It would not be long – her father would not pass this opportunity up, she knew that already. The entrance hall was warm, still, lit by a dozen candles and the fireplace in the corner. The rooms were empty though, none of the men returned. Niamh collapsed there, sobbing onto her hands. Helligan might even be dead already, and she had heard nothing of the others yet. At once, two of the younger temple sisters came running with fresh, warm clothing and a cape. Niamh allowed them to strip her of her dirty, bloodied clothing and slip the new robes over her head. Just as they finished, dressing her right in the middle of the entrance hall, the door swung open again. Niamh spun about, her breath almost a pant, to see Kilm half-dragging, half-supporting, an injured Morkyl in through the entranceway. Blood dripped down onto the straw, but Morkyl glanced up as they entered, conscious enough.

'Kilm! Morkyl!' Niamh gasped. 'You're alive?'

'My lady, I am sorry… we have failed…' Kilm spoke.

'No! It was betrayal?'

'Aye, that bastard McClaven!'

'McClaven?' Of them all, Niamh would have put him last on her list of men to rebel against Helligan.

'Aye... took us all for a shock! Musta had a deal with the old king for summin but we don't know what or why – never will now! I put me own axe through his skull!'

Kilm limped further in and dropped Morkyl to the ground where he sat panting.

'My queen, Helligan fell...'

'I know it, but he is alive – just!'

'You saw from up there?'

'No, I came down to the battlefield. He had me take him to the sacred glade.' Niamh said, then ushered the sisters who had tended her towards Morkyl, 'see to his wounds, sister? My Lord Kilm what of Jarlsen? Where is he?'

'Also dead,' Kilm said. 'Poor old bastard took an arrow fairly soon in, then last I saw was trampled under their horses.'

'Definitely gone, then?'

'Yes, my lady, I am sorry for it.'

One of the sisters moved in and began to fuss at Kilm but he brushed her off. Morkyl seemed to be strengthening under the care of the other, though and was accepting some milk-soaked bread. He looked up to Niamh and in his eyes she read not defeat, but stubbornness and that look was enough to make her stronger again.

'Come,' she said, 'let us make our way upstairs for now and rest whilst we can! It's going to be a long night – we're not done yet!'

Later, as the skies began to darken in earnest, Niamh, Kilm and Morkyl sat in silence in the chamber which was close by the east entrance, the one used by the servants and lowly guests. The soldiers were amassing about outside, and Niamh knew it could not be long before they were under attack. Enough of her own men had returned with Kilm to give some level of defence, and with the gates locked tight it would be a siege –

but already she knew it to be one she could not win. Hours had passed in this strange, strained silence, hours enough for Morkyl's wounds to be patched up, and for Kilm to eat three men's rations of food. Niamh didn't mind that; they'd not be there long enough to run out of rations.

'I reckon we can hold em off for a time at least,' Kilm said, pacing back into view – a habit formed since his return, pacing and talking and eating, and then more pacing.

'We'll be hard pressed, most of our men's run…' Morkyl replied, he was still bent over slightly but food seemed to have revived him too. Niamh had not been able to eat at all.

'Aye, but at least they're safe… safer than us! I said we should have run into the forest with em…' he glanced at Niamh, 'begging your pardon, my queen.'

'No, I understand,' she whispered.

'Wouldn't leave you, though, not here alone to face em with Helligan dead and all….'

'Helligan's not dead,' Niamh repeated for the hundredth time. She struggled to find more words, to explain that Helligan was coming back, that he'd gone to heal, but she was interrupted by a scrabbling sound in the wall. She gasped and stood.

'What? What is that?' Kilm growled, his hand going for his axe.

'My queen?' Morkyl did not stand but pulled his dagger onto the table. Niamh stood to collect her bow from by the door.

'Passages?' Kilm said, turning to her, 'Hidden ways in!'

'I…' she was interrupted by a banging sound behind a tapestry close to the fireplace where a small flame burned merrily, unheeding the feeling of danger building in the room.

Niamh found she had clutched for Morkyl's hand, and he had given it without a word. 'How many know about the passages?' she managed to whisper.

'Not many, my Queen, but this is one of your father's houses, we cannot rule out that he himself would know of it.'

'And so, this might well be an invading force?'

'Yes. It could well be.'

Another loud bang rang out from behind the tapestry. Niamh shuddered but laid down her bow. 'My father is no fool, he would not send a mere handful of men.' She bent and slid her dagger from her boot, 'Morkyl... I need you to... if we are to be overwhelmed... I won't be a prisoner.'

'No, my queen, we will fight!'

'We cannot! If they take me...'

Morkyl's gaze darkened but he took the dagger from Niamh's hand. She moved closer to him, her body trembling. 'wait... wait until we are sure,' she said, 'but then be swift – you will not have very long.'

'My lady,' he said, then glanced across at Kilm who stood rigid and silent, sword and axe in hand. A final bang, and then the tapestry fell. Niamh closed her eyes, unable to bear the suspense, but as she opened them relief flooded her form,

'Helligan!' she murmured, 'Helligan, Oh! Thank the goddess! At last!'

Helligan's hand still bore the smoke from the fire he'd cast at the door. He looked ragged and had dark circles under his eyes, but he was very much alive. Across his face where the wound had been was a new scar, and when he moved forward he limped.

'My lady,' he said, 'I apologise for my manner of entry, your father's forces are gathering at the traditional entrance...'

Niamh let out all the breath she'd not been aware she was holding in and ran to embrace Helligan, he crushed her to him briefly, but then put her aside and looked at his two remaining warriors. Both nodded in respect and he returned the gesture but his eyes held worry.

'Well met, my lords!'

'Helligan, you give us a right fright!' Morkyl chuckled.

'We are missing two, the traitor and...'

'And Jarlsen Mantle, who is dead.'

'A pity! He was a good man. How long do you think it will take to lay siege to this keep?'

'A day at the most,' Morkyl replied.

'Then we need to retreat. The bulk of the golden army is already at our gate and so many of our men lay slain without.'

'We have taken heavy loses!'

'We have, but when I gave the order to retreat many also did flee. It is no massacre, despite how it appears. Now we have to regroup, and find a clean escape. You say we have but a day?'

Helligan limped, with Niamh's aid, to the old wooden table and pulled out the hard-backed chair beside it on which to sit. His skin was so pale, but still his eyes shone.

'We have lost, Helligan,' Morkyl argued, 'we might as well fight to the last! Only a coward flees!'

'We have lost the battle, not the war, man! We only suffered the losses we did because of a turncoat and most of our men fled when they saw it was defeat! There are many left who would fight against the tyranny of the golden reign – many more – but if we are all dead who will lead them? How will our cause be achieved? We must be humble and retreat now! Better to lose our dignity than die martyrs!'

'What say'th my queen?' Kilm looked to Niamh and her heart swelled for his loyalty.

'Helligan,' she said, trying to stand tall, 'Could you, with your magic, keep them from the walls?'

'No.'

She nodded; his bluntness appreciated. 'I trust your council, so there is no way to keep this castle?'

'No, my lady, perhaps if I were fit and at my peak, but I am drained and injured... I am no use to you, for the moment.'

'You are my trusted council, as are you others...' she glanced about the room, trying to seem queenly, despite how dry her throat was, how difficult the words. 'I say we retreat, if there is no way to win here.'

'Milady,' Kilm nodded at once, hooking his axe into his belt.

'We must have a care,' Helligan added, 'we can sneak out the way I came in, but we cannot take the household, the servants, the rest of our men... we would be seen.'

'Through the tunnels?' Niamh asked, a small smile forming, Helligan caught her eye and she saw the same memory in his eyes.

'Yes, as we did once before, sweetling.'

Niamh was struck suddenly with emotion and her words left her.

'Send a message to the men who remain to disband,' Helligan said, 'King Hansel is at the gate but they can go over the walls and meld into the forest.'

'Indeed.' Morkyl nodded.

'The Golden king's army would not molest a household of common servants, I think?' Morkyl asked, 'your father prides his reputation...'

'Agreed,' Helligan replied, 'but I say we take the sisters with us, I would not care to leave them to his mercy.'

'Agreed!' Niamh whispered.

'There is one more thing I need to do,' Helligan said, 'Perhaps Kilm, you could pack us a few supplies – we will be on foot so comfortable boots and warm clothing are a must!'

'Aye, I can do that. What have you to do?' that was Kilm.

'I have to...' Helligan paused and then lifted Niamh's hand in his, 'I have to marry the lady Niamh,' he said.

'Now? Surely there is all the time...'

'There is no time! If we are separated for any reason...' Helligan paused and looked down on Niamh's face, then gently laid a hand on her stomach, 'I do not want my child born a bastard,' he finished, 'I do not want to go to execution, should I be caught, without having shared the blood of my palm with the woman I love.'

Niamh's heart took up thudding, her breath hiccupped. With child? Surely not? She had no time to process though, there were a few moments of shocked silence, but then Kilm clapped Helligan on the back, murmured his congratulations to Niamh and then left the room, Morkyl limping at his heels.

'What do you say? Shall we be wed?' Helligan asked Niamh.

Niamh could not speak but managed a nod. Helligan kissed her brow and then took her hand firmly in his, 'Come, then, Sister Dora can marry us whilst Greta and Lil stand witness.'

The chapel was very quiet and still. Above the king's men amassed, all of them with murder in mind and not a single one who could have imagined the sweetly quiet ceremony which took place below their feet in the sisters' little underground catacomb chapel. Helligan stood opposite Niamh, his eyes boring into her face, his lips slightly parted and his left hand outstretched before him. Dora stood between them, whilst her two initiates stood as witness. Niamh placed her own hand into position, touching her fingertips to Helligan's. Sister Dora lifted up her silver athame and turned Helligan's hand palm up. He inhaled as she used the blade to slice his palm, deep enough to let the blood trickle free. Niamh's hand shook a little, her eyes on the blood which dripped down Helligan's fingers. No mere cut but a gash. The blade was sharp though, and the pain fleeting as her own palm was slashed. Sister Dora lifted both hands and spoke softly.

'Once alone, bleed together, bind in the sight of the goddess, and allow this gift to her to birth a bond which cannot be broken.' She moved their hands over a cup which stood on the altar, and then moved the hands together again, so that the blood mingled as it fell.

'Are you ready?' she asked of them.

Niamh nodded, and Helligan murmured his assent.

'Good,' Sister Dora placed the hands together, bleeding palm to bleeding palm, and then opened a box which lay before her. Inside was an old tattered piece of twine. This she lifted and used to wrap their clasped hand and wrist.

'Your vows?' she murmured, 'do you know them?'

Helligan nodded.

'Go ahead then.'

Helligan looked down onto Niamh's face, a gentle smile on his lips, 'Niamh... by bud and root, by leaf and stem, by hill and dale and sky, by the rushing of the river, and by the sand of the shore, in the brightness of day and the darkness of night, I, Helligan Darkfire, leader of the free men and mage of the high council, do ask the goddess to bless this union.'

Niamh trembled. Her arm ached and her gut was eating itself, but still she managed to somehow move her lips and begin to speak, 'Helligan, by all that is above, and all that is below, by the whisper of the wind and by the heat of fire's brightest spark, by the mountains and by the sweet yellow energy which runs through us all, I Queen Niamh of Aurvandil, daughter of the Golden King, ask the goddess to bless this union.'

Sister Dora closed her eyes, her head falling back as a strange glow radiated from her form. Niamh stared, she'd witnessed many a marriage in her time, but this was not a part of the ceremony she recognized. The priestess let out a low moan which was almost a gasp and then opened her eyes. The odd white glow did not dissipate.

'The goddess lends her blessing,' the sister whispered, 'and in her name, I proclaim you to be man and wife.'

Helligan, seeming unfazed by the strange magic around them, stepped forward and used his unbound hand to pull Niamh closer. Their arms bent, still bound, so that they were trapped between them as they kissed.

'Congratulations,' the sister said as they parted, 'we have no time for... the consummation ceremony... but I will swear on my life that it occurred, should I ever be questioned.'

'Thank you Dora,' Niamh whispered.

'Goddess lend you mercy, my child. For now the time to leave draws closer and my sisters and I must pray before that time is upon us.'

'Will an hour be enough?' Helligan asked.

Sister Dora nodded.

'I will return for you all in an hour, then,' he said. 'Add an extra prayer for me? For our child?' Again he rested a hand on Niamh's belly. Dora smiled gently and nodded her head once, then moved away leaving Niamh and Helligan alone in the small chapel.

'Well met, my wife,' Helligan said to Niamh, a traditional greeting after a wedding ceremony.

'Well met, Husband.'

'We need to go – are you steeled? I don't suppose the next few days will be easy...'

Niamh nodded, apprehensive but suddenly feeling like she could take on the whole world.

Chapter 17

The forest was dark, misty from the rain and somewhat foreboding. Niamh's nostrils were loaded with the scent of wet horse, her body trembling with cold, exertion and fear. Helligan rode a little ahead of her, not so far that she was left behind but far enough that she had to maintain concentration and speed to keep up with his horse's heavy footfalls. The other men had gone home to Helligan's house in the marshes to begin to regroup the army but Helligan and she had ridden on, heading towards Havensguard and Morgana where Helligan believed she'd be safer hidden. As they rode, Niamh felt her eyes begin to close, the rocking of the horse along with her own exhaustion rendering her body limp. Realising this, she forced her eyes open, but almost at once they began to droop closed again. At the third time of her eyes closing, she slipped and almost lost her rein, being forced to grab for it. This movement caught Helligan's attention.

'Niamh?'

'I am well.'

'You slipped?' He pulled rein and allowed her to catch up to him. His whole demeanour was slumped, almost defeated, but his eyes still showed his resolve.

'I fell asleep…'

'Oh sweetling, I'm sorry, it's too dangerous to make camp…'

'I know…'

'Your father's men will be looking for us and we are not to safety yet….'

She nodded.

'One more hour, and then we should be close enough to the Wolder lands to make camp…'

Niamh nodded again and steeled herself for another hour.

Eventually the trees thinned, the shadows becoming eerie figures rather than a dark mass. Helligan slowed and then dismounted, leaping from the horse in a way which made Niamh's heart pound considering his recent injury. He came to take her rein and indicated the clearing to the west.

'I can see what looks like a cave,' he said, 'we could shelter for the night.'

'Is it not too close? What if they travel this far looking for us? If we can ride this far in a day so can they!'

'I can hide us, if we take the horses in with us…'

Niamh nodded her assent and turned her horse, Helligan remounted and led the way across the clearing, through another grove of trees and then down to where the cliffs began to rise. Sure enough, somewhat hidden in the rockface was a little cave. Niamh paused a moment, half wondering at Helligan's eyesight to have spotted the cave at such a distance, but then rode down to the entrance and dismounted.

'Let me go first,' Helligan said, 'The last thing I want is you disturbing a bear or a pack of wolves…'

Niamh nodded but her hand took her bow from her back. Helligan smiled and held up his hand. All at once his fingers seemed to ignite, creating a ball of blue flame to light their way inside. The cavern was actually quite large, room enough to stand easily and stretching back into the darkness beyond where Helligan's light could reach. Niamh stood, bow in hand, whilst Helligan walked to the back of the cave and then returned.

'It's safe,' he said.

Niamh slipped back out and took up the reins of the horses, leading them inside not just to keep them hidden, but also for their own comfort – the rain was coming down harder now and the forest floor turning to slush. Helligan took a torch from one of their packs and used the flame from his fingers to light it, again leaving it bearing that odd blue flame which was born from the bottle he held about his neck. The torch he handed to Niamh, then held up a hand to touch the rock face. Niamh watched, her heart pounding, as one of the outcrops of rock suddenly seemed to extend and grow like a stone stalactite. To this he bound the reins of the horses, but then turned his attention to the front of the cave.

'I won't be able to close us off completely, 'he said, 'I don't have enough of a hand with earth magic for that, but I might be able to cast an illusion to hide us.'

'Will it last?'

'Yes, a night at least.'

'Good, do it,' she said.

Helligan nodded and moved to the entrance of the cave. As Niamh watched, his body seemed to tense, the muscles in his arms tensing up as his hands moved. This time he did not touch his vial, but laid a white hand on the grey rock of the wall instead. As she watched, the entrance of the cave suddenly seemed to flicker, to darken. Not gone, but noticeable either. Helligan exhaled suddenly and the illusion snapped into place, an almost solid-looking rock-face which barred the entrance to the cave.

'Not the best of illusions but it is adequate,' he said.

Niamh nodded and moved back to where the horses were tied. Using deft, educated movements, she unsaddled the horses and brushed them down as best she could with her hands, then pulled the packs nearer to the front of the cave. It was still cold, but at least with the body-heat of both people and horses it was beginning to warm up a little. Helligan took the packs from her and laid out bedrolls and the thin blankets that usually the horses wore under their saddles. They stank a bit of horse-sweat but at least they were warm. Helligan wrapped one about his own shoulders, and the other about Niamh, and then reclined on the bedroll, holding her to his chest.

'Are you cold?' he whispered, obviously feeling where she shivered.

'A little.'

Helligan shuffled so that he was half-sitting and pulled her to him with one hand whilst with the other he lifted a handful of dirt from the cave floor and blew on it, then made a motion of throwing it, so that the grains flew all about them. Niamh watched, growing sleepy as the dust did not fall, but began to float about them, glowing an odd yellow like glow-bugs. All at once, the cavern seemed to warm – not an intense heat, but a gentle warmth which spread through Niamh's limbs, over her body, like a silk veil. Helligan, seeming content, laid his head back on the stone wall behind them and put his other arm around Niamh, cupping her belly.

'That's all I have left in me, I think,' he murmured.

Niamh looked up to see the exhaustion on his features, the strain he used in keeping his eyes open. Still he nursed his stomach where the arrow had impaled him and she'd not be surprised if that wound festered a little. She shuffled a little, coaxing him down onto the bedroll.

'Come, sleep,' she said.

'I have to keep watch…'

'You don't! If they find us now we are trapped anyway. You might as well rest.'

'Not how I wanted to spend our wedding night…' Helligan said, a wry smile showing on his lips.

'Nor I…'

Helligan placed a hand on her belly, 'Did you know?' he asked. 'About the child.'

'No.'

'I sensed it, I thought you might be hiding it from me.'

'No. Why would I?'

Helligan put his head back against the wall and closed his eyes briefly, then sighed, 'Because I fear you doubted me, perhaps still do. Last night you sent me away and I thought that… that I had lost your affections.'

'I do not doubt you. Helligan I…' she paused, almost retreating back to a place where communication was difficult.

'Hmmm?'

'I… Helligan, I love you.' The words echoed, the whisper seeming almost too loud. Niamh's heart began to hammer, more so as he took a moment to consider before replying.

'Niamh,' he whispered, 'you say that as though you are afraid of the words…'

'Afraid that I am alone in my emotion.'

'Oh sweetling, if only you knew…' he murmured, then, 'My queen, I love you more than my own life, perhaps one day circumstance will show you how literally I mean that…'

'As your queen?'

'No, as my lover, my sweetling and now my wife.' He lifted his hand to cup her face, 'you have my life,' he whispered, 'whether you be monarch or peasant, always.'

Niamh found a small smile, the most she could muster on such a day, and leaned in to kiss him, Helligan slid both hands into her hair, gently cupping her face.

'Tomorrow we take on the world, as true husband and wife,' he whispered, and kissed her again, pulling her body to his and, despite the exhaustion which encompassed them both, tugging at the laces of her gown.

Chapter 18

Niamh's eyes followed the shadows, fear flooding her every cell and fibre. Helligan and she were closeted in a dark basement, beneath the house of a Wolder family in the village of Bridgeton, the second largest of the Wolder settlements after Havensguard. They'd been trapped there by her father's men for a siege of two days but from the screaming and sounds of battle from above, the king's men had broken through the Wolder defences. Helligan's arms held her tightly, his lips whispering prayers to the goddess for their safety but already Niamh knew from the sounds above, that those prayers would not be answered. In the weeks of exile, moving from settlement to settlement at Morgana's suggestion, several times her father's men had come close to finding them, but this time it was too close for comfort. Her breathing came in small panted breaths as the din of battle grew closer.

'Should we go up, before they begin to murder the villagers?'

Helligan said nothing but nodded. His whole body seemed tense, alert. Niamh lifted the bow from her back and hooked an arrow into the nock. Her hands shook though and she doubted that her aim would be true. Another cry came from above, but before they could steel themselves to make a move, the trapdoor lifted, sending down a shower of dust in the cold breeze which surrounded them. Niamh's eyes took in three men, all in the white and gold of her father's tabard. One was a man who looked in his fifties or so, the other two younger; all of them looked mean.

All at once, Helligan sprang into action. His hand gripped the bottle at his throat and then a bright blue light shot free from his hand. Niamh did not fire her arrow, if for no other reason than that Helligan stood between the men and her. The light bounced from man to man, causing screams of agony. Whatever Helligan had done, he'd not held back. As her father's men fell, Helligan grabbed for Niamh's hand and all but dragged her up the stairs. She allowed him to do so, tripping on the prone bodies as they reached the top of the stairs. Helligan's hand was firm in its grip, and Niamh felt her arm pulled taunt as he dragged her away. Upstairs, the woman who had sheltered them was dead, a spear through her throat just left dangling there. There was no sign of her husband and children but the whole room stank of sweat and blood. Niamh choked back a sob, her hands cradling her now noticeably swollen belly. Behind her, the men were stumbling back to their feet and a hand grasped her shoulder. Niamh spun about and let fly an arrow. It was not a direct hit, even despite the close quarters, but it speared the man's shoulder, sending him reeling backwards to collapse onto his companion.

Helligan spun about again, hand still on the bottle and Niamh saw the heat building in his fingers once more.

'If you do that, you'll burn the house down,' she gasped, recognising his flames.

'There is none left alive to claim it, anyhow' came his reply, and then the heat flew past her shoulder, another ball of bluest flame. Niamh's eyes burned for it, and her lungs screamed at the sudden heat. All three of the soldiers fell, burning, one tumbling bodily down the stairs into the basement. Helligan's neck muscles tensed and for half a second, Niamh saw a glimmer of blue glow in his eyes. Then he seemed to repress it and exhaled slowly.

'Come, if we go carefully we might be able to escape capture after all.'

'The villagers...'

'I think they are probably either fled or killed. I do not think your father's men would spare them – they have tried to hide us.'

'Then their deaths are on our conscience.'

Helligan closed his eyes for a long moment, then nodded. 'they are,' he whispered, 'and on your father's.'

Helligan opened the door and stepped out, but then froze. Niamh's eyes were blinded for a moment for the bright sunlight outside of the dark and dusty house but then her heart sank. Another group of her father's men waited outside for them, all mounted and in full armour. Helligan inhaled and then once more his fingertips flared in blue flame. He was going to go down fighting, it seemed.

'Get behind me Niamh,' he said, his arms trembled slightly with the restrained power. Niamh did as she was told, watching as once more Helligan flung out his magical flame. The men without, more prepared than the footmen had been, simply avoided it. Niamh slipped an arrow from her quiver, but before she could nook it, a strong arm came around her. She screamed, making Helligan spin about as she was dragged bodily backwards.

'Niamh!' he cried, but then spun back to fire again at the men who came down on him. This time his aim was truer, and the closest of them fell from his mount, sparks bursting into flames on the cloth under his armour, burning him alive within the metal plates. The other two, both younger, retreated at the screams but then pushed on again as Helligan turned to try to get to Niamh. Her captor, also clad in plate was relentless though and her bow lay on the floor between her and Helligan. The grip about her chest was almost choking, her feet dragged uselessly. Helligan fired something in their direction but it missed wildly, likely lost in his fear of hitting her. The men were almost upon him again so he had to turn back again, to defend himself. During this assault, Niamh's attacker had dragged her to the edge of the woods and there he too had a horse tethered. As he relaxed his grip on her, she fought, hard, but weaponless against a man in full plate, the advantage was not hers and before a minute had passed she was thrown up bodily onto the horse, her pregnant belly pushed uncomfortably beneath her and her hands bound tightly together.

'Helligan!' she screamed, but he was preoccupied in avoiding his own capture. Niamh screamed again and he turned. Panic took his features as he realised her plight and with what looked like a sudden burst of adrenaline, he started towards her. Too late though, far too late. Niamh's captor clambered up behind her and spurred on the horse whilst from behind, the last remaining soldier, or so it seemed at least, continued to try to ride Helligan down. Niamh struggled again to be free but with the way she was tied the most likely outcome would be being dragged along beside the horse and she did not wish to risk the baby she carried with such. Closing her tearful eyes, Niamh said a prayer for Helligan's freedom and resigned herself to capture.

Niamh was taken straight from the horse to her father's closed hall. She was taken in by night and so was carted unseen by the commoners of the city who might have cried for her. Inside, as she awaited her father, she was handed a cloak to wrap about her for warmth and was given a weak mead to drink. The servants seemed not to know what to do with the royal prisoner and so she was treated with courtesy. Noticeable too, however, were the tight lips of the ladies waiting on her, the sympathetic eyes as they rested on her stomach – not huge yet, but still obviously bloated somewhat with babe. Niamh wondered how many of the commoners knew of her condition, of how this gossip might spread. As she mulled, however, thinking of anything but Helligan and whether or not he was taken or dead, her father entered.

The old king looked much as Niamh remembered him. His blond hair was white and almost gone on the top, and his skin was wrinkled, especially about the eyes and above his beard. He paused a minute and cast his eyes over her, her face, and then her body, pausing at her belly, and then back up.

'My daughter,' he finally said.

'Sire.'

'Child I beg you now, and you have but one chance... tell me that you were kidnapped, that the babe you carry is the product of rape and that you had no part in planning the uprising these four months past.'

'Sire I cannot.'

The words echoed, lingered and then dissipated as her father sat down opposite her. He was quiet for a long moment, but then leaned forward, a fatherly hand on her arm.

'I put it to you again, child, as though I heard not the words you just spoke. You have but one moment to redeem yourself, to save yourself from the dungeons and a traitor's trial. Say it now and say it again before the council, that the commoners might hear you. Throw off Helligan Darkfire and his wild men, and return to the fold. Tell me, tell them, that you were forced, that you were broken by the terrible practices and unworldly tortures of those foul men, and that you have come home broken by your mistreatment and pregnant for the rape of your person.'

So that was his game then, to demonise the free men. Niamh's gut twisted at the very thought that she would ever say such things. 'Sire...' fear made her voice tremble but love shaped the words, 'Sire, I cannot.'

'You sadden me, Niamh. You who I nursed and cradled with my true-born children, you who survived the hell of our loss with me, at the hands of those you now serve. You, who I legitimised! Was it not enough to be second in line? Would you steal my throne now through your impatience?'

Niamh said nothing, breathing through her nose in fear as her father moved closer again to her.

'So you won't speak to me, to give an old man a reason why?'

'Ondreich Highlark,' Niamh said, shaping the words.

'Is that it? A war waged because a little girl does not wish to be married?' The old man chuckled, the sound almost the mirth it was intended to emulate.

'Not all. That was the final piece, that was why I left.'

The king eyed Niamh again, and then stood and put his hands on the back of his chair, moving behind it to do so. 'So be it. Your plans are foiled and your war is lost. All I need from you, a self-proclaimed traitor as you claim to be – is the location of what remains of your men. Where is Helligan the mage? Where are the marsh lords, and why is it that my men remain unable to unearth the location of the fabled Heavensguard?'

'I will speak nothing more on that matter.'

The king's expression changed so suddenly that Niamh was startled out of her seat. The mask slipped and the man beneath showed with screwed up eyes and a cocked lip. He grabbed her and shook her with his hands, furious.

'Oh, you will play it this way, will you?' he asked, 'you dare to anger me?'

Her father's face looked almost piggy for his fury, the eyes so small and scrunched that the normal benevolent blue was hidden. Niamh had heard tell of his temper but never had she thought to see it. Her father threw her back down into the chair, then sat opposite.

'Talk!' he snapped.

Niamh held his gaze with defiance, her eyes hard despite the fear.

'Talk!' he shouted, 'Talk now or I'll take you down to the dungeons and leave you there for a night or two! How do you fancy the dark hole, hmm?'

Niamh inhaled, her whole body was shaking but she could not speak. The dark hole was just that, a black, windowless tiny cell once used as an oubliette. There was talk that it was

haunted, and if not, it had held so many men on the edge of –
and crossed over into – death

'Oh! You think I am bluffing?' he snapped, then stood and
gripped the top of her arm. Niamh squeaked where the skin
pinched under his fingers but her father paid no mind. He
dragged her out, before the curious faces of the servants,
before even a few courtiers – a true sign that his sanity was
slipping, to allow them to see him thus unmasked. Niamh's feet
skidded and slipped as her father dragged her from the main
keep, down a set of wet stone stairs and into the foot of the
turret. There, he banged on the door with a fist and all-but
thrust her through it when it was opened.

Niamh stumbled but was given no time to fall as her father
grabbed her again and marched her before him through dark
corridor after dark corridor, a nameless and silent guard
following in their wake. At last there was another wooden door
and this one opened up to a rough chamber. Inside stood a
fairly young man, blond of hair and shirt, stout. He glanced up,
then did a double take and flew to his feet, bowing to the king.

'Malachi, I want this one thrown into the hole,' her father
said.

'But sire, this is… I mean she is… is your daughter? Sire?'
the man named as Malachi whispered, 'Surely you don't mean
to…'

'To proceed as though she were not,' her father said, 'yes,
I do.'

Niamh's eyes took a moment to adjust to the darkness. The
room stank, old blood and god-knows what else. Before her
there was simply a desk and the chair Malachi had been sitting
in when they arrived, but to her right was another heavy door
leading into a sub-chamber. Malachi eyed her up and down,
then looked to her father.

'Is this a true order?' he asked.

'Of course it is!'

'She is with child, sire.'

'I am well aware of that.'

'I… can't send a pregnant woman down there! She'll catch a chill, or worse.'

'You wish me then to find somebody who will, perhaps? Perhaps you yourself are curious to what it feels like to spend time as a prisoner in these dungeons? The lady Niamh refuses to cooperate and so I will see her detained in the darker cells, until she is better ready to speak to me on such matters as I require.'

Niamh still said nothing, her lips pressed tightly closed, nothing seemed real, as though she had one foot in reality and the other in this odd dream world. She pulled in a deep breath and released it slowly, steadying herself. Her father eyed her again, then turned to Malachi.

'I will do it, if you order me, sire,' he said.

'Go on, then…'

Malachi swallowed but then nodded and turned to Niamh. 'Madam, the hole is a dark and foreboding place. I would suggest that you unburden yourself of your secrets now that you might be given a softer prison.'

Niamh shook her head. There was more than just her life at stake now, she could not allow her father to enslave the free men.

Malachi swallowed again, and then put a hand on her arm, he pulled her to the door to the antechamber and then turned the key and pushed her through. There Niamh did faulter. Never before had she laid eyes on a torture chamber, especially one so well equipped. In the middle of the room was the rack, a vicious-looking structure with cuffs for the wrist and the ankle, its giant wheel showing the merciless pain it could cause. Beside this was a table filled with unspeakable instruments, some she recognised – a saw, a striker and a dagger – others she didn't – strange alien devices. A fire burned in the grate, and beside it a poker-stand with different pokers attached. Niamh doubted very much that they were for stoking the fire. A frame stood at the edge of the room, shackles attached to its peak. Her father lingered at the edge of the room for a moment, eyeing up the devices, but then nodded curtly and removed himself.

'Just through here,' was it Niamh's imagination, or was there an edge to Malachi's voice, a soothing tone?

'Sir...' she managed.

'No, come, my lady,' his voice was softer still as he led her through the torture chamber and down a set of stone stairs. The stairs were slippery but Malachi put out an arm to steady her. Niamh rested a hand on it, following hm down into the depths of the keep. Finally, the jailer pulled out a key and opened the door to one of the far rooms.

'My lady,' he said.

Niamh moved forwards but there she balked. The walls were of grey stone and there was no window to let in light at all. Due to the location of the cell too, the ceiling was very high, like a long thin tunnel leading up, this imagery impacted by the total lack of floor space; the room must have been no more than five-foot square.

'In... in here?' she whispered.

'Yes, I... my apologies my lady but yes, this is where you father would have you held.'

The room would be total darkness, Niamh realised, with the door closed. Not a cell but a cage for an animal. Her eyes cast about the odd oblong room, trying to spy anything to give comfort but there was nothing. The cold stone walls looked damp and rugged, the floor uneven stone.

Malachi put a gentle hand into the small of Niamh's back, softly but definitely pushing her into the room. She was shivering already, and terrified, but called on the last of her dignity to make that step forward into the room. Malachi gave her one last sympathetic glance and then closed the door behind him. A rusty squeal as the bolt was slid closed, and then she was alone.

'Goddess preserve me,' Niamh whispered, sitting down by the wall with her knees pulled up towards her chest, hindered somewhat by her pregnancy, but determined not to give into the crushing darkness. There was a void of sound too, the heavy door cutting out all that was above so that the lack of sound became sound itself, rushing through her ears. Niamh felt claustrophobia pull in. She was not overly tall but the cell was too narrow either way for her to have stretched out, a fact which was somewhat masked by the illusion of vastness created by the darkness. The walls were rough behind her, the floor cold and uncomfortable. Niamh had not even a cloak to wrap about her, or to bundle into a pillow. Her hands were like ice already but her priority was the child, hugging herself and trying to keep her torso warm.

As the hours passed, the darkness grew ever more oppressive. Niamh gave up her stance not to cry and allowed precious moisture to leave her body in the form of tears. She was parched, and hungry too but those feelings were masked by the pressure upon her form of the crushing darkness. The hours seemed to run together too, so that she was suddenly unable to gauge if it had been one hour or three, two or six.

The sound of footsteps on the stairs without was hidden from Niamh by the heavy door, and so the squeal of the bolt moving back was her first alert that somebody was coming. She scrambled to her feet, pressing herself against the back wall as the door opened, despite the dizzying feeling of moving about the inkiness.

Malachi stood beyond. His lantern was very dim, but still the brightness of it made Niamh squint in the darkness.

'My lady,' his voice was a whisper. 'How fare you?'

Niamh had no words, just gawped at him. The jailer stepped into the chamber and closed the door. Niamh pressed herself further back against the wall.

'Fear not, my lady,' he said, 'I merely wish not to be discovered.' He took his thick black cape from about his shoulders and offered it to her. Niamh just stared but then put out a hand for the garment.

'I cannot leave it,' he said, 'But I hope at least that it will warm you a little whilst I am here.'

Niamh murmured a dry thanks and pulled the cloak about herself. Malachi nodded, and then produced from his belt a pouch and a waterskin, food and drink. These Niamh took with more gusto, gobbling down the water and then unwrapping cheese and bread.

'Thank you, thank you sir,' she finally managed,' I presume you come against my father's orders?'

'I do. I am...' it was Malachi's turn to look uncertain, his eyes darting about. 'I am charged to inform you, my lady, that you do not suffer in silence.'

'I... what?'

'Your father's men smuggled you in but there are those of us who noticed. The common folk, and others, higher, do not like the way your father has turned to ruling since the food shortages, they do not like the changes wrought in battle after battle and they do not like the thought of our princess, heavy with child and all, taken prisoner in the cold dank dungeons. These are some, some of *us* who would see you freed.'

Hope, a delicate bird which had ceased to fly took up a fluttering once again in Niamh's breast. Malachi, her father's own jailer, put a hand over hers. 'I cannot take you now, my lady, but upon first light a meeting of the rebellion will be had, and then it is my hope that on the morrow, you can be removed to a place of safety.'

Niamh inhaled slowly and then let it out. Here it was, as evidenced as ever it could be, she was the people's princess, the choice of the common folk over her father or even Laurin. Gratitude and appreciation bubbled together, coming to hold hands within her.

'The goddess lives within you all,' she managed to whisper. 'Thank you my friend.'

Malachi the jailer knelt, his lips moving to her hand and then his head bowing low. 'It is an honour, my sweet lady,' he whispered, and then stood again. 'I must depart, I cannot stay overlong without suspicion falling upon me. Here, hide this about your person,' he handed her a candle stub and a small silver-look tinder box. Niamh slipped them into the folds of her gown where something of a pocket had been sewn in.

'May your Goddess preserve you,' Malachi said, opening the door once again.

'And may she bless you,' Niamh said, welling up.

The night seemed to draw out forever. Niamh sat, alert, on the hard stone floor with her candle in her hands. She did not dare light it, unsure if it was gifted to be a saviour from the darkness, or needed for whatever plan Malachi had to release her. As she waited, her resolve hardened again, her stomach growled but she ignored that, she was hungry but not enough so to render her weak thanks to Malachi's bread and cheese. The time passed in a strange daze, hours and hours which could have been days or mere minutes in the darkness. Niamh's hands worried at the wax of the candle, her body aching for sitting so upright. She remembered how, as a child, she'd yearned to be allowed to come and explore the murky dungeons… the irony was not lost on her. A sobbing fit threatened again, but she repressed it, squeezing the candle stub in her hands in order to physically repress the emotions. There was no time to cry now, she was no longer "Idiot Niamh" the king's bastard, now she was The Lady Niamh, Queen Niamh to some – queen of the rebels and wife of Helligan the Mage. She was no snivelling child, and she would not give her father the satisfaction of her tears!

A rattle caught her attention, and then a click at the door. Niamh leapt to her feet, ready to go, but the visitor was not Malachi. The king eyed her with distaste, but then smirked. 'I have come to inform you that you go to trial tomorrow, he said simply, 'your companions, including your commander, have been arrested.'

'What… no!'

Her father said nothing more, but turned away. Behind him stood two guards and Malachi, the guards were expressionless but Malachi caught her eye and mouthed the words "I am sorry" before turning away and allowing the door to swing closed again.

Chapter 19

The royal reception chamber of the Golden Keep was much as Niamh remembered it, ornate and richly furnished. Her father's golden throne now newly stood up on a dais, and two tables had been pulled to the side to make up a makeshift court, the men of her father's council standing behind them. Niamh was dressed in a white ragged gown she'd been given – her own clothes confiscated. She wore no underwear, nor shoes, and realised that she already looked much like a condemned woman on her route to execution. Her hair was loose and tangled, her body trembling for the cold despite how she kept her head high and faced her Father with a bravery she did not know she possessed. Behind her Helligan and Morkyl too stood in shackles, condemned men, with guards on either side of them. At seeing her, when they had been brought in, Helligan had fought to get to her side and so suffered yet another wound above his hip from a guard's spear. He was dressed still in his own clothing but his fine leather jerkin was gone. Morkyl too wore his own clothing, his beard long and scraggly under his chin. He too had the residue of blood about his face leading Niamh to guess that they had both fought hard against capture.

'And so my absent child stands before us all, face flushed with rebellion, unchaste and fat with a babe of her own,' Niamh's father spoke at last, commanding the attention of everybody present. 'Tell us my dear, which of these wild men,' he indicated them both with his hand, 'if either, is the father of your bastard?'

Niamh stood her ground, silent. It would seem her father knew not of her marriage and she could see no benefit in informing him thus.

'Oh, I see you have lost your tongue again? Strange how that happens now, but you had no trouble in speaking out your treasons against me and my men!'

'I spoke only the truth, as did these good men behind me.'

The king looked long at her, but then his eyes softened and a sadness took his features. 'My poor child. So much like your mother,' she said, 'do you remember your mother, Niamh?'

She shook her head.

'I thought not, you were very young when she died. She was a whore from a house near the Golden Keep, in its heyday, skilled in the art of seduction, manipulation and of pleasuring a cock – it would seem you are very much her child!'

Still Niamh said nothing but her top lip curled, just slightly. Behind her came the stirring of Helligan's moving, shuffling, she prayed he'd not do anything rash and buy himself a harder death.

'But what to do with you,' her father mused, and then looked to his advisors.

'What proof do we have of the guilt?' An older man asked, Niamh thought his name was Western but couldn't quite remember – it seemed an age since she'd left that life and already the faces and names of her father's companions were fading.

'We have too much evidence to even warrant a trial. Witness statements, from all from courtier to peasant. Even my own son,' the king nodded towards Laurin who sat silently by his father's side, the new queen sat on the other side, 'saw the mage Helligan set siege to a town and brutally murder half of the occupants.'

EMMA BARRETT-BROWN

'I did.' Laurin's voice sounded high of pitch next to his father.

'Niamh, my daughter, and Helligan the mage are both defectors of my own court, a councillor of the highest order and a princess made legitimate at my own kindness. Niamh took with her the plans for a battle and more – thus thwarting our advancement and causing the suffering of many more of the common folk.'

'The question is not of whether of not these traitors are guilty,' that was Jahlyn Carver – the old knight who had once bounced a baby Niamh on his knee. 'Their guilt is undisputable. More the manner of punishment…'

'The two men *must* lose their heads,' Nordemunde said, moving forward to stand before the king. 'I beseech my liege not to show mercy to the girl either, lest this court be perceived as weak.

'The girl was ill-led,' that was Josynne Shale, ever he had had a soft spot for her and Niamh glanced up to see his eyes were dull, his lips pressed, 'ill-led and ill-advised, sire, I beg you to reconsider any harsh punishment as you would for a simple girl's actions.'

'Whilst I agree that she was so,' the king said, 'her crimes are vast, Josynne, I cannot pardon her completely.'

'Burn her as the traitor she is,' came a voice from beyond, another of her father's advisors. Niamh wobbled on the spot, her arms cupping her unborn babe. She didn't dare turn to see the impact the words had had on Helligan. This suggestion, however, caused a murmur to go up, hard to decipher, but seeming to come in her defence.

'No! Mercy! Father! Mercy!' That was Laurin, bless Laurin!

'Son? You would be merciful?'

'She is my sister still, and your daughter too!'

'Poison out the child perhaps,' another voice, 'or bash it's brains out upon its birth and if she survives, send her to the new temple as an initiate – if you would have mercy!'

'A more favourable suggestion, any others?'

A rumble of noises as all and sundry spoke at once, but then suddenly there was silence as the new queen, Magda, stood from her seat beside Niamh's father.

'I say that my liege should behead the girl with her lover,' she said, her voice gentle and soft amongst the harsh tones of the male advisors. 'Alive she is a danger to us all and despite cries for mercy, she must be treated as any other traitor. There is no need to resort to brutality, though, with burnings and the like – simply treat her as though she were any other sentenced of these crimes and allow her to be executed with dignity.'

Again, voices rose as people bickered. Niamh glanced down at her bound hands above her stomach. Helligan's child – never to see the light of a broken morning, never to play or to prance. She pressed her lips tight and forced her face back to neutrality.

'I think we must adhere to the wisdom of my good lady,' Niamh's father said, 'I sentence you to die amongst your friends, my daughter, and I do so with a heavy heart. Executions will take place on the morrow out on the green, you can all face death together, just as you have plotted your crimes. The scaffold need not be built, as I have commissioned it some weeks hence in anticipation of your capture.'

'No!' that was Lord Shale, an exclamation which seemed to echo, he looked ashen and gaunt suddenly. 'Sir to execute a woman laden with child…'

'I pity you for your kind heart Josynne, but I am firm, the princess, hereby to be stripped of that title and so thus the Lady Niamh once more, will die on the morrow with her companions.'

Niamh staggered, almost falling but a movement behind her and then a strong arm holding her up despite its bindings. Her father glanced over her head to where Helligan had moved to catch her.

'I thought as much…' he muttered, and then turned and swept away, followed by the queen and then Laurin. The rest of the court followed suit, leaving the three prisoners to the three guards. The only one to glance back was Lord Shale, his lips pressed tight and his eyes angry. Niamh wished she had the words to thank him, at least he had tried to save her.

'Come,' the elder of the three guards said, his voice soft, 'you will want to eat and to pray for your spirits to be accepted by your goddess on the morrow.'

Niamh glanced up at Helligan, then over to Morkyl who was almost grey with fear, silent and grim.

'Will we be executed together?' Helligan asked.

'You will, as the king decreed,' the guard replied.

'With time to meet again, before...?'

'I am sure, yes. You will be allowed your goodbyes.'

'Who... who first?' Niamh whispered.

The guard shuffled, his bushy red eyebrows showing his discomfort, 'Milady, you are first in rank...'

At least she'd not have to watch Helligan die, that was some relief!

'Come,' the guard said again, 'there is no sense in dawdling.'

The morning fell too quickly. Niamh spent the night in almost luxury, not a dungeon cell but a locked chamber up in the main keep. Her chamber was no dank and cold cell, but was softly furnished, with embroidered tapestries to keep out the drafts and a soft bed which was wasted on Niamh. All through the night, the new temple priest in the antechamber burned incense and chanted for Niamh's soul, that of her unborn child. As some odd mercy, she had too a sacred sister to tend her, to wash and anoint her when the time came and to pray for the safety of her soul. The woman, youthful and pale, stopped often to sniff too, and to wipe her eyes and mutter that it was a crime but Niamh could think of nothing to say in response. Too wrought and terrified to coffer comfort to the young priestess.

The dusky orange of morning came too quickly. A maid arrived with a gown of black velvet and a white cap. The gown she helped Niamh into; it was snug about her belly, enhancing the bump – surely not her father's choice of gown. The maid too was press-lipped and pale. Unhappy in her task. She brushed out Niamh's hair with flower-scented perfumes which were surely smuggled in, and then knelt to wash her swollen feet. Niamh's brow furrowed, her heart pounding. This was not as she had expected but she could not find the words to question the gesture.

Eventually she was clean and dressed though. A thin cord was bound about her hands, securing them, and a fine cloak draped over her shivering shoulders. Some words were exchanged through the door and then Niamh was led from her chamber, down two flights of stone stairs, and out of a wooden door. Niamh swayed, panic gripping her heart and rending the ordeal somewhat hazy and drawn out. The light was too bright, Niamh murmured aloud, blinking, but then felt her shoulders taken by soft hands, leading her, one by the maid, the other by the sister – both of whom had been allowed to accompany her down to the scaffold.

The scaffold itself was a large wooden stage which was set in against the rough brick wall of the tower. The grass beyond seemed very green, bright in the already warm sunshine of the day. From the tower, was an outdoor stone stairway which led to the wooden structure, and there were another six steps leading up to where the executioner already stood. Niamh's father and his new wife, as well as a red-eyed Laurin sat on a tiered seating arrangement towards the end of the platform, this lying up against the far wall. Before them, on the lower tiers were her father's courtiers. There were no common people in place yet to watch the relatively private viewing, but even as Niamh descended the stone steps, her cape pulled tight about her despite the heat, she saw that the wooden gate at the edge of the circle was opening.

As Niamh descended, stepping out onto the grass for a few steps before mounting the scaffold, a door across the keep opened and guards marched out Helligan and Morkyl.

Helligan's hands were not only bound, but covered by a thin cloth too – a defence against his being able to use his magic, Niamh supposed. Helligan caught her eye as they all but met in the middle of the green, but was then hidden from her as her own guard pushed her up onto the stage.

The block stood in the middle. There was a hangman's noose situated at the end, but there was no rope attached, nobody was going to hang today. The block was a small wooden structure, set onto the floor so that one had to kneel before it, in the blood of those before them if they were unlucky enough not to die first. As a princess, Niamh would not have to kneel in Helligan's blood, but she was suddenly very aware that he would have to kneel in hers. At the top she paused, watching as the men moved about to accommodate her. The guard lifted away the warm cape which covered her shoulders and put it to one side. Her black velvet gown was dusty already – she'd not even knelt yet! – and the wind pulled on her hair, making the strands tickle her neck; her hair was loose but would be bound into the little white cap her maid carried before she was executed. Niamh half-expected to be dragged straight to the block, but instead she was left standing to one side of it whilst Helligan and Morkyl were brought to stand beside her. Helligan glanced down at her, perhaps seeing the panic in her eyes, he closed his and took a long, deep, breath, then murmured something she did not catch.

'Hmmm?'

'Act on my command,' he seemed to say – the words lost in a murmur, and then looked out at the crowds again.

Before them, the circle was now filled with people. Normally for an execution, the crowds would jeer and call out obscenities but this crowd did not speak, not to utter a single word. A sea of statues, all with eyes of disbelief, lips pressed.

'Plead your belly!' one woman suddenly cried out, confirming Niamh's suspicion that her unborn child was likely reason enough for this consternation. Had she ever witnessed, or even heard of, the execution of another pregnant woman? she thought not!

'Plead your belly, Princess!' The cry was taken up by another and then another before the king stood and motioned for silence. It fell almost instantly.

'My ladies, lords and gentlemen,' he said, 'I am sure that this execution must make you feel distaste, as it does us all, but I beg of you to remember when you look at my daughter, that this is no frightened child, as she appears, but the woman who is responsible for leading these savages from the woods, marshes and fens, out into our civilised world! She is the reason your sons and husbands, fathers and grand-sires lie in their graves!'

The crowd was still strangely silent, not jeering still, but no longer crying for Niamh either.

'The spawn she carries, is the spawn of that savage standing there! That man who did not kidnap her, but to whom she went willingly! Together they sought to overthrow your king! Your civilisation! The golden age in which we once lived! Pity her if you must, misled fool, but do not cry out for her freedom unless you turn your back on all those who died at her hand! A clean death is too good for these people, and yet my queen, with a tender heart, begs for such and so I will oblige!'

He stood back and viewed the crowd but Niamh could see they were still not convinced completely.

'Come,' the king said to Niamh's priestess.

'May I unbind her, sire?'

'You may.'

A sharp blade cut away the rope which bound Niamh's hands together, dropping it to the floor.

'Kneel,' the sister said, gently.

Niamh did so, her knees trembling. The sister smeared a little oil onto her forehead, and then onto her chin, murmuring as she did so. She then knelt before Niamh.

'Will you donate your hair?' she asked.

Niamh nodded, unsure but too confused to refuse. The sister moved behind her and with a pair of shears she snipped away at Niamh's golden hair, slipping the locks into the bag. The sound of the blade so close to her head was a torture of its own but finally she was shorn, her hair tucked away for goddess knows what purpose. The temple-sister then took from Niamh's sobbing maid the white cotton cap which she slid over Niamh's now shorter, clipped locks, and tied into place under her chin. The silence thickened and with it the atmosphere which drew in closer and denser. The crowd were not happy, not at all. This was certainly no usual execution. The temple-sister put out a hand to help Niamh to her feet, and then stepped back. Niamh glanced up at Helligan again. His face was very pale but still his eyes shone. As she caught his eye, he made a subtle nod, then glanced down at the bottle on its cord about his neck.

Niamh frowned, not understanding. Panic was starting to grip her again, especially as the guards were now coming forward to lead her to kneel at the block.

'Helligan,' she moaned, her first word since those she'd spoken before her father's court the night before. The guard took her arm and tried to pull her away. Helligan inhaled and then exhaled quickly, his hands were still bound but he moved forward a step, closer to Niamh. At once the guards were moving in, shouts for Helligan to cease his movements.

'My Lords,' he said, his voice low and calm, 'my lords, ladies and common people here before me, it is customary, I think, to offer a reasonable last request to those about to die?'

A murmur went up as the king stood. He eyes looked over Helligan and then to his guards. He shook his head. For the first time, Niamh saw near-panic in Helligan's eye.

'My lords,' Helligan's voice at least did not show the fear, 'My ladies, I beg of you please, I want but a final kiss from my beloved. Enough that you would have me watch her die, enough to know my child dies with her final breath! …but without a final kiss, a final goodbye? Sire,' he turned to the king,

'Surely your heart has not hardened so to the Lady Niamh? She is your daughter, and she is terrified – heavy with a child which will never be born to us, allow me a moment to help her calm, to face her death with honour? It is not so very much to ask?'

At once the crowd began to shout again, some going so far as to boo the king, to shout for Niamh... and Helligan's... release. The king's face turned a shade of red and his hands clenched to fists.

'Never... never let it be said that I am not merciful,' he stammered, and then nodded. At once Niamh felt herself released and flew to Helligan. He was bound with his hands behind him still but Niamh embraced him, clutching his bound arms in her hands. Helligan leaned to kiss her, and then nuzzled her neck with his face, Niamh tensed to be pulled away again, but even as Helligan caressed her with his face, he whispered the words, 'Break the bottle,' into her ear.

Niamh's shoulders stiffened but there was no time for questions, her hands grasped the leather thong and even as she did so, Helligan bowed his head, allowing the necklace to be pulled off. Behind her, strong hands grabbed for her again and the crowds once more roared their displeasure at seeing Niamh and Helligan pulled apart. Niamh threw the bottle to the ground, oblivious to it all, and raised her bare foot. Bracing for the pain, she threw the foot down onto the bottle.

The pain was almost enough to make Niamh scream out. The bottle was heavy glass, strong enough to make her foot bruise before her weight went down on it, cracking the glass and driving a shard up into the pad of her foot. Niamh fell to her knees, grasping the foot and blind to the chaos around her. Then a blue flash, almost blinding in its intensity, burned her eyes, she put up a hand to shield her face, and felt herself released as the guards did the same. There were shrieks from the crowd but they seemed suddenly distant, echoing. Niamh tried to stand but fell to her knees again, her arms instinctively going about her stomach. She moaned, fear walking its bony feet up her spine. Then chaos as the platform began to sag, a thud, and then another sound, an odd growling roar. Still the air was too hazy to see though, a mist almost which encompassed them all. Niamh felt a hot breath on her face, and looked up into a deep-slit yellow eye about the size of her hand. She screamed and kicked at the beast, but it did not attack, merely stood watching her as the mists began to dissipate.

'Helligan!' Niamh screamed, scrabbling from her position on her knees and looking for him but then, as her vison cleared, her heart began to hammer at the inside of her chest.

Stood on the platform in place of her lover, was a blue-scaled dragon. It stood about twice her height, with wings which rose higher still. Its scales were rugged, unlike snake scales with their smoothness. The face was long, thin and contained those odd yellow eyes. Niamh inhaled a long breath, more so as the beast bowed its head to her.

'Helligan?' she moaned, 'Helligan… where are you?'

The beast stood still, holding her eye.

'Oh… god! Helligan?'

Still the beast did not move, but slowly lowered its head before Niamh.

'What…' she said, but understanding was dawning. A voice shouting beside her pushed her on, Morkyl, faithful Morkyl Braithwaite, still bound, running for her, grabbing at her with his bound hands before him and pushing her towards the beast. Niamh just stared, she was in something of a trance for the shock.

'Get up!' Morkyl shouted, 'Go!'

Niamh's knees shook and her chest was so tight it hurt. Morkyl pushed her again and then her feet were moving, scrabbling to clamber up onto the back of the dragon which had, until just moments earlier, been the man she loved. Morkyl scrabbled up behind her, struggling to find a grip with his bound hands but somehow managing to. Niamh put her arms around Helligan's neck, her swollen belly somewhat in the way but not so much that she'd fall. Morkyl sat behind her, hands gripping scales but his body protecting hers. The sound of the wings was immense as they began to flap and Helligan lifted up from the platform. As they rose, Niamh looked down to see her father and the queen running from the platform back to the tower, a guard on either side As she watched, her brother faltered, staring up and then shouting out an order to take them down. He raised up a bow – her bow! The last Niamh had seen of it was when the kings men had dragged her up onto the horse – her capture. How had her brother taken possession of her bow then? Niamh's chest hurt – not Laurin, poor blind Laurin! Surely he'd not led the men who'd taken them? Surely he was not her original captor? The bow in his hands said otherwise. Another arrow went up, and then another and another. Helligan seemed unfazed until the fifth arrow flew close enough to make Niamh gasp, the tip scratching her face, almost taking off her ear. Helligan paused in the air, almost seemed to double-think it, but then let loose a gust of blue flame from his snout. Niamh closed her eyes, a wail escaping her lips in the knowledge that suddenly she was alone to survive her father's children. No man could have lived after being exposed to that fire. She did not look down though, did not pause to watch the prince fall.

Helligan roared again and let loose another jet of flame, this one aimed at the wall of the tower where Niamh had been held. The old stone resisted but the wooden fixtures took light again, bursting into a combination of blue and orange flame. Niamh's hand trembled on Helligan's throat, the fire making it hot to hold onto as it shot up from his belly. He was nearly done though, his final exhale almost swallowing her father where he stood distraught, trying to get to the body of his son – it would have taken him had his advisors not grabbed him and pulled him away, running for shelter.

Helligan roared a final time, but then turned away, the swish of his wings taking them up and up into the air.

Chapter 20

The woodlands were dark, cold and unwelcoming. All about was an odour of peat and pine, a strange combination of scents localised only to very specific woodlands. Niamh, still dressed only in the robes of execution, shivered and wrapped her arms about herself. She was limping heavily for the wound to her foot where the glass of the bottle had pierced her skin and her other foot ached for the rough ground of the woodlands. The dragon which had been Helligan had settled here only long enough for the passengers to tumble free, and then had risen again, abandoning them in the unknown thicket. Morkyl was just ahead, his shoulders very straight but his form seeming somehow more fragile without his battle-axe strapped to his back or laid at his feet. He was dressed in the stinking rags of his clothing, bare-armed against the chill of the night.

'Do you have any idea where we are?' Niamh whispered, coming up to meet his step.

'No, my queen, other than that Helligan wouldn't have just left us if we were not safe.'

'What… was that really…'

'Helligan? Yes.'

'You knew?'

'Not entirely, but I have suspected for the entire time that I knew him that he was not human. I had him pegged for a beast-shifter.'

Niamh's shoulders sagged. It hardly seemed possible, as though she'd somehow slipped into an odd dream and had no way to waken herself. Morkyl watched the emotions on her face for a moment, worry in his own eyes, but then seemed to blank his expression again in a way only the Wolder had. All about, the trees pressed in close, giving Niamh the feeling of being watched. It stuck her suddenly that she was alone in the woods with just Morkyl, but that despite having been brought up to view to Wolder as savages, she felt safer with him than she would have with any of her father's men, save perhaps Josynne Shale, and even then it was a close thing.

'Come, this way,' Morkyl said, parting a group of rough ferns just ahead, 'there is a crude path. Come, lean on me, mind that foot.'

Niamh and Morkyl walked in silence for nearly an hour, but then found the path becoming more open, like a dirt road. All about them the trees whispered as their boughs rubbed together like eager hands, but the sensation of being hemmed in, of being watched eased back off again as the path widened. The air was cold and Niamh's foot ached terribly but she pushed back the feeling, marched on rubbing her hands on her arms to give herself some warmth. She kept her head high too, her lips pressed as they walked, determined not to make a fuss about her injured foot, her tiredness. Morkyl glanced over at her,

'I had my doubts about you, when Helligan first brought you in,' he said, 'I won't lie, I thought you were just a girl that had caught his eye... quiet and innocent mute that you were. But he saw in you the potential for the woman you have become. I am proud to call you my queen.'

'Oh... I... I am glad of it.'

'Do you need to rest?'

'No…'

'Your foot is bleeding….'

'I know, but my heart craves safety first.'

'So be it.'

As they walked on, though, Niamh felt an odd familiarity starting up. 'I… I think I know this place…'

'Aye, me too, as I reckon, we're just entering Havensguard from the north.'

Relief flooded through Niamh. Of course, Helligan would take them to the safest place, somewhere totally unknown to the king and his lords. Morgana's home, the village in the mists. She paused in the road and drew in a few tearful breaths.

'My queen…?'

'I am well. Relieved.'

'Aye, and me!'

Niamh smiled with something of a wry expression, she could well-imagine that it was a burden to have the safety of the queen to be firmly in your own hands.'

It was a relief to finally reach the village, to walk through amid those ever-suspicious eyes and then to fall into the embrace of the old witch and be held to her rose-scented, musky chest. Morgana did not speak at first, but her arms were welcoming and her body soft to hold. At last though, she pulled Niamh away and sat her on the fur pile in the corner, then went to the old pan over the fire to begin the boiling of water.

Morgana's back was to Niamh but she seemed to be at work and a spiced, comforting smell began to emanate from the stove, cloves and ginger, cinnamon; sweet.

'I take it she knows, then?' she said to Morkyl, knowing better than to try to speak directly to Niamh.

'Aye,' the old man said, still stood awkwardly at the hearth, 'she's seen 'im now, as have half the bloody kingdom.'

Morgana paused and glanced over at Morkyl, 'he showed form?'

'We were captured by the king's forces. They were planning on executing us… her…' Morkyl nodded at Niamh.

Morgana did not turn about but remained paused for a moment, then went back to her work. 'Figures,' she wheezed, 'foolish creature…'

Morkyl continued to speak, filling Morgana in on what had happened but Niamh just lay back on the furs, allowing the softness to embrace her. She wasn't ready to dwell on what had happened yet though, still the idea of how close she had come to death was chilling, and that was before her mind brought her Helligan's great revelation. Instead she closed her eyes and tried to repress it all, consider that she was safe now, there was no need to panic, at least for the meanwhile.

Footsteps came closer, shuffling so that Niamh knew they were Morgana's. The old lady put a beaker to her lips and she drank, trusting completely. The thick liquid was sweet with a burst of honey and spice. Niamh didn't even open her eyes, but allowed the witch to feed her the drink, then relaxed as the cold metal was removed from her lips. A hand smoothed her hair away from her face, and then there was nothing but blissful darkness.

The sounds of the bustling village came first to Niamh, a chuck crowing outside, the slamming of the blacksmith's hammer in the smith just across the dirt track from Morgana's house. Voices, laughter, the squawk of another chuck or maybe even a goose. Niamh stretched, eyes opening slowly to wince at the brightness of the sunshine flowing in through the window opposite where she lay, still on the same pile of furs in the corner of Morgana's tiny cottage. As she stretched, her body seemed more supple, less achy and sore. There was no pain in her foot at all and a glance showed her that it was bandaged tight against a mush of herbs, just as once before her arrow wounds had been.

Then the smells began to break through, sweet tea, bacon and bread through the hazy scent of thick incense which permeated every corner of the cottage. Niamh's stomach growled and she sat up, eyes searching out the food source.

Morgana sat on the wooden chair by the fireside, a pan balanced over the flames giving off the bacon scent. Morkyl sat on the bed in the far corner, a wooden plate of bread and the fatty salty meat already before him.

'Ah, you've decided to join us for breakfast,' Morgana said, her deep voice vibrating the words a little, 'I wondered if you might. Here, eat!'

Niamh found a plate thrust her way with two hunks of bread coated in what looked like a pale butter and two rashers of the bacon. She nodded a thanks and put the food to her lips – it was nectar, especially followed by a mug of strong herbal brew which burst with a taste of citrus that Niamh had not experienced since she'd fled her father's keep.

'Good morning lass,' Morkyl said, 'looked like you needed that sleep.'

'Indeed,' Niamh whispered, licking the final few crumbs along with their greasy snoutlet fat from her fingers. She felt immensely rested and motivated to action. Morgana sat for a moment longer, her own cup to her lips, then spoke.

'The lads of the village know you are here as do the maids at the temple. They think we are shrouded enough to prevent your father from penetrating but I cannot be sure of that. Kilm and his wife arrived a few days past, and have made house here, as have many others who fled your armies.'

Niamh nodded.

'You are welcome to rest here too, but you have a higher calling for the future.'

Niamh nodded again, her mind whirling.

'You'm no use to me in your state, but I can offer you a roof whilst you plan your next move.'

'That is kind of you, mother,' Morkyl said.

'I need not tell you, your situation is dire. You need to rethink now what you plan to do next. You have little of an army and that now scattered. You have a mission without means and a queen without crown or army. I see a great future, still, but the edges grey. You also need to locate Helligan now…'

'We do!' Niamh whispered. 'I don't know… how…'

'He's a ten-foot tall blue dragon trapped in form, possibly injured and definitely furious, living in a patch of woodland which is no more than three miles across – how difficult can he be to find?' Morkyl snapped.

Niamh found a smile, it was small and delicate, but still a smile none-the-less.

'He'll be hiding himself,' Morgana returned, 'And unless he wants to be found, I doubt very much that we will be able to locate him. Dragon magic is far superior to anything you've witnessed before.'

'Even in human form, he is so powerful,' Niamh said.

'True, and yet if any can find him, if any can penetrate his shrouding, it's you, girl.' Morgana said.

'Mother, is it true?...' a voice suddenly came from the doorway. Niamh jumped at the sudden unexpected sound, but then gasped with relief to see the face of Kilm peering in.

'Kilm! Oh!' she cried out, leaping to her feet and running to embrace the clansman. Kilm pressed her tightly for a moment, and then murmured, "My Queen" under his breath. It was the most emotional Niamh had ever seen the old goat.

'Come on in, Son,' Morgana said, 'There is room at my fire for another still.'

Kilm did as he was told, and clapped a hand with Morkyl before settling himself by the fire.

'How do you come to be here?' Morkyl asked. 'The last I saw of you was when Helligan and I were taken! I presumed you'd perished with the rest!'

'Brother, I am sorry I left you…'

'It is of no mind! I am gladdened to see you survive!'

'I do! I heard the ruckus as you and Helligan were taken, and slid back into the shadows – there was little I could do to save you, one man amongst the multitudes, so I knew I must travel the marshes, mountains and dales, and begin again to rouse an army! Before we were just the marsh lords, but with Helligan's execution scheduled, and yours too my queen, I began to rouse lord after lord... the clans are merging and the army is vast. Then news came to my ear that your executions were moved forward. I set the men to the road but we already knew that we would not be in time. I was ready to give it all in, but then a messenger brought a tale to me of a scene at the execution, of a dragon...'

'Helligan showed form,' Morkyl said, 'just as we suspected.'

'He is draconis?'

'Yes. A younger blue for the size of him.'

'Goddess save us all. Where is he now?'

'We don't know?' Niamh replied. 'He left Morkyl and I, and flew off somewhere.'

'The vial which holds his essence is broken,' Morkyl added, 'He won't be able to change back... I'd imagine he's hidden away somewhere in the mists licking his wounds.'

'What of your army?' Niamh asked.

'Ready and awaiting our command, My Queen,' Kilm smiled, 'it is time to take down your father, and we shall manage it properly this time!'

The woodlands were daunting. Tree after tree so closely knit that it was almost impossible to find a path through, especially as the dusk was beginning to fall. All about there was no sound, and the only scents were those of trees, peat and fir. Niamh had been walking for nearly an hour. Ought but a ball of twine to mark her path. If she didn't find Helligan soon, she would likely be so lost in the trees that she'd never find the path again but she couldn't mind that. Morgana's instructions were not heartening, either.

'Intuition will guide you,' she'd said. 'Take a strong pair of shoes for your feet, water to keep you from parching, and your own head. You will find him.'

In Niamh's hands were the twine, given to tie about the tree boughs to mark a path, and a clouded glass bottle. A spell of sorts which had been handed to her with stopper in place.

'Helligan needs somewhere to store the dragon essence,' Morgana had explained, 'any bottle will do, with the right incantations.'

Niamh paused and took a swig of water. It was a nectar. Her feet hurt more than ever she'd known, already swollen from her pregnancy. She was frightened by the falling darkness, but still there was something soothing in the forest, something safe. She paused again and recapped the bottle. An odd feeling, almost a pull overcame her. She pulled in a deep lungful of air and glanced to the west. There, almost missed in her determined stomping, was a small half-concealed path into the trees. There seemed to be more light that way at least, less trees. From above an owl hooted; another sign that night was fast drawing in. Niamh glanced back the way she'd been walking, only darkness. Trust your instinct, Morgana had told her, well here was its first stirring.

Niamh moved onto the path, and, after a few minutes, was pleased to see it opened up to a glade. Her body felt energised, awash with a strange electricity. The clearing was surrounded by an odd blue aura, so tangible she could almost see it. Her hand closed tightly on the vial Morgana had given her. This had to be it, surely? She paused for a moment, then slipped through the trees, stepping into the clearing. At first, the mist seemed to rise but then, as she moved further into the clearing, it thinned enough for her to make out the shape of the slumbering dragon which lay before her. Niamh knew with a strange certainty that nobody else would have been able to see him.

'Helligan?' she whispered.

The beast stirred, causing the mist to move in an unnatural swirl. Niamh stepped closer again to the form, pausing as it lifted its head to cast that bright yellow eye upon her.

'Helligan,' she whispered again, 'my love...'

The dragon snorted, a gust of hot air escaping from its nostril. Niamh paused, but then firmly stepped closer again and held up the vial.

'Helligan I... I don't know if you can understand me,' she said, 'but this... this is to replace the one broken. Morgana... Mother gave it to me... I am to uncap it but I... I want you to be warned...'

The dragon's head lifted slightly, that unblinking eye solidly fixed on her. It did not move to prevent her from acting though. Niamh took in another long deep breath, and then let it escape her. She, following the instructions that Morgana had given her, shook the bottle so that the water within was a swirl, and then uncapped the vial and held it out to Helligan. At first she feared it hadn't worked, as nothing happened, but then the blue light began to build around Helligan's form. This soft azure deepened and thickened to a peacock mist which swirled about the dragon, much as it had on the executioner's stage where she'd broken the last bottle. Niamh gasped but gripped tightly to the vial, terrified it would drop and break. The wind swished her cape from her shoulders but she barely noticed, concentrating on holding tightly to the vial. In her struggle, she dropped to her knees, hunched over and trembling. Then it passed, as suddenly as it had begun. The wind died down and the mist began to evaporate. Niamh stifled a sob and with trembling hands, capped the bottle with the cork stopper.

For a long moment there was silence. Niamh remained crouched, unable to move for the fear of what she might see. A step behind her, a human footstep, and then the warmth of a body cupping hers. Niamh turned and put her arms about Helligan's neck. He, completely naked, pressed her tight to his chest for a long moment, but then released her and knelt, Niamh touched his face, kissed his brow, and then stood and glanced about for her cape. The blue wool was caught in a tree a few paces and so she ran for it, returning with it in hand to wrap about Helligan's shivering form. Still he had not spoken, and as she wrapped the warm cape about him, Niamh noticed the tiredness in his eye, the way he slumped.

'Helligan, are you with me?' she whispered.

'I am,' finally his deep tone. He put a hand about hers and pressed it gently. 'I... it takes a moment to adjust to a new form.'

Niamh could well imagine. She said nothing but lifted the vial which once more simply looked to be a bottle of clear water. Helligan took it and slipped the leather thong it was attached to about his neck.

'Thank you,' he whispered, then, 'Not just anybody could do what you have just done.'

Niamh bowed her head but did not reply. Helligan took her fingers in his and kissed them. He seemed tired.

'Thank you,' he whispered, 'I dread to think of how I might have fared, had you not come to find me.'

'And if you had not done as you did, both myself and our child would have died. Your sacrifice was noble, Helligan, and I thank you.'

Helligan tugged her to him again, laying a kiss on her brow. 'And now you know...' he whispered.

'That you can take the form of a dragon...'

He paused, looking down on her face with a mixture of indulgence and concern, 'Sweetling, no, you have it backwards,' he murmured, 'I cannot take dragon form... that form is my own. I am not a shapeshifter; I am Draconis... a... a dragon...'

Chapter 21

The walk back to Morgana's cottage was one taken quietly. Helligan leaned fairly heavily on Niamh, shivering despite how he was wrapped in her cape. The sun shone with feeble rays down onto the earth, enough to brighten but not to warm, and the ground remained frosty even as the hour approached noon. Finally, the trees thinned and they came upon the old falling-down wall which denoted the edge of Morgana's shack. Helligan was limping, pale, and beginning to stumble by the time they arrived at the door. Inside, Morgana had the fire roaring whilst Morkyl seemed to be at work cooking. Morkyl exclaimed as they entered but Morgana did not bat an eyelid, simply shuffled over to allow Niamh to lead Helligan to the edge of the furs, into the warm.

Helligan's body slumped, and there he knelt for a moment, warming his hands. Morkyl seemed to view him for a long moment, his eyes taking in the form of his commander, but then half-smiled and nodded. 'I'll go and find you some clothes, brother,' he said, leaving the stove and escaping from the door.

'There's stew in the pot,' Morgana said, 'It will revive you both.'

Niamh moved to the stove and inhaled the scent of rich gravy and beef. Suddenly she was ravenous. She served up two bowls but by the time she turned around, Helligan had fallen into a doze.

'Leave him be,' Morgana said, 'the change of form is a difficult magic. He is exhausted.'

Niamh nodded but moved to sit at his side with her own bowl of potage. As she sat the baby moved, planting a kick towards her back and making her wince.

'A healthy boy,' Morgana said, watching her, 'He'll be born in conflict, but he will live.'

'And will he be human… or?' the question was almost painful.

'Goddess knows, child, Goddess knows.'

Niamh fell to silence, eating her stew and watching the light from the fire flicker onto Helligan's face. Her heart was full for him, especially where he seemed so vulnerable, but still she knew once he was awake again, she had questions she needed him to answer.

Helligan slept for most of the day. Morkyl returned not long after with a pile of tatty male clothing, alongside a chest-piece of fine hide. Obviously Helligan was still well-loved among the Woldermen. These items Morkyl placed down beside Helligan but he too was silent.

'Any news?' Niamh whispered.

'They are scouring the countryside for us lass, but rest assured, this place is one of our best kept secrets. Helligan can explain further about the whys and hows of it when he wakes up, but they won't find us…'

'What will we do now?'

'That I don't know…'

'What of Kilm and his army?'

'It's hopeful, lass, maybe, but they will be reluctant to fight after the slaughter of our last attempt. We must tread with caution.'

'That wasn't your fault! Alfric turned coat! He betrayed us all!'

'And yet to them,' he ushered generally, 'Alfric too is a Wolderman, and Helligan the mage led Wolderman against Wolderman.'

Niamh's jaw set at the unfairness but she did not argue. She only hoped Helligan's reputation would save them, that and the news she was sure was spreading of his true nature.

'Why... why is he here? I thought they all... all left? I mean, so the stories say...'

'That is something you'll have to ask him.'

Helligan slept for most of the day and following night. Morgana seemed content to lie at his side though as darkness fell and so Niamh made herself comfortable on the rugs beside the bed. As the morning dawned, Morgana left again to go about whatever her business was, leaving Niamh to make the morning porridge ready for when Helligan opened his eyes. It was not far after daybreak though when he stirred and then groggily sat up.

Niamh wordlessly put the bowl before him and his eyes examined her long before he put his spoon in to eat the spiced, stewed oats. She sat herself back down by the fireplace.

'I never really believed that your kind existed,' Niamh finally said, playing with her own porridge. 'I grew up with the stories but I never... never really believed in the Fae.'

'That is no accident. When we left, we used our magic to dull the memory of us. A thousand years is not long enough to fall to legend, and yet we have, due to the mists we shroud ourselves in.'

'Is anything I know true?'

'I know not of what you know?

'The stories tell only of a great war betwixt the Fae and the mortals which ended when your kind left for another world.'

'Your stories were written by us,' he said, putting down his bowl, easing himself up from the rugs and moving to a chair with the movements of one whose limbs are sore and achy. 'Most of what you speak is true, but we never really went anywhere, we simply obscured our sacred forests and mountains from your view. There is no "other world", as you call it, Niamh, there is no such thing. We simply vanished from your view, and there we have lived since, hidden from humanity by the veils of our magic.'

'In this world?'

'Yes.'

'This... kingdom?'

'Yes, sweetling.'

'How can that be? We have maps... explorers...'

'The obscuration we use, much like I once used to hide us from your father's men on... on our wedding night, is more than simple visual trickery, it's a confound as well. As your cartographers drew up maps, they would not have even realised that the aspects were incorrect, they simply drew the maps as they have them. Your explorers walk to the edge of one of our forests, and then find themselves at the far edge, unable to pass through and unknowing of how they have just been transported. The problem began when your father's scholars uncovered an ancient map... that, of course, would not match up with what your modern maps say. Vast stretches of land unmapped, missing even, from your modern maps.'

Niamh stood and paced to the window, looking out. 'And where we are now – this is obscured, thus why you are so confident we will not be found here? Why it took so long for my father to locate you before?'

'Yes. This is the outer edge of one such place, yes. The Woldermen live on the very edges of our world, they are the footmen of our mind, our mortal go-betweens.'

'But.. when we met! They... I thought they had killed you...'

'Those men knew not what or who I was. It was not until they brought me here, to Morgana, that my identity was realised.'

'I... I see... And the glade where I... I found you yesterday...'

'That was further into our lands. A mortal should not have been able to tread such, but I theorise that the load you carry might have had... some bearing on your ability to enter, as well as your ties to me.'

Niamh put a hand down to her stomach, over the baby. It trembled there. All at once she felt lost for words again. Her eyes scanned Helligan's face, trying to see a sign of his heritage there, a clue, but there was nothing. Never had anyone looked less reptilian, less ethereal or Fae. Within, something began to tremble, starting in her belly but working up to her torso and arms. Tears welled and, tired of repressing them, Niamh allowed them to fall. Helligan watched, his eyes following the water, and then stood and moved to her side. He did not embrace her, but put a thumb up to catch the water at her eyes. His skin felt soft, human, it only made her want to cry more.

'Niamh,' he said, and his voice sounded a little hoarse, 'I never wanted to lie to you. There is a code amongst my people, never to come back here, never to be seen or have our presence on your world known. I was only permitted entry to the mortal lands because I was chosen for a quest, a mission. I was chosen because, of all of us Draconis, I was the youngest and still the most human.'

'And what is that mission? I still know not why you have come here!'

Helligan sighed, his eyes turned cagey.

'Helligan, please...'

'What I tell you now, I break a code to utter,' he said, 'Nobody else may know, not even Morgana, not even the Wolder...'

Niamh nodded.

He sighed again, and moved a little closer, 'There are, amongst my people, those who have the sight – the foretelling. They speak of a day when the mists will fall, and the war will begin again. Those days come closer, but we fear them, we fear the loss of our mists, of our hidden world. When your father began pulling down temples, uprooting sacred trees and searching out items such as the artifact he now holds, my people came to fear that the end times were nigh. I was sent to gather information from the mortal world, and to... to stop your father, if it was in my power...'

'Stop him?'

'To end his reign, and to put in his place one who would be more sympathetic, less likely to wage war on my kind...'

'You... you have been using me then, for these ends?'

'Admittedly, at first... perhaps... you make a gentle, intelligent leader, you make a fine queen...'

'Soft!'

'No! Not soft! You are a warrior through and through, you have shown me thus! I fight for you now because I love you, not because of what I was told to do. I fight for you from love only! Please, trust me in that if nothing else.'

'Can a dragon love?'

'Wholeheartedly... and in this form I am human in mind as well as body! A dragon may love, but so might a human man and I am both.'

'I have to... walk...'

'Go then, but do not harden your heart to me, I beg of you!'

Niamh nodded, but moved to the door. She took up her cloak and wrapped it about her, then stepped out of the cottage, squinting a little against the cold wind, bright winter sunshine. She said nothing as she walked away, her body shaking but her feet firm. She walked right to the end of the village and then out into the misty forest, knowing now that her steps were privileged indeed. The forests were eerily quiet. If, as Helligan asserted, they were populated by the various races of the Fae, then they were either not at the edges thus, or hid themselves well from the sound of a mortal's footsteps. Niamh walked a little further, mindful not to get lost, and then found herself at the edge of a small pool. The light through the trees reflected off of a thin layer of ice which crusted the top, making patterns in the frosty surface. There she rested a moment, her hands pulled up inside her cloak, and her body caked in sweat of her exertion despite the cold. She gasped in a few more breaths and then cupped her hands around her belly. Dragon-kin. Another word which had fallen into legend, the child born of dragon and human. If the stories were to be believed, most of them had died in the wars, slaughtered by both human and Fae alike, as were the other half-Fae offspring of human and magic-dweller alike. Her child would be alone in his birthage, completely alone in the world, an abomination by human and Fae standards both. The tears flowed faster, the sobs choking her and making her shoulders rock but she remained standing, refusing to fall prone like a foolish damsel.

A footstep came from behind and Niamh tensed, using her hand to clear her face of water.

'It is only I, my love.'

Niamh turned to face Helligan, the light from the feeble sun's rays glinting off the frozen pool in a manner which made her squint her eyes. He stood a few paces away, his shoulders relaxed but his eyes burning with repressed emotion.

'You should not come out here alone,' he said, 'it could be dangerous for you…'

'I…'

'Please,' he put out a hand, 'walk with me, if you must walk?'

Niamh did not take the hand but moved to his side, falling into step but allowing him to lead them away from the frozen pool.

'You are so quiet again, sweetling,' he said at length. 'I worry that I have lost you completely now?'

'I cannot comprehend this,' Niamh said, and for the first time in so long, the words really were difficult.

'I know.'

'Could… could you not have… have told even me? Not even after… everything?'

Helligan shook his head. 'It was forbidden. That was a part of the arrangement, that I never utter even a whisper of what I was. It would put you in danger and I never wanted to do that. I have broken a grave rule in allowing people to see me in my true form now.' Helligan glanced almost apprehensive into the forest but it remained eerily silent.

'So you were never going to tell me?'

'I hoped I would never have to tell you, no.'

Niamh paused ran a hand over the thick bark of an old willow tree. They were closer to the village now, safely on the outskirts of the forgotten lands. Her whole body shook but she was struggling to find the words to explain the hurt within. Helligan stepped closer and lifted her other hand and kissing her fingers. Despite it all, he seemed more personable than ever he had before.

'Niamh, my princess,' he murmured, 'From the moment I laid eyes upon you, I knew you were somebody of note to me. I allowed myself to be captured, all those years ago, that you might escape. I have taken you to my bed, and I have put a child inside of you – a dragonkin where none have been born in so many generations. I did all of this against the orders of my people. You may consider my lack of candour and my original motives a betrayal, but already I have... I have done more than I should have, broken so many rules, for you.'

Niamh said nothing for a long moment, gathering her thoughts, but then sighed, 'You just seem like a man to me,' she said, 'the very best of men, but a man still.'

'When I am with you, sweetling, I feel as though that were the case. You ground me, you fill me with love.'

Niamh caught his eye, 'You do love me then, Helligan?' she asked.

'Do you doubt it?'

She didn't doubt it, she realised, she knew he loved her, despite it all. She shook her head 'No, I know it. What next?'

'We have to stop your father, any way we can...'

'I mean, for us?'

Helligan held out a hand and she took it, finally allowing herself to be soothed. He pulled her to him and laid a kiss on her hair.

'I will have to go back to my people once my mission is complete and answer for my crimes, beg forgiveness…'

'And then you will return?'

Helligan paused, a fraction too long. Niamh pulled away from him again, turning angry eyes on his face, 'You *will* return, Helligan?'

'If it is a choice given to me, then I will return in a heartbeat and live out this human life with you before resuming my life amongst my own kind… but…'

'But?'

He paused again, 'my people are forgiving,' he said, 'but I have broken so many laws and commands since I arrived here. Not small indiscretions, but fundamental laws. I alone have shown humanity that we of the Fae live still… and that is the greatest crime one of my kind can commit. None other of my people dare to come through to get me, but should I go back – not here on the edges, but properly back, to my own lands, I will do so at risk of my freedom.'

'You are a fugitive?'

'I am.'

'And the punishment?'

'I could be stripped of my wings for this, crippled and unable to fly, to change form. My magic will be taken from me and I will become nameless. That is if they allow me to live.'

Niamh's heart pounded. 'Can you not just hide? Stay here?'

'No, sweetling, no I cannot.'

'Why?'

'Several reasons. I am honour bound to return, that is why they do not come for me now – they know by my honour I will return when I can. My mission is too important for them to stop me now. Secondly, the elders would find me, if I did try, they wield magics far superior to mine. And if they were to find me, with honour broken, the penalty would be far worse.

Thirdly, and perhaps most importantly, somebody will need to return the sphere of Gual to my kind…'

'But… what of our child?'

'I swear that if nothing else, I will see him born.'

Niamh began to weep again, more full hiccupping sobs. Helligan pulled her back to him, one hand holding her head to his chest whist the other cupped the bottom of her back. He said nothing, simply held her as she cried. When she looked up, his eyes were darker still, his lips pressed. Niamh moved away and Helligan put a hand to the bottle at his throat, the dragon essence, and then closed his eyes. Niamh watched as he allowed the blue flames to dance over his fingers again, becoming a ball of flame. He closed his eyes and inhaled, and before Niamh's eyes, the flame began to freeze. It was the strangest thing, the icicles forming alongside the flame but without extinguishing it. An impossible feat. Once the entire ball of flame was frozen, Helligan closed his grip, shattering it, but then reopened his hand to show Niamh what looked like a clear glass crystal, the edge of which was tinted blue.

'Dragonglass,' he said, 'When my son is old enough, have a dagger or sword cast for him, with this set into the hilt. Wherever the sword is wielded, if I live, I will feel it.'

Niamh took the sliver and slipped it into the pouch at her waist, then dried her eyes on her sleeve. When she moved her eyes up to Helligan's again, they were once more filled with resolve. 'I will ever ensure he knows of you,' she whispered. 'I promise.'

Helligan kissed her brow again, and then put up a hand, 'Come,' he said, 'We have work to do now.'

Chapter 22

The gathered men in the tavern of Havensguard reminded Niamh a little of the old battle-meetings back at Helligan's house in the swamps. The thought made her a little uncomfortable. The group that Kilm had gathered were a little rougher around the edges than the marsh lords had been, but with Morkyl and Kilm being the only surviving of those, and the rest of the armies scattered, Niamh could understand why these new, less civilised commanders had been brought in. Of them, she struggled to keep atop of who was who. A giant of a man with a black beard and hair of ash, another who had wilder red hair, two of an age with her – or so it looked – the twin commanders of the Whites, far south. Names eluded her, just face after face, and yet despite their gruffness, every single one did his duty and knelt for her, pledging swords, axes and even a weak spluttering green flame spell from one.

'We need as many mages as we can muster, even fledglings,' Helligan whispered to her, out of the man's earshot, 'So many of those I called my brothers perished, they are rather a rare breed, but it is not a choice, it is by birth and so new will come into their rights every year.'

'By birthage?'

'Yes. All mages have fae blood,' he smiled. 'and those who work with fire are likely the descendants of my kind.'

'I never knew it,' she whispered, but found herself smiling more kindly on the lad with his green-tipped fingers and lop-sided smile.

'How are we for troop numbers?' Helligan asked of Morkyl and Kilm, when the others had given up on war-planning and were engaged in becoming as intoxicated as they could manage on Niamh's bar tab.

'Not what we had, it's true – and wilder, less disciplined men.'

'And we already lost once,' Helligan mused, his eyes scanning the room.

''We have you, too,' Niamh whispered.

'The girl's right,' Kilm butted in, 'and I think the queen under-estimates her own armies still.'

'I know my people will rally…'

'Have rallied,' Morkyl said, 'as I hear it. Sent out word via the sisters who remain whilst you were looking after 'im – those who would muster for the lady, were to begin to gather. Last I heard it was up in the thousands of men and growing still.'

After two more days, Niamh and her party rode out of Havensguard with the Wolder army in tow. Twenty-thousand strong, she was told, all armed to the teeth and with high morale after three days binging on food and ale. At her side rode Morkyl and Kilm, with Helligan leading the army by just a fraction, his honour as her captain. They rode in a noisy clutter through the old forests where she and Helligan had lain together in their early acquaintance, passing the inn where once they'd fled. The inn-keep stood at the door as they passed, hat in hand, and Niamh was pleased to see how his eyes widened as they rode past. Once out of the forests which offered the Wolder their safe haven, things felt more dangerous, but they went un-molested in the bright and hot sunshine for another three miles, past the River Sy and to the base of the hill beyond the now burned out Anglemarsh – her father's men had pillaged the keep, rather than reclaim it.

As they reached the crest of the hill, Niamh's chest seemed suddenly to expand and her hands shook on the reins of her horse. The army which had gathered for her stretched further than the eye could see across the valley, camped throughout the ruins of her old home and off into the fields beyond. Common men all, most on foot but the odd one mounted on a farm-horse or nag. Pikes and swords were raised alongside makeshift weapons, rusted rapiers. Ash branches turned to vicious points, and here and there the rusting old steel which was probably pillaged from previous battles. The men had dressed in the best armour they could find too, and this too varied from stolen plate to handmade leather and hide items. Helligan slowed his horse to stand beside hers, his eyes lit over the crowds and then moved to Niamh's face.

'See how they gather for you, my queen,' he said, 'see how they love you.'

'Helligan I…'

'Hush! I know! I am somewhat overwhelmed too. It makes my little Wolder army look small in comparison.'

Niamh glanced behind at the smaller army Helligan had mustered, less than half the men, but the Wolder were at least trained for battle, fierce soldiers. For the first time since the defeat on the edge of the Golden Keep, suddenly Niamh felt hopeful of victory.

'There are a handful of lords who have turned for you too,' Morkyl said, pulling up his horse on the other side of her, 'Lord Marks, Lord Harris and Lord something else… you have a few knights too, and one of your father's council but he's been detained until we can understand his motive.'

'One of my father's? Which?'

'Lord Shale – Josynne Shale?'

'Oh! I know him,' Niamh murmured, her mind bringing her the dark-haired beautiful Shale – the man who had found her bow, and the only one who had spoken for her at her trial. 'Release him! He is definitely trustworthy!'

Morkyl nodded and then indicated the valley again, 'will you go down milady?'

'Is it safe?' Helligan asked.

'As safe as ever it can be. You can use your magic to put a barrier about our lady, should anybody try to harm her.'

Helligan nodded, his eyes protective.

Niamh glanced over again, barely able to believe that these crowds really were there to fight, and maybe to die, for her. 'I should go down, my people love me because I am like them, born of a commoner and relatable, it does my cause harm if I consider myself too important to walk amongst them. That is how my father behaves.'

'A fine point very well made, my queen,' Morkyl said. 'We are agreed then.'

Niamh nodded and then pulled her rein. The horse began its careful descent down the valley. The party was about halfway down when suddenly a cry went out, "Fair Queen Niamh!" "Blessed Queen Niamh!" All at once, this cry became a din as the men shuffled closer, each one hoping to get close enough to touch Niamh's skirt or hear her words. Niamh paused, nerves pausing her, but then pressed on until she was flush with the crowds. A strange tingle caused her to pause again, but then she realised it was just Helligan's protective spell falling down on her, invisible to all but her. She pulled up her reins before the crowd but then to her shock the man closest fell to his knees, and then the next, and the next until the entire field knelt in the dirt before her horse.

'Good...' Niamh paused and looked to Helligan who simply nodded for her to continue. 'Good people...' she said, a little louder. 'I cannot.... I can barely express my gratitude and happy surprise to... to find you all here thus, for me...'

Smiling faces looked up at her from her kneeling soldiers, despite how surely no more than the first row or two could have heard her. Niamh put a hand to her belly, hoping that the move did not seem calculated.

'I… I beg of you all, your… your forgiveness that I will make you fight, and I… I extend that plea to your good womenfolk, some… some of whom will find themselves lost of loved ones in the days which follow. I…' she paused again and sucked in her breath, 'My… my husband and I thank you all. Your faith in me gives me hope, and any sacrifices made will be… be made in the quest to… to rid this kingdom of this so-called Golden King, and to bring in a reign of… of fairness to all, no matter your station!'

A murmured cheer came from the men at the forefront, the sound moving backwards through the crowds in an odd game of Chinese whispers.

'I… I intend a kingdom run in fairness, a… a place where the Woldermen need not hide, and the common man need not fear them. I…' again she paused, nerves stilling her, but then pushed on, 'I will ensure every man has food on his plate, and a roof over his head, with taxes which whilst still necessary, will not cripple… all I ask, is for your support now.'

As she spoke, a familiar face in the crowd caught her eye, she broke off but then beamed, 'Malachi?'

At once, faces turned to where she looked, to the figure of her father's torturer standing flushed amongst the men. He wore proper armour, likely stolen from the armoury as he left, and wore a fine sword at his hip. The crowd parted so that Niamh could run down to embrace him. Malachi stood shocked and did not embrace her back but when Niamh pulled away his face was pink and his eyes glowed.

'You came to my side, as you said…' she said, joy making the words easy.

'Yes, my la… my queen. As I said I would. I led a group out with me,' he indicated a rabble of men about him, all similarly clad in fine armour and weapons. Niamh wiped a happy tear and then paused. Everybody was looking at her, every single face. At once, she felt embarrassed for her childish reaction, how it must have looked to the men. Not very queenly or dignified. Unable to find words again now, she turned to face Helligan. He was smiling and as she turned he nodded just once. She paused, then realised that her familiarity with Malachi had probably actually been a good thing. The people loved her for her common ties – it made her as one of them. If her speech had not ingratiated her to her men, her reaction and embrace of a commoner certainly had done. Helligan held out a hand and she went to him, putting up her lips to kiss his. The crowds cheered.

'Come,' Helligan said, 'Let us travel through to camp, I want to meet with this advisor of your father's.'

The hovel where Lord Shale was being held was all but a ruin out on the edge of the main ruins of Anglemarsh, near the woodlands – perhaps a groundkeeper's hut, once. It was heavily guarded, but Niamh could see that half of the roof had fallen in and there was no door. A fortunate ruin rather than an allocated prison. It was close enough to the woods to have that heavy scent, the starting of the mists which Niamh could now see as clearly as she could see the trees. She steeled herself for another fond reunion but as the guards parted, Lord Shale did not come forth to greet her. Niamh stepped inside, allowing her eyes a moment to adjust to the darker shadows of the little cottage and then looked about for him. Lord Shale was shackled at the arm and leg, a chain securing him to a wall. His eyes met hers though and his lips fell into a small smile.

'My lady,' he rasped, his tongue obviously dry from lack of water. His clothing was ripped too, his long hair loose and dirty.

'Unchain him,' Niamh said, her chest hurting to see her friend in bondage.

Helligan glanced in through the door, and then to Niamh, 'Is he safe? You are sure?'

'I am, please! He is loyal and a friend, I will not reward such loyalty thus… with chains!'

Helligan motioned to the Wolderman who guarded the building and he moved at once into the room. It seemed to Niamh that he fumbled for an age, but finally the chains fell away. Josynne Shale stood, seeming a little shaky, and stepped forward until he was before Niamh.

'Ah, there you are at last,' he said.

'Lord Shale, you have my upmost apologies…'

'Ah, no need for that,' he interrupted, still raspy but with relief on his features, 'I would have been concerned if you were guarded with any less vigour! You have my bow, my queen… when it is returned to me, at least…' and with that he fell gracefully to one knee, his head bowed and his eyes cast down.

'I…' Niamh choked on the words, unable to finish her thought.

Lord Shale stood again, half-pulled up by Niamh, but kept his head bowed.

'My queen,' he said again, sounding overwhelmed himself. 'My sweet princess.'

Niamh still could not speak but instead stepped forwards and put her arms about his neck, a tight embrace just as she had Malachi not long before. Lord Shale's skin and clothes smelled of damp, of unwashed body and grime. Niamh didn't mind it, just relieved to have yet another familiar face in her camp. Lord Shale stiffened in shock but then put his own arms about her and hugged her back. Niamh kissed his dirty cheek but then stepped back and nodded to him.

'My Lord, Helligan,' she finally managed, looking back to her husband, 'may I present one of the few people in this world who has my entire trust: my oldest friend and advisor, Lord Josynne Shale, commander of the east armies and lord of the wetlands. Lord Shale, may I present to you my husband, Helligan Darkfire – commander in chief of my armies, mage of the high council and leader of the free men.'

'My Lord,' Lord Shale said, bending his elbow with hand offered in the gesture of solidarity amongst Lords. If he was surprised at how easily Niamh spoke, he did not show it. Helligan did not take the gesture. His eyes were still distrusting.

'Helligan?' Niamh whispered.

'Forgive my reluctance. I know only that you have been a faithful servant of the king since before my time on the council. I respect your friendship with our lady, but I have yet been given no cause to either trust, or mistrust, your loyalty, My Lord.'

'Helligan the mage,' Lord Shale put down his arm, but still held a smile on his features, 'I remember you, you know – even amongst the mages, you were an odd one. I understand your reluctance, sir, but understand now that I have not been loyal for many years. Since Niamh was a babe, I stayed at court only to protect her.'

'An odd claim my Lord, and why should I believe thus?'

'Because I knew and loved her mother…'

Niamh's heart pounded in her chest and her eyes moved to meet Helligan's. Still he was unreadable, cautious. She moved her eyes instead to Lord Shale, 'my mother… the whore?'

Lord Shale shuffled slightly on the spot, favouring one leg and making Niamh worry that he'd been injured when they'd captured him. He held her eye, his face suddenly serious.

'My queen please disregard such notions as given to you by your father in his venom. Your mother was nothing of the kind. Might I suggest that your *dungeon* is perhaps not the best place to have such a conversation? I am chilled through and thirsty…'

'Indeed, my apologies,' Helligan suddenly seemed to snap back to politeness, 'Come to our tent and be refreshed!'

Helligan led the way back, but his step fell in with Lord Shale, his eyes still suspicious although his shoulders were less stiff. Niamh walked slightly behind him, allowing him to lead for the moment whilst she gathered her thoughts. Back at the tent were wooden chairs laden with furs and it was a relief to sit, to rest a hand on her heavy stomach and put her swollen feet inside the warm fur rugs. Helligan indicated a chair opposite, and Lord Shale sat.

'Perhaps have food sent for too?' Niamh said, pouring a goblet of wine and handing it to Helligan, and then another for Lord Shale. Helligan nodded and whispered a few words to one of the guards at the edge of the tent, then came and took his seat at Niamh's side. She offered her hand and he took it, caressing her fingers.

'Sir,' Lord Shale spoke, 'I do understand your caution and it warms me to find my lady so well protected. I approve even, and if that means that ever you distrust me, then I will not take such as in insult, for I know it is born of your love of that sweet lady.'

Helligan simply nodded.

'You spoke of my mother?' Niamh whispered.

'I did.' Lord Shale's smile cracked slightly for the first time, and he took a deep gulp of his wine. 'My lady, what your father said to you about your mother during your trial was not only unkind, but entirely untrue. Your mother was no whore, she was... was the most wonderfully sweet creature I ever knew. We met her during the first Wolder wars, before you were born Niamh, but I am sure Lord Helligan remembers.'

'I do. It was before I stepped through the vale to this world, but it was part of the reason I was sent through.'

Lord Shale eyed Helligan again with caution. For the first time, Niamh found herself wondering how the common folk must perceive her husband. 'Indeed,' he said at last, then turned back to Niamh, 'My queen, your father likes the people to forget the time before the golden age, but in truth that is hard done – it was a difficult and bleak time. The wars had raged for hundreds of years, battles at the edges of the kingdom where the land becomes contested. Wolder shrines and sacred places were being destroyed by your father's men, sometimes for settlement or building materials, but often more for your father's distain in and disrespect for the old gods. I was but a squire to your father then, a young man not even a score in years. I suppose I never really pondered the implications behind what we did when we slaughtered them, burned out whole villages where we could. Your father was a young man too then, ill-adept at fighting such a war...'

'I cannot ever imagine him a fighter or commander, even now.'

Helligan remained silent, but his eyes showed he was at least listening to what Lord Shale had to say.

'Indeed, my queen. Finally, through sheer destruction, your father and an old Wolder lord, one of the lords of the mountains, drew up the treaty for peace – that your father would leave their sacred spaces to be, but in return, Wolder armies would disband and no raiding parties would be sent out into the borders.'

'A treaty which was broken by both sides, multiple times,' Helligan said.

'That is true, my lord, but a treaty which was adhered to enough that it allowed for the golden age to begin. It was after the signing of the treaty, as we turned our horses for home, that we found Niamh's mother... It was I, in fact, who found her. The entire army was camped around a small village still near the borders. I was drunk, we all were, celebrating what we considered a victory. I had to... excuse my saying so, my queen, but I had to piss and so wondered off to the edge of the forest to do so. There, standing by the edge of the trees was a woman. She was slight of form, with golden hair and green eyes which pierced you. A Wolder woman, by the dress, by her wild hair. Her eyes widened when she saw me, but she did not flee or scream, merely stood with those green eyes upon me.'

Lord shale paused in his narration and swigged another mouthful of wine from his goblet. He played with the article in his fingers and then glanced at Niamh.

'She never spoke a word, not one,' he said, 'in the whole time I knew her.'

Helligan and Niamh exchanged a glance, Helligan's face grim, Niamh's thoughtful. 'Go on,' she managed at last.

'I… I spoke to this woman, asked her name, asked where her menfolk were and why she was out alone. She simply came and put a hand on my arm. I asked her if she wanted for anything, food or shelter, I tried to be kind, gallant as the knights of old… Still she did not speak but there was something… something ethereal about her… her eyes seemed to glimmer from blue to hazel, her hair was alight and the more I looked, the more beautiful she seemed.'

Niamh caught Helligan's eye again. He nodded, then cast his eyes down. 'She wasn't Wolder…'he said.

'No, my Lord, I don't think she was – I began to realise the truth when you… when you showed us that the old stories were all true… if… if dragons could truly exist…'

'Then so could others of the Fae,' Helligan finished. His fingers tightened around Niamh's, offering her support as she digested what Lord Shale was telling her.

'It was I who brought her back to camp. I thought to have her in my bed – I see no shame to tell you thus now, I was just a yellow boy with a bellyful of good beer and she was… erm… affectionate in her touches of me. It was not to be though, for as I walked past the royal tent, the king himself was coming out, probably for a similar purpose to mine. He saw me with my nymph and I suppose he wanted her from the first. He demanded to know who she was and so I told him what I knew. He took her wrist in his hand and pulled her to him. She…' Lord Shale closed his eyes for a moment, then opened them and looked over to Niamh, 'she struggled, my queen, I am sorry to say this to you, but what happened that night was not for the want of it by your mother… I could not fight for her – what squire would raise a sword to his king over a wench?'

Niamh's eyes spilled tears over her cheeks but she remained without words, she could not have formed them if she tried.

'What happened, later?' Helligan asked. Niamh glanced up to see his eyes were more trusting now, his expression less guarded.

'The king kept her with us for the entirety of the journey home. She was bound about the wrist by a golden chain, wrought with the magic of the First Mage, Lord Tarquinn Rush, and the king called her his "offering", convinced that she'd been gifted to him by the Woldermen to sweeten the treaty...'

'Disgusting,' Niamh whispered, clutching tight to Helligan's hand. He did not reply by more than another gentle squeeze of her hand, listening with pressed lips.

'Once back at the keep, the woman was transferred to a chamber of her own: still a prisoner and with her belly already rising with you, Niamh. I was given permission to visit her – of course the king had already grown tired of the silent girl by then – and so I used to go and visit with her, to sing to her, play my lute. I always felt my presence soothed her and sometimes... sometimes she would kiss my hands. I loved her. I never used her – I loved her innocently and sweetly as only a boy on the cusp of manhood loves.'

'How did she die?' Helligan's voice was deep, his arm fingers crushing Niamh's.

'She... after Niamh was born, she grew listless. Even my lute could not soothe her. She had no interest in the child, and seemed agitated and frightened... I... my queen, I am sorry, I am so sorry. She escaped her luxurious prison when Niamh was less than a year old. She made her way to the battlements and flung herself off. I... I did not know until after she had done it! Had I known how desperate she had become, I would have done anything to help rescue her from her prison. I swore then and there, that I would mind her child, care for you and protect you. It was I who convinced your father to legitimise you, I who commissioned your bow, spoke for you at your trial... I did what I could to watch over you, my queen, because I... I loved your mother...'

'I...' Niamh tried to speak but broke off, wiping away the tears which wet her whole face. She shook her head to indicate the words wouldn't come.

'If I might ask, what happened to her body?' Helligan asked instead. 'Was she returned to our people with dignity at least?'

'She was. The king was… neglectful… in offering her a final rest and so I… I took her back out to the edge of the marshes and I left her body there, laid out amongst the reeds, in hopes that she would be found and returned to her… to your people. When I returned the following day, she was gone.'

The silence echoed as Lord Shale ceased his speaking. Helligan let out a long, audible breath and then stood. He moved to Lord Shale's side. He bowed a head to him, and then bent his elbow, hand extended. Lord Shale stood and clasped the hand, making the traditional step forward so that the men stood chest to chest, hands clasped between them, and then raised their spare hands to each other's shoulders. The weight on Niamh's chest lessened a little. Helligan was the first to step away, coming back to his chair and sitting back down, resting his head against the back of the tall chair. His eyes closed and Niamh saw his hand go to the bottle which contained his essence.

'Is there anything else I should know?' Helligan finally asked, opening his eyes to look over at Shale, 'anything else at all.'

'Yes, yes there is. The very thing which pushed me to defect… which pushed all of us from the castle to come here. The King's scholars have learned how to use the artifact….'

The dining tent was too loud for Niamh. With both Helligan's soldiers and hers – a concept that still felt unreal, to have her own army – the noise level had reached the point of din. The soldiers were seating by ranking, with Lords at her and Helligan's table, both Wolder and Common; this included Jos Shale from her men, and both Morkyl and Kilm from Helligan's. The common soldiers were tolerating the Woldermen, but still, they themselves were a rowdy bunch and seemed to be on their absolute worst behaviour, to Niamh at least. Niamh broke a crust of bread and absently dipped it into a honey pot. The taste was sweeter than she liked, but there was no Pomple Jam to be had at the camp. Helligan, sat by her side, chuckled.

'Hmm?'

'You've the manners of a Wolder now, it would seem,' he murmured, indicating the jar. Niamh glanced up to see the eyes of some of her soldiers upon her, mostly with affection, but one or two with disapproval that she'd dipped the bread rather than use a knife.

'I will have a care,' she whispered back to Helligan. It was well to have quirks, but she did not want to risk alienating the common men. They were after all, the base of her army. She made an effort to lift her knife and scoop out honey for the second slice, in the spirit of manners.

'My Lords,' a voice to her right, 'I have a messenger here...'

'Bring him in,' Helligan said. He barely ate, Niamh noticed, his plate holding just half a chuck leg and a sliver of bread which he seemed not to be of a mind to actually eat. Helligan caught her eye again. Messengers generally carried threats from the opposite camp. Niamh tried a reassuring smile and put a hand over the growing bump of her child. Seven months in now, nearly time to give him birth if she was to carry for a normal human cycle, another thing which nobody could confirm or deny either way.

The messenger was a lad of about seventeen. He was no common boy but a well-dressed squire with plentiful yellow hair and a velvet doublet. His eyes moved about the tent as he entered, resting with fear on the Wolder Lords.

Helligan stood, lending Niamh an arm to do so.

'You have a message for me, Boy?' Helligan asked gently, 'I suggest we go somewhere private?'

The boy's eyes finally rested on Helligan and it was not difficult to guess his thoughts when faced with the dragon, even in human form.

'Come,' Niamh said, beckoning the boy. The less the people feared Helligan, the better for all in the long run.

The boy followed Niamh through from the dining tent into a smaller anti-chamber. They were followed in kind by Helligan, Jos Shale, Kilm and Morkyl. Once within, Niamh pegged the door and pulled out chairs for them all, not forgetting the boy.

'Who are you and what is your message?' Helligan asked, Sitting and learning forward to engage with the young squire.

'Sir I...' he paused and cleared his throat, 'I am the youngest son of Lord Shelby, of the king's court, squired currently to Lord Glenn.'

Niamh nodded, both minor knights in her father's court.

'I know your father well,' Lord Shale said. 'He ever struck me as a good man.'

'He is, sir...' My father and my lord both wish to leave King Hansel's court and come to...to yours, my lord, my lady... I er... my queen...'

'Tell them they are welcome,' Niamh said. Any man could join them, trust would be earned once they arrived.

'I... thank you, my queen. My father sends... sends tidings, from Aurvandil, word that might... might not have reached your ears yet...'

'What is it boy?' Kilm snapped, causing the timid creature to flinch again. He'd need to toughen up if his family were going to join the rebellion!

'Sire, my queen... my lords...' the boy stuttered, 'there is a new... a new law just passed in Aurvandil and to be spread about all of Rostelis... the... my lord, my queen, the old religion is now... now illegal in all parts of this country. The move to the new religion is now complete. The temples have all... all been desecrated and the sisters... the sisters slaughtered. Most of them have been executed... some died during the purging.'

'It cannot be!' Niamh murmured, grabbing for Helligan's hand. He gripped it tightly in his own and held on to it.

'And this is throughout Rostelis?' Helligan asked.

'Not yet, my lord, just in Aurvandil, but the royal decree is that it is to be thus… there is more…'

'More?' Niamh asked, she felt an anger she'd never before known building up in her.

'Your father, my lady… my queen… your father is not just… not just executing them, but he is burning them as Heretics… my sister, my lady…' a tear formed and rolled down the boy's cheek as the reasons for his family's abrupt turn of loyalty became clearer.

'Take your time, lad,' Lord Shale said but his voice wobbled. Niamh examined his face, watching as his colour grew paler and paler.

'My… my sister was executed this morning alongside all of the captured sisters from the temples. The… the patrons were… Lord Shale, I am sorry, the patrons were all burned too, as heretics.'

Niamh looked back to her friend, confused. He pressed his lips and nodded. 'Thank you, boy.' He said, 'and… and my son?'

'Him too, sir… as he… as he tried to protect his mother from the soldiers… he was but a boy after-all, and did not understand the danger.'

An odd, painful silence fell about the room. Lord Shale seemed to deflate. His skin was grey and his chest heaved.

'Lord Shale?' Helligan asked.

'My… my wife, Bertha… she is… was, I suppose… a patron to the western temple and a fervent follower of the… of the old religion… I… I wanted to bring her but I… I.. thought it would be too dangerous here for her and I… I thought she'd be… I'm sorry, I…Niamh, Helligan – will you excuse me?'

Niamh stood and took both of his hands in hers.

'Jos, if I can do anything…'

'Thank you, my sweet queen,' he said and kissed her hands, then turned about and left.

Chapter 23

Niamh's armour, newly made as it was, fitted ill over her increased girth. Uncomfortable and unyielding despite being of leather rather than steel. It made her back ache and she knew she'd be in agony by the end of the day. Her mount was a new one too, a black destrier which was massive compared to her little dappled girl. The baby was moving a lot, adding to the discomfort, making Niamh wish she'd agreed to Helligan's pleas for her to wait with the sisters again. Not this time! After the last defeat, she could not stand to watch Helligan go out alone, even knowing he was more than capable of looking after himself! Niamh held fast to her reigns and moved the beast out to meet Helligan and Lord Shale in the field. The Marsh Lords, what remained of them, were further out, in the edges of the forest. There would be no parley this time, no niceties, the king and his men were prepared for battle, and so were they. Helligan glanced over at Niamh, worry in his eyes.

'You look fit to drop that baby in the field,' he said, 'you really shouldn't be here.'

'I won't get too close to the actual battle and if I start getting pains, I'll leave.'

'Please mind at you do, you are carrying a precious load and so close to dropping it now…'

'I'll be careful,' Niamh whispered.

Lord Shale glanced over too. Still he was pale, obviously stricken by grief, but his eyes showed steely determination. Niamh hoped he'd not let his emotions get the better of him on the field where he was to lead the archers.

'Right, let's do this…' Helligan murmured, suddenly pulling his horse onwards. Shale signalled for his longbowmen – escapees from her father's army – to follow. At the gate, the siege was interrupted by the opening of the gates and the first wave of her father's troops emerging. No siege this time, but full on bloody warfare. There must have been several hundred at least within, now spilled onto the land before them. Helligan glanced to Niamh and went to speak, but then suddenly he gasped, putting a hand to his chest.

'What? What is it man?' Shale shouted as their first wave of longbowmen let off a volley into the army below.

'I… I don't know…' He shook his head, then began to indicate where the men should position themselves, still in some discomfort. A sweat began to show at his brow, a dullness to his eyes.

'Helligan…'

'Get back, all of you. Niamh, listen to me now and make your way back up. Shale, you take her. Send in the men but… but make it quick…'

Niamh didn't argue, something was terribly wrong, she realised. Lord Shale gripped her rein and all but pulled her onwards as their men and the men below finally began to merge. The sounds of the battle were more than Niamh could ever have imagined from her previous positions during the actual fighting. Not just the clanging of metal on metal or the shouting, but the footsteps of so many men, the screams as they went down. Niamh glanced to her right to see Kilm bringing his clansmen in from the west flank, whilst Morkyl had still not appeared. The siege ladders were up already, but being countered by hot oils and flame. Suddenly it all seemed to be a chaotic blur. Niamh couldn't breathe.

'Come, My Queen, it'll be well,' Lord Shale said, a soothing beacon as he led her away from the fray. 'Come, the battle doesn't need you now – the goddess Helston must take over from here.'

Niamh allowed herself to be led a little further, then looked back to where Helligan was beginning to attack the wall with his ice bolts. Still he seemed in discomfort, his magic not quite so focussed and his mount skittish beneath him. Her heart thudded. Helligan was a damn good horseman, something was certainly not right. Despite that, however, the magic he aimed at the wall of the keep seemed to be having some effect; the whole wall was buckling, crashing under pressure. Her father's men seemed to see this too, suddenly fleeing from that parapet. Lord Shale put up a hand again and more arrows rained down from her archers. Other than Helligan's strange behaviour, things seemed to be going as they should. The Woldermen had taken the sides too, her father's men being fast surrounded. Niamh found a smile, her hand clutched tight about her bow despite that she'd yet to fire a single bolt. They were winning! She could hardly believe it… but then Helligan caught her eye again, almost doubling over in his saddle. He put up a hand and gripped the bottle holding his dragon essence. Niamh moved in slow motion, turning her mount, but Josynne took the rein and held it fast.

'No, Niamh!' he shouted, 'It's too dangerous!'

Helligan's hand, from what Niamh could see of it, seemed to lift the bottle. Inside, the smoky liquid was bright shining blue, much more so than usual.

'W…what?'

'Your Father…' Josynne muttered, 'Damn!'

'My father?'

'The sphere! It… it controls dragons!'

'But he's in human form!'

'I don't think it matters…'

Helligan roared, a sound of anguish and pain, and ripped the bottle from his neck. Even as Niamh screamed, he pulled loose the stopper. Josynne gripped for her reins again and all but dragged her mount away from the battlefield, making her grip at the mane with sweaty hands. Behind them, she could hear the flap of his wings beginning.

'Oh! No! Josynne!' she sobbed.

'Move back! Come on!'

'No! I need the bottle…'

'He is too far under the control of the sphere! He'd kill you if you went down there now!'

'No! Oh! Oh by the Goddess!'

Josynne dismounted from his horse and pulled her down from hers which had grown skittish as the dragon pulled up into the sky behind. His hand was rough beneath the metal of his knuckleguard but still she grabbed it, running with him as their horses bolted.

Lord Shale dragged her to the edge of the battlefield and then lifted a hand. A wave of arrows flew then, her own men, firing at Helligan. Niamh screamed again and tried to fight her way back.

'Niamh, you cannot help him now! The king has him in his thrall!' Josynne said, 'we have to take him down before he kills us all! Those were his orders… if this happened!'

'And I order you not to,' Niamh sobbed, pulling on his arm, 'rescind the order, please! No!' her voice turned to a scream as the first volley of arrows flew upwards, towards Helligan! 'No!' she screamed again.

'Niamh! Stop!' Josynne was almost beside himself too, panicked, covered in sweat and frenzied so that his eyes looked wild. 'Somebody… somebody remove the queen from the battlefield! It's not safe here and she's hysterical!'

'No!' Niamh screamed as two hands gripped her arms, 'don't you dare! No! Helligan!' another volley of arrows went up, causing the dragon to spin about, letting loose a jet of flame into their own army.

'Let go of me or I swear… I swear I'll have you all arrested for treason,' Niamh sobbed, 'My love! Please! Save him!'

Josynne put down his bow and ran to Niamh's side, pushing the two men who had apprehended her aside, he pulled her into his arms, crushing her tightly. 'Niamh, my darling please be reasonable! We have two choices, to take Helligan down or to surrender... he himself ordered us to do this! He himself wanted us to push on!'

'I cannot live without him,' Niamh sobbed, 'I cannot stand and watch you kill him.'

'Then give the order... you are our commander now. Surrender to your father... against Helligan's command, against my council! Give up on it all to save him, or close your eyes and let us take him down!'

Niamh slumped to the ground as yet another volley of arrows went up. Helligan roared, pain and fury. Niamh put her hands over her ears, closing her eyes against the sight of her lover flailing in the air. Her sobs were stilling though, as the monarch within took over. The heat and noise of the battleground were suddenly overwhelming. Her own body ached all over, her swollen feet pinched in the boots and her back aflame from standing upright so long. She couldn't surrender. Not now that they had the capitol city! It was just the Golden Keep to take. If she surrendered now she'd lose her supporters, lose face. She'd just be another weak woman, ready to sacrifice victory for love. Unfit to rule! If she did not surrender, Helligan would fall... but they didn't have to kill him, she realised, and he was a strong healer...

'We will not surrender,' she said at last, drying her eyes. 'Take him down but restrain him, do not kill him!'

Josynne nodded curtly and moved back to repeat her order to the men.

'My father is our main target,' she said when he returned. 'He thinks to distract our army with Helligan. We need to show him we cannot be so easily distracted! We do not know how the sphere works, but if we can at least acquire it...'

'Agreed! Where would your father go, to be safe?'

'You know better than I... you were one of his main advisors...'

Josynne frowned, then glanced behind him to where Helligan had ascended right up into the sky, beyond the scope of the archers.

'The west tower,' he said, 'I'd wager that device needs to be directed at its target so he'd need a window or a battlement. The west tower is hardest to access...'

'Send Kilm with the ladder-men!'

'Good thinking, my queen.'

Niamh looked down over the battle, the walls were breached now and her men were swarming through. They didn't need to defeat Helligan, just outlast him. Niamh felt herself relaxing, allowing the panic to recede but then another cry came, one which chilled her to her very marrow.

'Flank! Flank!'

Niamh spun about as though she'd be able to see the army behind but there were nothing but trees in her view.

'What? Where?' she gasped.

Josynne kissed her hand, 'I'll find out!' he said. 'Stay here!'

The panic instantly began to build again but Niamh quashed it. Her back ached, reminding her that she was alarmingly close to giving birth and should in fact be locked away in her confinement, not out on the battlefield. She moved to the edge of the trees, hoping to find shade and slump, just for a moment, when suddenly the sound of horse's hooves burst through from the woodlands to the south. Niamh glanced up, then gasped to see her father himself riding in, his own personal guard surrounding him.

'There! He roared, 'the traitor!'

Niamh tried to run, even as the screams of the sisters rose about her. In the distance she saw Josynne stop and spin about, but already she knew it was all too late. She made it as far as the trees before a hand gripped the back of her gown. She fought, striking up, but then gasped as what could only have been a contraction cramped her stomach. Niamh fell to her knees, suddenly surrounded by men. A lone arrow flew past her, impaling the ground close to her hand, one of Josynne's no doubt, aimed at her father. A thud beside her and then her father stood above, sword in hand. Niamh covered her face with her hands, bowing down to the dirt, convinced that this was to be her last memory, but her father knelt beside her and lifted her face to his,

'You are defeated, surrender.' He said.

'No! I might die here but my army is victorious!'

'Your dragon is mine and you are captured. Your men are about to fall into a trap. You are defeated child! Surrender!'

Niamh closed her eyes, then gasped as another contraction began. A wetness drenched her feet.

'By god, the mighty queen has pissed herself!' that voice could only be Lord Nordemunde but even her father showed distaste at his words.

'That's not piss,' he said, 'she's in labour! Sound the horns, tell the men she has surrendered!'

'No!' she gasped but her words were lost in the echoing sound of her father's war horns.

Niamh was bound, lifted onto her father's horse and carried through the battlefield. Stopping only so that her father could stoop where Helligan had been stood and pick up the now-empty bottle he'd carried. Her men, those who were not dead, were knelt in irons all over the battlefield. She'd lost! She'd surrendered, despite that she'd never once uttered the words. As they approached the Golden Keep, the gates opened, allowing them admittance. Behind her, Josynne Shale walked in irons where he'd been taken in the shock of her apparent surrender, and behind him were Kilm, others she knew to be Helligan's elite. Her father marched them into the middle of the grass before the keep, his own soldiers moving with them to form a ring of spectators. There was no gallows, no block, but that her father was taking her to her execution was obvious. The contractions were coming closer now, enough to make her stumble as she was dragged into the middle of the green. There she was forced to kneel, Josynne at one side and two of the captured sisters on the other. Both of the women were sobbing and even Josynne was deathly pale. He put out a hand to Niamh and she gripped it tightly in hers.

'If this is the end, I am proud to die by your side my queen,' he said.

'Silence!' a voice from behind barked but Niamh couldn't even bring herself to turn about. How had it all fallen so quickly! What had happened?

From above came the sound of wings swishing and through her tears, Niamh saw Helligan land. He was a little battered up, arrows poking through his hide but he walked without a limp into the circle, the king's soldiers moving to give him entry. Niamh's father stepped forward and showed her the sphere, set into the hilt of his sword. It glowed blue.

'Luckily for me, my torturers were tardy in cleaning up after your lover was… questioned… upon his arrest,' her father said, 'it would seem that the missing ingredient was the blood not of just any dragon, but of the one you wish to control… Helligan Darkfire is mine now. Any who doubt thus are about to witness the extent,' he said.

Niamh looked up at Helligan, he was impassive in form, his yellow eyes focussed on her father, his nostrils moving with the exertion of his frenzied battle with his own people. Suddenly he seemed completely alien, not Helligan but a mere beast with his personality stripped, repressed.

'Helligan,' she whispered.

'He cannot hear you. He hears only me,' the king said. 'he is bound.'

As the king spoke, Niamh noticed men in the background bringing forward what looked like large wooden flagpoles, these they were fixing into the ground. Niamh glanced away, looking down at the lushness of the green grass on which she knelt, still damp with dew. Josynne was speaking again, but she couldn't hear him, couldn't concentrate on anything but the turmoil in her mind and body. Another contraction made her gasp aloud, bending almost double.

'Niamh!' Josynne cried, 'What's wrong with her.

'She's in labour,' a voice from behind, Niamh turned to see that Sister Dora had been brought in behind her, Kilm too, although he lay in a pool of blood. Still alive, but bleeding out. Both were shackled.

'My Lord, have mercy! Have mercy on her and let her birth her child in peace!' Josynne appealed to the king. 'I beg of you!'

'No child will be birthed here this day,' the king said, then moved to speak to his lords.

'Treason is a difficult beast to root out! See her, my old child! The golden princess who I nursed as my very own despite her bastardy! See how she tried to attack, like a cuckoo in the nest of a swallow! She has led these wild men to our very bosom, murdered our people and laid siege to our city! This pretty little girl! This princess who is so beloved! Here, bear witness, though, that my mercy is not infinite! Men, take them to the stakes!'

Niamh scrabbled about, confused, as two arms lifted her to her feet. She tried to struggle, but was carried anyway, weakened in her current situation. Josynne fought, and Niamh watched as he was subdued, and then carried unconscious. The men took them, and the others – Kilm, Sister Dora, the other two temple sisters... Morkyl, who she'd not seen until that moment. All were taken to where the poles were driven into the ground and Niamh's panicked eyes took in the cuffs hanging there.

'No!' she murmured, finally realising her father's intent! His most lethal weapon, stood before them snorting little puffs of smoke from its nostrils. 'He'll never forgive himself! Father you can't!' Her hands almost pulled free from her captor in her panic, but then another contraction ripped through her, weakening her so that her hands could be forced into the cuffs. Beside her, to her right, an unconscious Josynne was cuffed to his own stake, and to the left one of the Wolder Lords, and then the younger of the sisters – Greta – who was almost hysterical as she too was affixed in place.

'Dora?' Niamh called, 'Sister Dora?'

'I am here!' came a voice from her right. Niamh turned to see the sister was held on the other side of Josynne.

'Pray! Pray to the goddess for our souls,' Niamh sobbed! 'I beg of you! That she might take us as we burn!'

'Helligan, move in,' the king commanded. The dragon came closer, walking in a slow, heavy gait.

Niamh forced her eyes from Helligan, to the spectators. Mainly the king's army, but a few women from the keep now showing their faces too.

'Witness this travesty!' She choked out, 'See the truth in your *golden king!*' the tears began to fall again as she turned her eyes back to Helligan, now moving closer still under her father's control. 'I forgive you, Helligan' she sobbed. 'If you ever regain yourself and this memory, remember that I forgave you!' She could not continue, broken with almost hysterical sobbing as Helligan moved to stand before them.

'Helligan, burn the first prisoner,' The king commanded.

Greta, the sister on the first stake, began to scream. The terror in her tone was paralysing. Niamh closed her eyes, whispering her own prayers along with the ragged tone of Dora, who prayed aloud for their souls. The heat was unbearable, even yards away from where the jet of flame touched the stake, silencing the screams of Sister Greta almost at once. Niamh's breathing turned to ragged gasps as the woman twitched and then fell into a charred silence, her body hanging limp as it burned. Beside her was one of the new Wolder lords – Niamh didn't even know his name. His skin turned very pale as the king ordered his death, and it came swiftly. Niamh was close enough that she could smell the burning skin, feel the heat of it blistering her hands. Helligan turned to Niamh.

'I love you,' she sobbed, giving up her struggles in the knowledge of their futility, 'I love you Helligan. I forgive you! I forgive you! I love you!'

'Burn the traitor queen,' The king commanded. Niamh's eyes cast out frantically over the spectators, desperately hoping for a reprieve but despite the obvious discomfort amongst the men, none were going to come to her aid. She closed her eyes then, whispering her prayers in her head and waited for oblivion.

It did not come.

Helligan stood before her, his head raised and his yellow eyes looking directly at her.

'I said burn her!' The king repeated, 'You cannot resist me Helligan Darkfire! Burn the traitor queen!'

Helligan staggered. He was fighting the command! Niamh's heart thudded.

'Helligan! Helligan it's me,' she said, 'I am in labour Helligan! I am having our child! As we speak!'

The dragon lurched again, it's lips snarling to reveal sharp teeth.

'I command you!' The king all but shouted, anxiety showing in his tone.

Helligan looked again to Niamh, his chest expanding as he did when he was about to breathe his fire. Niamh closed her eyes again, but then the sound of the people's screams came to her ears. She opened her eyes and there she gasped. Helligan had breathed his fire, but not at her. The king danced on the spot as the flames encompassed him, setting aflame his flesh, his hair. His face seemed to be melting, his golden etched armour melting onto his body in a molten wave. Her father had not screamed though, had not had time to in the attack. It was the people gathered who screamed, who fled as the beast whipped its head from side to side.

Niamh began to struggle again, kicking her feet up to try to pry her hands away from the cuffs. It was fruitless, but then, realising they were no longer prisoners, her men began to move, throwing off their repressors. A commoner she did not know by name came to Niamh, cutting down the ropes which bound the cuffs to her hand. Between them was just more rope rather than a chain binding the manacles so once that too was cut, Niamh could use her hands despite the cuffs.

'I thank you!'

The man nodded and then moved to the others freeing them too.

'Dora, see to Kilm's injuries,' Niamh gasped, trying to regain control. 'Where is Helligan's vial?'

'Josynne will know! He was taken with you…'

Niamh ran to her friend where he was just regaining consciousness. 'Jos! Helligan's vial!' she said, 'What happened to it?'

'The king…' he said groggily, trying to sit up.

Niamh nodded and ran to the still burning body of her father.

'Please don't be melted,' she repeated over and over in her head, 'Please Goddess guide me!' The body was badly charred, beyond recognition, had she not seen him standing there and known his identity. Niamh's skin blistered on the hot metal as she searched his body, but then finally came up with the glass vial – oddly unharmed.

Niamh murmured in triumph and bent to ride through another contraction, this one powerful enough to make her gasp. She let out the breath with a hiss and then uncapped the bottle and muttered the words Morgana had taught her. At once the blue mist came down again, and Niamh felt her exhausted body falling to the ground now that she knew victory was assured.

The floor beneath her was cold, hard. Niamh groaned and splayed her hand on the hard stone. Stone! But she'd been on the grass. Her eyes flew open. She was indoors, in the great hall of the Golden Keep. She was laid on the floor, her gown hitched up and something, somebody, behind her, holding her upright. A pain ripped through her, making her scream as it felt as though her womb were escaping her body.

'She's awake! A voice from behind.

'Oh! Thank the goddess! That's it, push, my queen! Push!' The voice was Dora's, the one from beyond unknown. Niamh's vison began to return properly bringing the swimming figures into focus. Dora knelt between her legs, she was rubbing something onto her ankles. Her burned hands were bound with leaves and her back supported by flour bags. Two other sisters loitered beyond. Niamh glanced up at the figure behind her and found Helligan's eyes looking onto her face.

'Helligan…' she murmured.

'I'm here, sweetling! Listen to Sister Dora and push!'

Niamh did, then screamed as more pain ripped through her. Reality focussed more though, the realisation that she was not dying, just in the throes of the final stage of labour.

'Breathe! Breathe! And now push!'

Niamh did as she was told, throwing her head back with the effort and allowing another scream at the agony. Once more, and then an odd slippery sensation. For a moment there was silence aside from her ragged breathing, then suddenly the wail of a child echoed within the hall. Niamh's eyes filled with tears as Dora, also panting slightly, laid a precious bundle onto her belly

'Oh, by the goddess!' Niamh breathed as the little thing, still attached to her by the cord, wailed and threw its arms about.

'It's a boy,' Dora said softly, 'My Queen, My Lord, you have a son.'

Niamh touched a finger to the baby's cheek, then spilled a hand about him and pulled him up closer. Dora used a dagger to cut the cord so that Niamh could hold the child properly. 'Helligan… Just look…' she breathed.

'Our baby, with us at last. What shall we call him?'

'He must have a good name! A strong name!'

'Alistair?' Helligan asked, 'Prince Alistair?'

'A dragon name?'

'A half-dragon child…'

Niamh's eyes closed. Within her, something pulled again. She opened her eyes and glanced fearfully at Dora. The old sister just smiled and knelt back down, 'just the afterbirth, my queen,' she reassured.

Chapter 24

Niamh stood at the edge of the glade looking out into the mists. She had worked long and hard on being able to see them, and now could just about make out the shapes beyond, in the fae part of the forest. A movement here or there but not enough to alarm her anymore. Her body was healed now from the birthing, just about, but still she tired easily and still her stomach ached, monthly blood yet to return. Helligan stood by her side. Her hand held tightly in his as he too looked out towards his own lands. In his other hand was the box which contained the deadly artifact, her father's sphere.

'Must you go? In truth?' she asked.

'I must, my love, I have waited too long already. Your kingdom is secure now, and the last of the resisters subdued. You will rule well, and long.'

'You will return, though?'

'If I might.'

'What sentence awaits you there?'

Helligan glanced down at her. 'The sentence for revealing our kind to yours is death,' she said, 'but my people are not savages, and my reward for returning the artifact will be mercy.'

'Please, it is not worth the risk! Allow another to take it?'

'There is nobody! Besides, if I do not return to face my penance, they might come for me, and that would be worse... so very worse.'

'How will I know how you fare? Of your sentence?'

Helligan's lips pressed and his eyes showed his emotion for just a moment. He put a hand to his vial, the one containing his essence, and there pulled free a small blue ball of light. This twisted in his palm, then shrunk into a small lump of stone, not unlike the Dragonglass he'd given her previously.

'This contains a sliver of my essence,' he said. 'Whilst it glows, I live... it is little enough, but it is something...'

Niamh took the stone from him. She bit her lip and forced herself to serenity.

'How can I rule without you?' she whispered, 'I can barely speak when I am wrought!'

'And yet you have won this war, my love. You – not I. You will rule because it is in your blood. You will be a gentle and kind ruler, over your people and the Wolder. Bring them together now, my love... that is your main objective.'

Niamh dropped his hand and moved so that she was against his chest. Helligan's hands pressed her tightly to him, his lips caressing her hair.

'Never forget,' he whispered, emotional, 'despite what I am and whatever happens to me now, never forget that I love you with everything that I am. If I can return, I will, it will be my only thought. If I am absent now, it is not because I wish it, and I vow to you that one day I will come home to you.'

'I love you Helligan. I will be waiting,' she whispered, 'with your son...'

Helligan inhaled the scent of her hair one last time and then stepped away, handing her the box. He put his hand about the vial, paused, and then uncapped it. All at once the blue fog came. Niamh stood still through the tears, through the pain in her heart, until the great beast stood before her once more in his place. Helligan stepped closer and there bowed his head, Niamh opened the box and removed the sphere, slipping it into a bag and putting that about his neck. The vial, which had been snapped from its chain as he changed was on the ground at her feet so Niamh picked that up too and added it to the bag.

'Goddess…' the words choked but she persisted, 'Goddess watch over you, Helligan Darkfire, and bring you home to me.'

The dragon bowed its head just briefly, and then turned and walked into the thicket leaving Niamh sobbing in its wake.

Then there was quiet. Niamh sat herself down on the grass, the pulsating blue stone in her hands. She allowed the tears to fall, allowed herself the pain, but then forced herself back to her feet and turned. Josynne Shale stood at the very edge of the glade, the reins of her horse in his hand. As she moved forward he held out a hand and Niamh took it, allowing him to help her mount. He did not say a word, he needed not and they both knew Niamh was too wrought to reply anyway.

Before them lay the great walls of capitol city – a city still celebrating the death of a man once thought golden, but who was shrivelled and cold inside. Niamh had already heard herself named the Golden Queen, it was a nickname she was determined would not take hold. Let her be the dragon queen, let her be the Wolder Queen or the warrior! Even "the idiot" was better than this odd homage to her father.

Niamh flicked the rein and her horse began to move towards home, towards the new challenges and adventures she would face as queen of the realm.

About the Author

Hi, I'm Emma. I'm an author and local historian from Plymouth, in the UK. I write under various genres: Historical Romance, Supernatural Romance, Dark Fantasy and Historical Fantasy. My background in Psychology (educated to Msc) combined with my love of history, (educated to Ma, PhD underway) influence and intertwine in everything I write. I am local to Plymouth, Uk, and both work and study at Plymouth University. My PhD is focused on insanity and asylum care in the long nineteenth century.

I started writing at a fairly young age, 18 or 19, but didn't publish my first novel for some years. Ella's Memoirs was released in May 2014 and after a short social media campaign, it was found to be a success, making it into the top 10,000 best-selling ebooks overall on kindle for new releases, and the top 1000 free ebooks on kindle during a free promotion shortly after release. This led then to the full proof and edit of novel number 2, The Blood of the Poppies. Unfortunately, due to the death of my father, this novel was somewhat delayed. However, it was released a year later than planned in the May of 2016. Since then, I have released the sequel to Ella's Memoirs, "The Black Marshes" as well in 2018.

This novel, The King's Idiot, is my first in what is a new genre for me. Book two is currently in writing, as is another novel set in the same world.

https://www.facebook.com/EmmaBarrettBrown/

Also by this Author:

Ella's Memoirs
The Blood of the Poppies
The Black Marshes

Printed in Poland
by Amazon Fulfillment
Poland Sp. z o.o., Wrocław

59992592R00155